Long Time Dead

Tony Black

W F HOWES LTD

This large print edition published in 2011 by
W F Howes Ltd
Unit 4, Rearsby Business Park, Gaddesby Lane,
Rearsby, Leicester LE7 4YH

1 3 5 7 9 10 8 6 4 2

First published in the United Kingdom in 2010
by Preface Publishing

A CIP catalogue record for this book is available
from the British Library

ISBN 978 1 40746 705 4

Typeset by Palimpsest Book Production Limited,
Falkirk, Stirlingshire
Printed and bound in Great Britain
by MPG Books Ltd, Bodmin, Cornwall

Long Time Dead

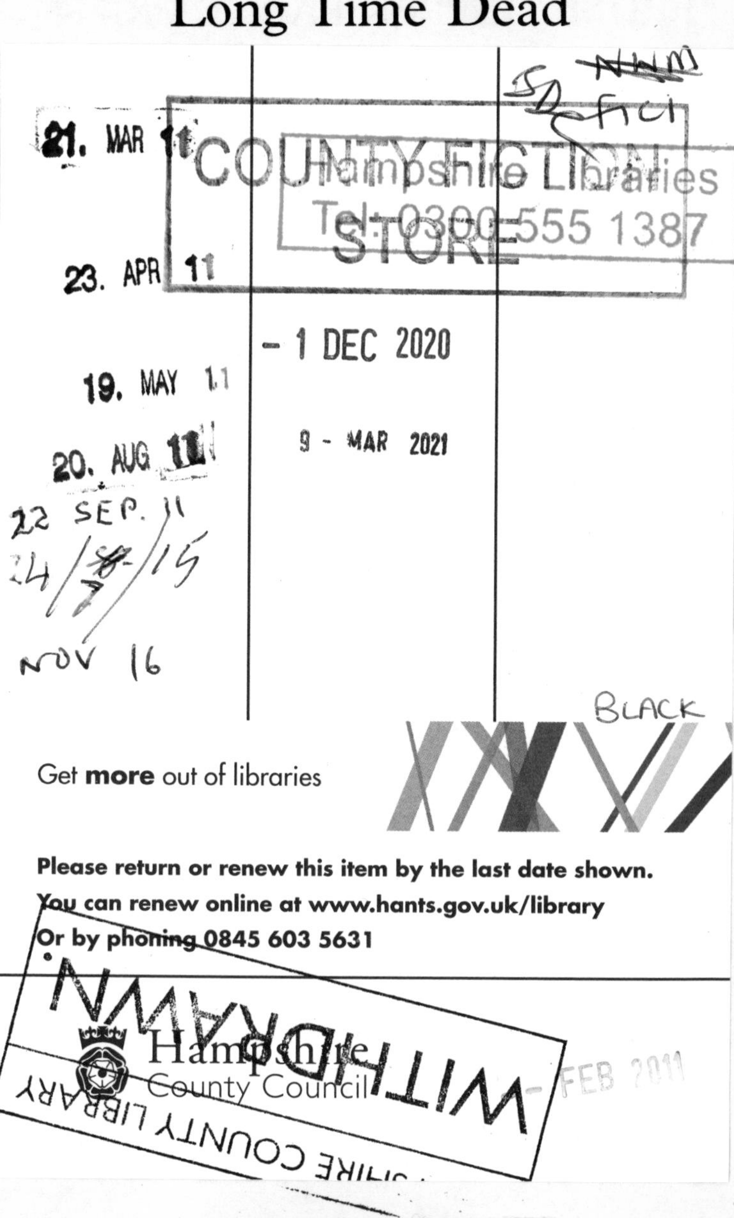

ALSO BY TONY BLACK
FROM CLIPPER LARGE PRINT

For Matt 'Doc' Neal

CHAPTER 1

The doctor was a no-nonsense west-coaster, type that called a spade a shovel and if you didn't like it would add, *You got a problem with that?*

Problems I had. In spades. Or should that be shovels?

'What were you drinking?' he said.

'Black Heart.'

'*Rum* . . . the condemned man's tot.'

Like I'd argue. He laid hands on my head, tilted my face to the light, opened my eyelids with his thumbs.

A *tut*.

'Pardon?'

No response.

He motioned me stand, said, 'Open your shirt.'

The unbuttoning was a trial. My hands shook like fluttering starlings. The doc looked at his watch.

'You in a hurry?' I asked.

A frown. 'Are you?'

I got his meaning. Didn't answer.

The stethoscope felt cold, made me flinch. What

made the doc flinch, I could have done without knowing.

'You're dangerously underweight,' he said.

I hadn't been on any scales that I could remember, said, 'You weighed me with your eyes, did you?'

He took off his glasses, frowned again. 'Mr Dury, I can count your ribs.' He put back his glasses, stood fists on hips. 'You're malnourished.' Then the killer: 'How frequent are the hallucinations?'

I hadn't told anyone about those. Either this guy was good or moonlighting as a stage hypnotist.

I sat upright in the bed. 'Halluci – *wha'?*'

A hand on my shoulder, was meant to calm me. 'You were flapping arms on Princes Street like Freddie Krueger was after you . . . You're a sorry state, son.'

My heart stilled when he called me son. My own father had never shown such concern. I grabbed the crisp white linen of the bed sheets, lifted them up to my throat. I could remember nothing. 'How did I get here . . . I mean, what happened?'

The doctor exhaled slowly. I felt as if I was back at school, in the headmaster's office after some dust-up or a smashed window. 'An old lady on a mobility scooter ran into you. She must've been going at a fair clip, mind . . . put you into the window of Burger King. Out like a light you went.'

He didn't even smile; I had to fight to suppress a laugh. Well, if you can't laugh at yourself, you really are in bad shape.

'She's okay, by the way,' said the doc.

Like I gave a fuck – she put me in hospital; lied: 'Glad to hear it.' I touched my elbow; the skin was broken and reddened. As I looked at my fingers I saw they were stick-thin, yellowed by nicotine and black under the nails. I was plugged into a saline drip. I looked, and felt, like complete shit. Worse, I was choking for a drink.

The door behind the doc opened. I caught sight of Hod. He held out a bottle of Lucozade, bunch of grapes. He was motioned in. Doc said, 'Try talking sense to him, eh . . . He's living on borrowed time.'

I'd heard it all before. Been to the meetings, the therapy, the interventions. The ex-wife couldn't help me – what made them think anyone else could? I felt like a man at the end of a long road; I was tired. Done. I needed no more looking after than I could give myself, and that wasn't much. I didn't care, though, because I'd lost all cares. As you stare down that dark well of despair, there's the most astounding sense of relief, a release almost. A surrendering. A feeling of putting it all in the man upstairs' hands. Fuck it, like anyone could do a worse job of it than me. I looked at the clock on the wall. It said 3 p.m. I'd be off by half past, if I could get a drink in me.

'What's this?' I said to Hod.

'Lucozade.'

'You serious? Nothing else . . . ?'

Hod bridled. 'Gus, your liver's fucked. You're up

Shit Street, and you want me to bring you sauce.' He shook his head, sliced the air with his hands. 'No can do, buddy.'

I tried to get out of bed. My head swam.

Hod flattened me back with his forearm. 'Don't be so fucking stupid.'

Oh, I was that all right: ran over by an old grunter on Edinburgh's main drag – this was a new low, even for me. I wanted out. I wanted a bottle to climb into. I wanted to wash away the contents of this banged-up head of mine. I needed out, away. Anywhere but here. I struggled with Hod, but I didn't have the strength; I was piss weak.

'Okay, okay . . . you got me,' I said.

'Are you quite settled?'

'Perfectly.'

'Good, because I need you to get yourself together pronto.'

Hod's eyes widened. He had that stare of his on, one that says, *Whatcha make of those apples?* He had my full attention as he handed me a copy of the evening paper. Front-page splash was a story about a hanging at one of the city's universities.

'The fuck's this?'

Hod snatched back the paper, read aloud: 'Lothian and Borders Police announced the death of nineteen-year-old Ben Laird at a capital press conference this morning . . . *blah-blah* . . . His mother, the actress Gillian Laird, dismissed police claims of an erotic asphyxiation accident and pledged to spare no expense to root out her son's killer.'

'Erotic . . . what?' I said.

'Asphyxiation . . . Think they call them gaspers. Y'know, tie themselves up to get turned on.'

Sounded like too much work to me. I took the paper back. 'This him?'

Got nods.

I could see the family resemblance now: the lad's mother was Scottish acting royalty, but she'd been front-page news herself recently. 'Hod, this is the chick that came out, yeah?'

A grin spread over his chops. 'That's the one . . . Left her husband, some big film director, for a twenty-year-old glamour model.' He put open hands in front of his chest to mimic a sizeable rack.

'She just dumped the film guy and swapped sides?'

'He was a bit of a swordsman, lives over in the States now. Put it about for years. I'd say she got fed up and took the *dramatic* course of action.'

I shook my head. 'Some family . . . The glamour girl was a pole dancer, yeah?'

'I dunno what nationality she was!'

'Ha-fucking-ha . . . The one she's sleeping head-to-toe with, she's the one the papers ran the scoops on: had worked in the Pubic Triangle, and been a junkie and all that.'

'Aye, aye, aye . . .' Hod clicked fingers at me, shook his head, rapid-style. 'Look, that's neither here nor there, mate. What you need to know is,

Gillian Laird is looking for someone to go and poke about in her son's murder, and she's paying big money.'

He had my full attention.

I was flat broke. Jobless. Hod had lost his last means of income, the Holy Wall pub, which I'd sold to him. The last thing I needed was any more grief in my life, but shit on a stick, I needed something. Fast. My situation was worse than a fly sliding down a razorblade using its balls as brakes. Something had to give here – could this be the something?

Said, 'Go out that door and keep shoatie, Hod.'

'Come again?'

'Till I get dressed. You don't want me creeping out of here in a hospital gown, do you?'

Hod grinned. 'Nae danger . . . Let's get ready to rumble, eh.'

'Yeah, whatever.'

On his way out the door, Hod spoke: 'Seriously, Gus, you won't regret it. I have a good feeling about this.'

I'd heard those words from him before; nothing ever shitted me more.

As I picked up my trousers the belt buckle rattled so much in my shaking hands I was like a leper with a bell, said, 'Fucking hell, Gus, what're you thinking?'

I was in no state for this whack. I was in no state for anything.

CHAPTER 2

I tried to pull out the needle attached to the saline drip, but my vision wouldn't focus. Be fucked if my hands would work either – shaking like a jakey with a tin cup.

'What's up?' said Hod.

I didn't let on. Big mistake.

'Aahh . . . *fuck*.' The needle broke in my hand. I almost leapt through the wall.

Hod was grimacing. 'Jesus, Gus . . .' He ran over, grabbed up my arm. 'You've made a right cunt of this.'

Like I needed telling. 'Just pull the thing out would you!'

He grabbed hold, tried to steady my hand, couldn't do it. It flapped about like a power hose on the loose. 'Can you keep still?'

'Does it fucking look like it, Hod?'

Three-quarters of the thick needle was poking through the skin and blood was oozing from the now sizeable hole it sat in. 'Christ on a cross, Dury! Will you ever learn?'

I thought that was one of those questions that required no answer, even the obvious one. As Hod removed the needle, flung it in the sink, I folded my arms and tucked hands under my oxters. Figured the flapping was on for the day; they wouldn't settle. Had it come to this? I thought. What was next, shitting in a bag? Sleeping on cobbles and waking blind after a night on the meths? I had reached the end of a very long drop. My heart wept at what my mother must think of me. I could care less about the kip of myself, but I couldn't bear putting more hurt on anyone else; I'd made an art form of that already.

'Right, I think you'll live,' said Hod. He shot up an eyebrow. 'For a wee while longer anyway.'

He opened the door, looked out into the corridor. Was empty; he motioned me to follow. I was unsteady on my pins, my knees bucking on every step. There was a cement mixer going in my stomach, and I knew that had I eaten anything of late I'd be spraying the walls. My head hurt, but I couldn't remember when it hadn't so that made no difference to me. The real pain, though, the real heartscald, came from the realisation that I was walking back to reality, going into the real world. The song of drink called to me with every step; I needed a swally. A quick one or ten. A good bucket. I needed to put the lights out, shove my head under the pillow and wait with blessed relief until the magic wore off. I was hurting.

In the lift I caught sight of myself in the stainless-steel doors. There's a film, *The Machinist* with that Christian Bale bloke, think he went down to about eight stone for the role . . . He looked the picture of health by comparison to the image before me now. I'd watched my physical deterioration over the years with a kind of detached wonder . . . wonder at how I could let myself get so fucking bad. But now the wonder was replaced with flat-out awe. It was nothing short of miraculous that a human being could get so close to death's door without knocking; mind, I didn't have the energy.

Hod placed a hand under my elbow, said, 'You okay?'

I jerked my arm away. 'Get off, would you . . . I don't need looking after.'

He shook his head as the lift juddered and the doors pinged open.

An orderly in a pale blue smock and a pair of Dunlop Green Flash was waiting with a mop and bucket. The smell of the strong disinfectant made me dry-retch. I brought a hand up to my nose and tried to hold off the stench, wasn't working. Hod sensed my unease and put an arm around my shoulder. I was too faint to argue now, let him guide me past the reception desk and out the front door.

We got a few steps into the car park when I was clotheslined by the sunshine.

'Some day, eh?' said Hod.

'Won't last.'

Frowns, bit of a headshake.

'But you can enjoy it whilst it's here.' A broad

smile crossed his face. He clasped palms together and headed for the car. How could I argue with him? Was a given I felt more comfortable in the dreich, grey rain pounding down like stair rods of the Edinburgh I knew.

Hod spun the tyres, seemed anxious to get rolling. I watched the city go by in a blur as we made it out onto the main road and headed for Porty.

'We'll hold up at my gaff for a bit,' he said, 'just till you get yerself on your feet again.'

I turned to catch his expression, said, 'That better not be what I think it is.'

'What's that?'

'Your usual caper . . . keeping an eye on me!'

He smiled again, a fake one. 'Gus, calm down. We have a job on.'

Hod had got himself mixed up in my previous jobs for want of anything better to do, for kicks, a nice break from the office; slightly more of an adrenaline rush than snowboarding or rafting. With his property business going tits up, I guessed he had nothing better to do. Was that likely to play to my advantage? Was it hell as like. Hod on Rambo-action mode was like a Ritalin-deprived six-year-old with a Super Soaker. He needed more looking after than I did, and that was saying something.

'Look, Hod . . . what's the go here?'

'Come again?' He pulled out, floored it as he overtook a shit-heap Astra.

'I mean, why the fuck are you getting all hyped up about some posh bint's son copping his whack?'

He cut the revs, steered round a parked white van with the blinkers on. 'Look, Gus, it's not a case of me taking an interest in the Laird boy's murder—'

'Whoa, whoa,' I cut in, 'you don't know that it was a murder.'

'Bollocks. You going with the papers, with plod?'

I felt an urge to cough; I was craving nicotine. 'Look, the way you fire up, mate, I'd be taking the dogs on the street serious before you.'

Hod shook his head, gripping the wheel tighter. Saw I had him: there was more to this than he was letting on.

I ferreted out a crushed ten-pack of Regal from my jacket pocket, sparked up. 'So, what's yer angle here, Hod?'

'My angle? . . . Did you read that paper?' He tapped the dash. 'Look, I saw yer Laird woman on the news the other night – she's fucking dripping in bling and living in a castle!'

'And?'

'*And* . . . she's putting up serious poppy to get to the bottom of this murder.'

I didn't bother correcting him again. 'And that's your sole interest, is it? Making a nice little wedge? Cos I know you're a fucking action junkie, Hod, and if you think I'm getting dragged along so you can play at being Richard Branson on his balloon race with my time and dime you can forget it.'

He brought the car to a halt outside his block

of luxury flats, turned the key in the ignition and opened the door. As he eased out he looked back to face me for an instant. 'Gus, I need this payday like you wouldn't believe.'

He closed the door. I got out and eyed him across the car roof. 'What do you mean?'

As he turned I saw his pallor descend several shades of grey to rest at white. 'Get inside, Gus. We need to talk.'

Hod managed another three steps before he was T-boned by a burly biffer in a black suit. He placed a hand on Hod's chest. 'We've been waiting for you.' Another suit, shorter, but heavy in the neck, emerged from the passenger door of a pimped-up Merc. He started to put leather gloves on as he strode towards us. I couldn't see his face but I recognised the gait. Looked the kind of swagger I'd seen on more than a few widos from this town: the strut that said, *You messing?*

'The fuck's this?' I said. My heart was pounding, didn't do my head any favours. If either of them breathed on me I'd fall over. I knew I'd be no use in a pagger.

'Get back in yer fucking hole, Dury,' shouted the wee man. He pointed a black leather-clad finger as he put the bead on me. Now I recognised him. It was Danny Gemmill. A bottom feeder, but connected. He'd been a Hibs casual back in the eighties, back when they'd sharpened the tips of their golf brollies and gone looking for eyes to stick on them. He was a skelf with a serious wee-man complex. Had worked a rep as a nut-case after Stanley-knifing a few faces. After the casuals had carted the Samba and Pringle sweaters, though, Danny had moved into the more organised stramash, ran with a few mobs in the town; some of the bigger ones of late.

Hod held up his hands in submission. 'Okay, okay . . .'

Gemmill quickly patted him down, thrust hands in his pockets. I'd seen Hod in some shit in my time, but this was the first I'd seen him roll over. The wee pug found what he was after, shook the car keys in front of Hod's nose and smiled. 'Don't think you'll be needing these, eh.'

Hod drew swift breath, his deep chest inflating. I could tell there was a thought brewing, maybe a swift kick to the knackers and a few jabs to the jaw as a follow-up, but he clocked me pressing a palm to my aching ribcage and started to slowly exhale. 'Nah, don't suppose I will,' he said.

Gemmill placed a paw on Hod's face, leaned in. 'Don't think this buys you much time, boy. You've got a fortnight to come up with the rest.' He spun on the tarmac, tossed the keys to his mate, who took off for Hod's Beemer laughing like an asthmatic hyena, seemed to be putting that in *my* direction; wondered why.

I watched the pair drive off. Hod caught my gaze, shrugged.

'The fuck's that all about?' I said. I couldn't get over seeing him cave like that.

Another shrug, hands thrust in pockets. 'Come on, let's get in, eh.'

I reached out to grab his shoulder as he started away from me. 'Hod, you just handed over yer car to a pair of fucking mugs! What's going on?'

He turned. 'I'm in for a few bob . . . to Shaky.'

'Fuck me! *Shaky*?' Boaby Stevens specialised in brutal violence, loansharked on the side. Not even Hod was that stupid, or desperate, surely. No wonder Gemmill was laughing his arse off – he'd hit the big time now.

Hod removed a hand from his pocket to scratch his chin. This was altogether a new expression for him. He didn't do whipped dog well. Went, 'Let's get inside, eh . . . I'll fill you in.'

I found myself staring open-mouthed. As he turned again, I sprang at him, surprising myself with the force I contained. 'You're in to Shaky! That fucker'll cut yer hands off, y'know.'

Hod checked to see there were no curtains twitching in his neighbours' windows. 'Gus, can we get inside?'

'There's nowhere to hide from him.' I pushed past. 'You daft cunt, Hod . . . You fucking daft fucker.'

CHAPTER 3

Thank Christ it was summertime – the place was as cold as a witch's tit. For luxury apartment in Edinburgh, read: flung-up-in-five-minutes new-build. Bit of a view. Maybe some chrome on the balcony. If the estate agents were being honest they'd describe it as fucking shonky. Might make reference to plasterboard walls so thin you can hear your neighbours taking a piss and maybe a wanky Shaker-style kitchen from Ikea that's the latest must-have on the ideal home front. If I'd seen one of these low-on-style, soulless shitholes, I'd seen a hundred. They were, as a whole, the boldest metaphor for what this city of ersatz culture had become. The architectural equivalent of gonorrhoea, only spreading faster among the Pinot Grigio-drinking smart set. Trendy yuppies – can't get enough of them.

I'd kipped at Hod's gaff before, been a guest more times than I cared to remember . . . but never once did it look like this. As we entered the hallway my Docs clumped heavily on the exposed floorboards. I say boards – can you call chipboard slabs floorboards? The walls were bare, the light fittings had been removed, the one concession to homeliness was a cheapo Argos slim phone, sitting disconsolately on the ground with its cord twisted and kinked into all angles.

Hod held schtum, closed the door behind us and motioned me to the living room. The carpets had been lifted in here too, every stick of furniture had been removed. On the wall where the plasma had hung was no more than a depressing oblong outline that looked as though it had been drawn in charcoal on the wallpaper. Hod caught me staring open-mouthed and turned away. He took off his jacket and flung it on the fireplace. The fireplace had once been in the wall; now it was on the floor, no doubt on its way to the car boot sale.

'Hod, what the fuck has happened here?' I said.

He stalled. 'Want a coffee?'

'Do you even have coffee?'

'Erm . . . actually, no.'

Hod walked the long steps to the kitchen door, opened it, pointed in. The kitchen had been stripped.

'Where's your kitchen, man?'

He put his hands behind his head, ruffled his hair a bit then threw them up with a great exhalation of breath. 'Gone to the yard.'

'Come again?'

'Flogged it . . . Was Italian marble – needed the wonga.'

I felt my hand rising to my forehead, don't know

why; is it the universal symbol for disbelief? Hod had been the one safe port in my stormy existence. He was successful in a way most people can only dream of. He was stable. Sorted. Had a Nectar card, for Chrissake. This was off the scale.

I walked towards him. 'Hod, mate, time to spill the beans.'

That sigh again. Huge chestful of air departed. 'I got into a bit of a rut there with the pub . . .'

This I did not want to hear. The Holy Wall had been bequeathed to me by our mutual friend Col. With all the business acumen of Del Boy I'd promptly set about running it into the ground . . . Then Hod had stepped in.

'I knew I should never have let you buy me out—'

Hod sparked up, 'It's not what you think. It's, well, finances were stretched across the whole business.'

'Bedsitland by the Sea . . . Thought the student digs were doing all right.'

'Were . . . look, the long and short of it is I ran out of credit with the bank and . . .'

I saw where this was going. 'Went to Shaky.'

'No, no . . . not really.'

This was promising. Maybe he might get to keep one hand; a few fingers, anyway. 'Go on.'

'I went on a bit of a spree. Actually, went a bit high-roller for a while there.'

'Shaky doesn't touch casinos. How did he get in the picture?'

Hod's head fell back, landing on the jamb of the door. He looked out towards the Forth. 'It's a bad debt. Shaky buys bad debts . . . Willie Gallagher from the casino sold Shaky my debt.'

'The cunt.'

'Oh, aye . . . he's that.'

'Did he not give you any time to pay?'

Hod raised palms. 'Few weeks, days . . . Everyone's short of poppy, need to get cash flows moving. Can't blame him for that.'

'But Shaky. Fucksake, Hod, man's a mad bastard.'

Got a soul-deep stare, 'Tell me something I don't know.'

I dug in my pocket for my smokes, lit up. Kip of the place, didn't think there was any need to ask first. 'So you've sold all your stuff?'

Nods. 'Everything . . . pub's gone too.'

That was a belt; Col would be spinning in his grave. 'What about the flat?'

He reached into a cardboard box at his feet, pulled out a stack of letters from the bank, all printed in red. 'Already started repossession proceedings. Matter of time before the locks are changed and I'm flung out.'

This was not good. It was hard to see a man of Hod's stature felled like this. I had come to rely on him as one of the few constants in my life. Hod was the man I could have been if I'd got my shit together. Held down a job. Held on to my marriage. Holy fuck, I was hurting for him. I needed a drink, more than ever.

'I've got to whet my thrapple, mate . . . Been too long on the dry bus.'

Hod arked up, 'Are you off yer nut?'

'Whoa-whoa . . .' was I the one up to my sack in shit here? Well, yes, but that wasn't stopping me playing the heavy hand. I needed a drink desperately now. 'I'll take no lectures from Porty's answer to Stig of the fucking Dump.'

He marched over to the other side of the room, dragged out another cardboard box. It was full of cartons of UHT milk and packets of Complan, the build-up drink. 'This is all you'll be drinking, Gus!' He picked up the box, started ripping into the contents.

'Complan . . . What the . . . ? Are you serious?'

'Need to build you up, Gus, it's part of the plan!'

'What fucking plan?' I wasn't having this. I didn't want any more looking after. I'd had enough of that from Debs, and look how that had ended – her walking out, leaving me nothing, not even the dog. The thought stung, but I knew she was better off without me.

'Here, look, it's strawberry. Who doesn't like strawberry milkshake? Get it down you, come on . . . You'll be well on the mend after a few of these shakes.'

'Hod, I have enough shakes as it is!' I couldn't believe my ears. 'Have you no Grouse?'

He walked forward, thrust the glass tumbler into my hand. 'Drink!'

'*No*!'

'Do I have to hold your nose and pour it down your throat?'

'You could fucking try . . .'

He did.

Hod's strength seemed superhuman to me; I couldn't even muster a struggle. When my pathetic put-up was over, I had a frothy mouthful of milk-shake left, which I spat at him. Didn't have the power to put any force in it, though: the lot leapt in a low arc for a millisecond before landing on my shirtfront.

Hod laughed. 'That's piss weak, Dury.'

'Fuck off.' Pink bubbles came out my nostrils.

He went off again: 'Piss weak . . .'

I pulled myself together, tried to land a punch on his arm but my wrist collapsed behind my fist and I ended up shrieking like a schoolgirl, shaking out the pain of it. 'Ahh, Christ.'

'Look, cool the beans, Gus. I have a plan.'

This I did not want to hear. All Hod's plans, with few exceptions, had seen me setting up shop on Shit Street. They invariably involved broken bones, time inside, and a bundle of regrets.

'I don't want to hear it.'

'Shut up.' He strolled out the room, returned with a manila envelope. There seemed to be something bulky inside.

'I hope that's dosh.'

Wide smiles. 'Good as!' He chucked me the envelope.

As I ripped into the contents, I couldn't believe what he had handed me.

'Tell me this is a joke.'

'Joke?' Hod crossed his brows. 'Fuck no . . . this is our only hope.'

I put my hand in the envelope and took out one of the small white cards that read, *Gus Dury, Private Investigator*. I put it back, said, 'You have to be kidding.'

'No way. This is primo.'

I held up the cards. 'Hod, tell me, how many packets of Bazooka Joes did you need to save for these?'

He looked wounded, stood rolling on the balls of his feet. 'I thought they would help with the case . . . y'know, the actress, Gillian Laird. She's paying top poppy, I thought—'

'No, Hod, you didn't fucking think . . . My days of running after rainbows are well and truly over. Check the nick of me – I'm done, Hod. And that's my final word on it . . . *Done*.'

CHAPTER 4

I left Hod and his grand plan to simmer. Grabbed a dusty cushion off the floor, drop-kicked it against the wall and sat. My mind was swimming. I knew I was at the end of my rope. A prayer away from the grave. The trembling began again in my chest. The whole cavity felt suffused with fire – like hot coals had been shovelled into me. I knew only one thing would cool it: if I didn't have a drink soon the bats would be back, swooping me, clearing the way for the vampire monkeys that always followed them. I started to shake. My head hurt – worse than usual – and a cold line of sweat was forming on my spine. I looked at my hands; they were in an all-out flap. Tried to sit on them but it only made my whole body tremble. Oh, sweet Lord . . . get me a drink before I die.

'Gus, look . . . I've never asked you for anything before.' Hod approached again, looming over me. 'I really need this.'

I looked up to meet his gaze but his head was turned the other way. Like Bogart's beggar in *The Treasure of the Sierra Madre*, he just couldn't ask another man for help and look him in the eye. I felt an enormous weight of responsibility descend on me. Hod needed me, but I also needed him.

I said, 'Right, do as I say, no questions, and I'll see what I can do.'

He turned to me. 'Okay.'

'Go out that door, down those stairs, and bring me back a bottle of scoosh.'

'Gus . . . I—'

'Hod, if you don't I won't last the fucking night!'

He looked down on me, dark eyes pleading, then the resigned face, well-worn by the loved ones of alcoholics, appeared.

He went for the door.

As he left I was suddenly surrounded by the blackness. I knew the hallucinations were coming back. I sensed them creeping up on me, like a child who expects nightmares. I had felt pain, real and emotional, in equal measure in my life, but this was a new form of hell. But then, hadn't my life turned down that track since Debs had left?

I had kept off the sauce, the bottle was corked and would have stayed so for good . . . if she had. We'd already split, separated and divorced, went our separate ways but something drew us back together. Love is a strange thing – can anyone ever understand it? Comprehend it, even? Not us. We were marionettes in its hands. Dragged dancing through some surreal times, but now the music had stopped. The lamps expired. We might both long for those headier days when we'd meant something to each other, but they were gone. Now we only wrought misery on ourselves; too much had happened, too many hurts. Neither of us had space left in our hearts for any more of that.

But endings, I don't do well.

My father threw himself into the bottle when his playing days came to a close. The mighty Cannis Dury, the hard-as-nails match winner, the sweeper with the silver studs. He never lost his desire to fight, he merely swapped his opponents – battered his wife and children into submission instead.

My brother Michael, dead and gone. Another end met unfairly. But what could I have done? Me, a washed-up loser. A hack who hadn't had a decent byline in the best part of a year. A burned-out fuck-up who'd stumbled upon a line digging about in people's dirty business. Gus Dury, he's yer man . . . Used to be a good investigative reporter, one of the best . . . Now he's the go-to guy for rooting out any half-dodgy caper in the town. Cheap too. Ply him with scoosh and he might just forget to charge you.

I appalled myself. I had gone beyond self-loathing; I no longer recognised me. This trembling, incoherent wreck of a man was no one I knew. No one I wanted to know.

The room grew dark.

Cold.

I heard the suck and wash of the tide, lapping at the beach.

A man in a black cape walked into the room. I couldn't see his face, but I sensed he was smiling. He held out a storm lantern. The light dazzled me, near burned the retinas out my eyes.

'Ah, get that the fuck away!' I yelled.

My arms flapped about my head.

The man spoke, but I couldn't comprehend him.

The light burned, right into the core of my being. I could see nothing but bright white light. Burning. Searing into me. And then, the bats came. Far off at first, but getting closer, louder. They swooped. I could feel the rush of the wind they travelled on. I could hear their wings, their screeching. I opened my eyes, their teeth . . . I saw their pointed, bloodied teeth—

'Gus, Gus, it's me, Hod!'

A slap across my face. Beads of sweat fell from my fringe. My eyes smarted. I couldn't breathe. I was panicked, kicking out with my feet, flailing arms like a lunatic.

'Gus, get a grip!' Hod roared. His hand on my shoulder shook me into submission. In an instant everything seemed still, becalmed. My vision returned, the room was bright again. I could see the whisky bottle in Hod's grasp; snatched it up.

I twisted the cap in my mouth and spat it out. My teeth stung but the sweet smell of whisky took away the pain. I felt my dry, dead body coming back to life; at the throat at first, then in my chest and the pit of my stomach. Clarity, a moment like no other. My head began to still.

My hands stopped flapping. I began to settle. I could feel my heart beating; it was a strange sensation, otherworldly. But I was alive. And that was something.

Hod helped me up, took me to rest on the window ledge.

'Thanks,' I said.

He shook his head. 'What for?'

That was a stupid question if ever I'd heard one. 'Look, I know you're in a bad way here, mate . . . I'm not saying I'm doing any better – Christ, worse probably – but I've got yer back.'

Hod pressed out a weak smile. 'Thanks.'

He eased himself off the window ledge, took out some papers from the inside pocket of his jacket. 'I got this drawn up.'

Looked like a contract, same lettering as on the cards was on the headed notepaper. *Gus Dury, Private Investigator.*

'Oh, Christ.'

'Gus, we need to do this right. We need to let this Laird woman see we mean business.'

I read the contract; it was a straightforward terms of engagement. He was hitting her for £400 a day, plus expenses.

'Jesus, aiming high, are you not?'

'She wants the best . . . The best charge.'

'I thought there was a reward?'

'There is, we have to show her we mean business, though.' Hod spun on his heels, broke into a trot as he headed for the bedroom. He returned with a large Oxfam bag in his arms. He opened it up, fished out a tweed jacket.

'Here, get this on.'

'You're kidding!'

He shook his head. 'Do I look like I'm fucking kidding? . . . I spent my last fifty sheets on this. Put it on, Gus, it'll help you look the part.'

'No way! I don't do tweed!'

'Why not?'

'For the same reason I don't buy Happy Meals – not my style.'

Hod lifted up the jacket, showed me the arms. 'Get it on, Gus . . . You're not going to meet Gillian Laird looking like some washed-up fucking jakey.'

'Hod, think it'll take more than a new bit of Harris to pull that off.'

His look of defeat said it all.

CHAPTER 5

There are some parts of the city I feel more comfortable in than others. I like Leith – I'm working class, it's in the contract. Drop me in the East End, up the Hibs park, even on match day, I can feel at home. But take me to the tourist-thronged Old Town, or the New Town with its wanky style centre, I feel ready to chuck.

We have hills in Edinburgh like you wouldn't believe. Climb any one of them and you can look down on the shambles of cobbles and spires with something close to wonder. The place looks the dog's. Pretty, even. But appearances can be deceptive.

'This it?'

It was one of the Georgian crescents off Palmerston Place, serious-wedge territory. The estate agents needed special sales signs to fit all the Bobby De Niros on.

Hod hoofed it to the front door, clocked the number, checked his little notebook, said, 'We've landed.'

'Thank Christ.' The schlep from the bus stop

had near ended me. 'We need to get some wheels, Hod.'

'Yeah, yeah . . . Mac has the van. I'll call him later.'

Mac too, another nutter on the job: could things get any worse? I shuddered to think. Wondered what I was getting myself into. Doorstepping high-profile Scottish acting royalty, a matter of days after the death of a child, didn't seem any plan I wanted to be part of. Especially dressed in tweed, looking like the fucking Man from the Pru, and with Hod clutching a contract in his mitt. It wasn't me. None of this gumshoe caper was me. What the fuck was I playing at? I'd been hoyed along on another one of Hod's hare-brained ideas, buoyed by his enthusiasm, his unremitting optimism that I knew was founded on squat. Zilch. He was up for this because he could think of nothing else. He was mad for it because he was fucking mad. But someone needed to sort him out – someone needed to pull his arse out of the fire. Didn't look like anyone else was stepping up to the job. Was gonna have to be me.

'Hod . . . mate, look, are you sure this is wise?'

'*Wha'*?'

'I mean, she's not gonna button up the back. She'll see through us, man.'

He dipped his head, rested his chin on his barrel chest. 'Gus, trust me.'

That was a laugh – I seemed to remember hearing that a few times before . . . usually preceding some kind of catastrophe: a door slammed in my face; good kicking; Debs packing a bag.

'Hod, I just think—'

He slayed that move by pressing the doorbell. Loud theatrical chimes sounded; three, maybe four little dogs yapped behind the glass.

A dark figure loomed, rattling keys.

Hod spoke: 'Remember, Gus, I need this . . . *we* need this.'

Did I need reminding?

'Shut the fuck up, eh.'

The door edged an inch, caught on a chain, closed again.

'Seriously, Gus . . . screw the nut. *Now.*'

As the door opened a ginger Pomeranian snapped at my ankles, then two other indeterminate bundles followed, barking and generally throwing a shit fit. Felt my 'please, God' face forming. Swept it aside. There was a bigger picture here: Shaky's name had been put up – Hod's card was marked.

Hod fronted the man in black, grey-haired and stiff-collared. Did people still have butlers these days? Holyfuckingshitballs. I was appalled how the other half lived. A few soap operas, slot in the *Big Brother* house, all the usual piss and wind generated by *Hello!* and *OK!* and suddenly you're living the *Upstairs, Downstairs* life. Not for the first time, I wanted to throw.

Hod spoke, 'Good morning. I'd like to speak with the lady of the house.'

Couldn't help it, had to laugh. Muttered, 'Lady of the house . . .'

Hod slit his eyes at me, put his hands behind his back and squared his stance. 'Is Gillian Laird at home?'

The suited gadgie turned up an eyebrow, was as close to incitement as I'd seen; screamed derision. I had this little arse-licker pegged as an adept in the art of greasy pole climbing. Would have been a shit-shoveller before ascending the stairs to the big hoose.

He peered down his nose, chipped, 'And you might be?'

I'd be fucked if I was pandering to this prick.

Easing past Hod, I fronted him. 'Look, bonny lad, we're here to speak to the organ grinder, not the monkey. Go and get herself, there's a good chap.'

That got his goat. His thin lips parted for a moment, revealing falsies that needed longer in the Steradent cup. He said, 'If you don't have an appointment, I can't—'

Enough was enough. I dipped into the pocket of the tweed, handed him one of Hod's newly printed cards. It took all my strength to stop myself posting it in his mush. 'You might want to tell her this can't wait.'

Jeeves took the card, made a face as if the poker in his arse had just twitched, then invited us to wait in the corridor.

The dogs followed us in, barking and yapping

all to fuck. It hurt my head so much I wanted to put fingers in my ears but they soon lost interest in us, started to calm. Hod was less relaxed. It unsettled me to see him so desperate, so unlike the Hod I knew. He'd always been so confident, so cocksure of himself. It was as though I was watching him dwindle before my eyes.

'What's up with you now?' I said.

'Did you have to noise him up?'

'Hod, the guy's a tool.'

'I'm only saying . . . Can we be professionals here.'

'Professionals . . . You think we're playing Bodie and Doyle, fuck off.'

'Gus, just cool yer jets, eh. At least till we've got her signature on that contract.'

I shook my head, turned eyes to the corniced ceiling, said, 'Whatever.'

There's a phrase, *through you like a dose of salts*, could tell from the off this chick was ready to put it into action. The heels came clacking on the tiled floor like sniper fire. She had a hard, drawn face that was softened only slightly by what looked like a Hermès scarf. You write the odd magazine feature in your time, you get to know the kip of the pricey gear.

Gillian Laird stopped a couple of yards from us. She wore long black trousers and a black cashmere top. When she put her hands on her hips she looked like a very familiar work of art. Fuck me, was I a bit star-struck? Told myself to calm down – she'd done *River City* after all.

She looked me in the eye, seemed to register disbelief, then her gaze quickly darted to Hod. She was weighing us up, no question. Said, 'Gus Dury . . .' then thrust out the card. Was I supposed to take it back? Leave?

Stepped up to the plate, nodded, 'That's my name.'

She took a deep breath, her cheeks pinching as she looked me up and down. Got the distinct impression she thought I was taking the piss. Her expression yelled: *There's a pikey in my house.* I inwardly cursed Hod for making me wear the tweed – felt like a Terence Stamp caught shoplifting.

'Should it mean something to me?'

Hod interrupted, 'Mrs Laird, we believe we might be able to help you with—'

She opened her mouth a little, lowered the card, then quickly folded her arms. It was a defensive stance. Her gaze flitted left to right as she barked, 'Help me with what?'

I could see Hod's anxiety rising. If I let him start yakking he'd be like a dog eating chips. I took the reins: 'I have some experience in dealing with the particular situation you find yourself in, Mrs Laird.'

An improbably tall blonde appeared at her back. She had a rack Jordan would have been intimidated by and a pair of lips set in a permanent pout. She looked groomed to within an inch of her life as she sidled up to the actress and put an arm around her waist. When she placed her head on her shoulder she reminded me of the models I used to see coming into the paper to shoot fashion spreads. They all looked like unattainable goddesses, until they opened their gobs and you realised they were schemies.

Gillian spoke: 'Is this some kind of joke?'

She handed the card to the blonde. She stared at Gillian for a moment and then said to me, 'I know you . . . Yer the reporter guy.'

There it was, the schemie inside . . . Who says you can't polish a turd?

Hod blustered, 'Mr Dury specialises in investigative work now.'

I could have given him a slap. The woman was on the verge of kicking us out; could this have gone any worse? What had I been thinking, taking Hod's word that this was a goer?

'*Does* he now?' said Gillian.

I watched her weigh up what looked like several possibilities. One was obviously calling the filth, but there was a flicker of desperation in there – as though she couldn't rule out anything, however weak. Or maybe she just thought I looked the part: rat catchers don't dress in pinstripes. She turned her head, spun on her heels, a shrill tone in her voice as she commanded, 'Follow me.'

Hod winked as we set off behind her. The blonde bit turned once or twice, drew a few daggers at us, but I figured her approval we could live without.

In an immaculate white drawing room, the black silhouette of Gillian Laird cut an incongruous figure. She looked bullet hard as she perched on the edge of a giant sofa, crossed her legs, patted the cushion beside her. 'Sit down, Tina.' Her friend did as she was told. I thought she was out of her league – what the Scots call *all fur coat and nae knickers*. But her face was her fortune; throw in the figure and she was commanding a tidy sum. Maybe Gillian thought she could knock off a few rough edges here and there, or maybe rough was a nice change.

'Okay, what's the story, Mr Dury?' said Gillian.

I felt as if I was put in the spotlight; an urge to rifle her shelves for a whisky bottle flashed. Calmed it, took hold again: 'I believe there's some case to doubt the official verdict on your son's death.'

'You do?'

She was hardballing me. I didn't buy that she was all granite, though. There was an artist lurking in there and that required some sliver of sensitivity.

'I believe . . . you do.'

She looked at Tina. I noticed their fingers had laced. 'My son was killed, Mr Dury.'

'The police said it was death by *misadventure*.' I'd spat it out, came too harsh and I immediately regretted it.

'They called it *breath-control play*! . . . Bullshit. I know my Ben, he would never . . . He was far too sensible, too smart to . . .' Her resolve dropped, eyes misted; but she pulled it in. 'Mr Dury, why are you here? I mean . . . what do you think you can do for me?'

'It's fir the money,' said Tina. She had a heavy accent, sounded Leith. *Christ*, sounded Leith Links.

Hod butted in: 'We're professionals, Mrs Laird. We have a track record that can be verified. We don't enter into any undertaking of this nature without serious consideration to the known—'

I stood up. 'If your son was killed, I'll find his killer.'

Tina put a long pale arm around Gillian's shoulder. I saw some bruising on her wrist; it was dark against the skin. She spoke loudly: 'You sound right confident, so you do.'

I held schtum. Wasn't getting into a barney with this bint. Felt my chest cry for nicotine. A finger went up to my collar.

'Gus is the best there is,' said Hod.

Gillian's eyes darted to him. 'The best?'

I walked towards the couch, crouched down in front of them. I was close enough to see the red edges of the actress's eyes, the tears welling. She needed help; I knew the territory. For the first time since I'd arrived my sympathies sparked. I knew I could bring some ease to that deep suffering. Made me feel useful – if not entirely capable. Hoped my health would hold out. I reached inside me for the right words. 'If you like,

I could look into this for you. I promise you this: things are never quite as they seem . . . If there's an answer that can ease your pain, I'll get it.'

She turned to Tina, nodded to her.

We all rose, stood in the middle of the floor facing each other like an AA meeting.

'Perhaps we can discuss terms, Mr Dury.'

Hod reached for the contract in his pocket.

I spoke up: 'There are one or two things I'll need to know first, Mrs Laird.'

The door to the drawing room opened. It was the butler again, showing in a young lad of about eighteen in a checked sportscoat. He had red hair that, despite a heavy application of gel, burned the eyes. He looked shocked to see Hod and I, but fought it. I looked him up and down – he turned away.

'Hello, Paul . . . Do you mind hanging on a minute? I'm just seeing to something,' said Gillian.

The lad fumbled his words: 'Oh, no . . . not at all.' Some sheets of paper fell from a folder in his arms. I watched him collect them up. He bumped his shins on the coffee table as he went about it. 'Sorry, I'll just get this tidied up.'

'Paul is a . . . was a friend of Ben's.'

The lad halted, a few more sheaves of paper fluttering to the floor. 'Ben was my best friend,' he said. 'We were on the same course.'

'Oh, really,' I said. Thought about telling him he might want to change course in that case, but got the impression a wisecrack might snap him in two.

Gillian took Paul by the arm, led him back out and asked her man to get him a drink in the kitchen; she closed the door behind him and sat back down. I made a mental note to have a word with young Ginge at some point in the future.

Was a mother the best person to go to for the rundown on her only son? Seriously doubted it. Christ on a bike, my own mam would paint a rosy enough picture of me, and I was pretty far south of any kind of respectability. Gillian Laird had shifted into default gear to tell me about her deceased boy, Ben. I knew she was hurting. I'd lost loved ones, knew the manor, but I got the impression our actress was laying on the histrionics a bit too thick.

'My boy was an angel.' She rose from the sofa, crossed the immaculate carpet to raise a silver photo frame from the dresser. 'He never had a bad word to say for anyone; never heard a cross word leave his lips.'

I caught Hod creasing his brows, rolling eyes up to the ceiling. Was one of those moments calling out for an elbow to the ribs; let it slide. Went with, 'Gillian . . . Do you mind if I call you Gillian?'

'No, that's fine.'

'Was there anyone who might not have . . . shared your opinion of Ben?' I said.

She looked startled, flustered. A pale hand rose to her cheek, then was clasped tightly in the fingers of her other. She looked rattled by the thought, genuinely thrown at the notion.

'No . . . no one . . . Ben was the most adored child.'

Her son was nineteen; that made him a man in my books. I was still young enough to remember what I was up to at that age – none of it was something I'd be opening up to my mother about. Late teens carry more secrets than the Masons. Had she never watched *The Inbetweeners*?

'Your son, Gillian . . . he was at the university?'

'Yes,' my words had hit her like arrows, 'he was a good student,' a laugh, feint one, '. . . when he put his mind to it.'

'What do you mean by that?'

Her eyes were wide, trailing some distant memory. They misted momentarily then dimmed. 'Ben liked to be the centre of attention . . . always had, since he was a child. My husband . . . ex-husband, always said he inherited my dramatic tendencies.'

I knew the type: show-offs. Class clowns. Needy kids. The boys and girls so lavishly danced attendance upon by Mammy and Daddy that the real world always fails to deliver a big enough audience. Edinburgh was crawling with them. Always had been. Throw in a leisured class, proliferation of public schools and the brats come ten a penny. Couldn't say I was warming to our Ben.

'He was popular?' I chose my phrasing carefully.

'Oh, yes . . . very popular.'

'With whom?'

That bit. She slit eyes, went hellcat on me: 'With everyone, of course!'

'Gillian, I don't mean to be disrespectful, but you and I both know that's seldom the case outside of maybe Gandhi and Elvis Presley.'

She arked up; her eyes became needlepoints, the thin slit of a mouth widened to a cavity ready to spew forth enough bile to blow me into the middle of next week.

'My boy was adored! . . . By everyone!'

Okay. Registered that one.

Was time to move on. I made a mental note to keep all emotive questions away from her; I couldn't rely on getting any kind of truthful answer anyway. This was a downer for sure, but there were many other ways Gillian Laird could make herself useful.

I pressed on. 'He was at university . . . What year?'

'Erm, second . . . he was in his second year.'

'Studying?'

'Media and arts.'

A typical pisspot subject for a spoilt little rich kid. Still, was one up on windsurfing and Beatlemania, I suppose, although a BSc in either would be as much use as a nun's tits in the current job market. I'm sure it worried neither of them.

'I'll need to see his timetable . . . and can you supply a list of his friends?'

'Yes, yes, of course. I am about to be made rector of the university, I don't know if that's something you know – it's not been released yet . . .'

I hadn't heard. This was a turn-up for the books.

Edinburgh Uni rectors had come down in standing compared to previous post-holders – the country's celebrity obsession had seen to that – but the job still carried some clout. Not least affording the appointee a nice profile. Sure that had nothing to do with her throwing her hat in the ring, though. Actors going for more press? Never.

'You are? When was this decided?'

'Erm . . . just now, well, within the last few days.'

Ben had died nearly a week ago now. I didn't think the two incidents were related; not in any obvious sense, anyway.

'Who told you about the . . . appointment?'

'Mr Calder . . . Joe, the head of form. He was coordinating my campaign with . . . Ben.' She gave in to emotion; her chin sunk onto her chest and she returned to the couch, head in hands. The blonde put a hand on her leg. She had very big hands; I figured she was the one playing the quasi-male role in this relationship. I almost sniggered at my lack of political correctness. Knew Hod was storing up a power of strap-on jokes to come.

'Ben was working on your campaign?'

'Yes . . . why?'

'No reason. Just trying to form a picture.'

'Surely the two incidents aren't related.'

I coughed on the back of my hand. 'Probably not.'

'Then why ask?'

I felt my lungs call for nicotine; my stomach was

calling for something else. 'Gillian, if I'm to get to the bottom of this case, there will be a lot more questions . . . some of them pretty uncomfortable.'

The blonde patted her back, clasped her hand tightly. As she leaned in closer I saw her belly button was pierced with a silver bow.

'I understand, I understand,' Gillian nodded.

'To that list . . . can you add all the campaign contacts, university staff especially.'

She nodded again.

'Of course. I'll let you have all those details, Mr Dury.'

Hod rose at my side; we'd covered all the ground we could, for now.

On the way to the door I had a Columbo moment: 'Oh, one more thing . . .'

'Yes?'

'How much clout at the university does this post of yours carry?'

'I'm sorry . . . what do you mean?'

'I mean, is it honorary, or can you throw some weight about?'

She flustered, 'Erm, I have some core responsibilities . . . It's mainly for profile, but I do get to sit on a few committees.'

I buttoned up my tweed, said, 'That might be very useful to me.'

CHAPTER 6

I took myself off for a tab whilst Hod presented the paperwork to Madam; had a feeling this wasn't going to be one of his better working relationships. Something about being lorded over by a snooty-nosed actress that got his goat. Call him picky.

The tweed was uncomfortable, had me shuffling shoulders to try and make the bastard wearable. I imagined a cloth-capped trail of my ancestors queuing up to chuck in the road. Christ Almighty, I'd be in brogues next, or worse, imperial collars and a dickie bow. What was I doing mixing it with posh twats? How little a fuck did I give for the loss of one more chinless rugger bugger with a trust fund and a silver spoon up his arse?

Thought: Not the attitude, Gus. I'd seen the look of hurt, real grief, on Gillian's face and it touched me. The woman deserved justice – however much she had in the bank. Blood was blood, and the loss of it wounds us all.

Hod was hurting too. This was a payday for the man who had saved my arse more than once.

I needed to screw the nut, put aside all my class prejudices and go to work. One thing was for sure: something wasn't right here. And that did have my attention. Call me creeped out by the whole lesbo affair thing, but that dirty blonde in there was hiding something. Pound to a pail of shite she'd sussed I was on to her as well.

Hod appeared. 'Right, let's mush.' He looked none too charmed. Pissed, even.

'Who stole yer toffee?' I said.

He marched off down the road, headed for the bus stop. There was no sign of the contract.

'Well, are we in business or not?'

'Y'wha'?'

I put a hand out, stopping him in his tracks. 'Are we on Her Ladyship's books?'

Hod knocked my arm away, slumped off again. 'Like fuck.'

'Eh? She didn't sign the contract, then?'

A grunt, bit of a tut. 'What do you think?'

'I'll take that as a no.'

Hod spun, fronted me, 'She's running the contract past her lawyer.'

'Well, what did you expect?'

'A bit more professionalism.'

'Sounds fair enough to me . . . Think because you get a few cards printed up yer Duncan fucking Bannatyne? Grow sense, man.'

Hod took off again. 'Yeah, well . . . that's the good news.'

Didn't like the sound of that. Had been put to

me as a done deal, easy money. Suddenly that image collapsed like a house of cards.

'Good news? What's the bad?'

'She didn't go for the expenses either . . . and our retainer's only two hundred a day.'

'Fuck.'

'Exactly.' Hod took out his phone, pressed it to his ear. 'I did push for a bumped-up bonus, though. Might be an idea to flush out a speedy result, Gus.'

Speedy result. This was a suspicious death we were talking about, not some fucking shunt and punt for Tam's Hot Car Lot. There was no quiet road to the truth, I knew that from bitter experience. This was added pressure I could do without.

'Yo, Mac,' Hod barked into the phone, 'get yer skanky arse down here and give us a lift, eh.' He gave out the location, hung up. 'He's on his way.'

Didn't fancy bussing it again, felt relieved. Sparked up a Lambert and Butler and watched swirls of smoke make for the sky. The sun peeked out through the clouds, put a few rays about. Felt unnatural. But the city always did at Festival time. Could almost feel the crusty carnival spreading down from the Mile; the rattle of piercings and Home Counties accents a heady mix.

Hod calmed, seemed deep in thought. He didn't look as if he was thinking about the case. It was a *my arse is on the line* expression.

Chugged on the tab, said, 'What about that performance in there, then?'

Hod scratched his chin. Held schtum.

I went on, 'Yon Tina's playing her cards close to her chest.'

He laughed, 'Like she's a choice . . . her arms are only three feet long!'

I welcomed the return of humour. 'You get the impression she's . . .'

'Got something to hide?'

'Yeah. Or maybe, I dunno, is pulling on an altogether different set of levers to Gillian.'

Hod put his back against the wall, sighed. 'So, what you thinking?'

I was thinking we didn't have much to go on, that I didn't know where to start. 'The university's gonna be pleased to see us.'

'They won't welcome any digging around, that's for sure. Stuffy old place like that, they'll not be putting out the red carpet.'

'Far fucking from it.'

Hod turned. 'You think they'll be awkward?'

I knew for sure they'd be that; what I didn't know was how I was going to get around it. All my previous encounters with academia had ended in abject failure; I'd have to work smarter – the nick of me, harder sure as hell wasn't an option.

'You see much of Amy these days?' I asked. Amy had been a trainee reporter of mine back in the day, till she got ideas about practising a little more than shorthand with me . . . on the company's time. She'd been punted, then resurfaced with a passion to pick up where she'd left off. But Hod had got keen on her and saved me the trouble of holding her at bay.

'Amy? . . . Not in months. Why ask?'

'Well, last I heard she was a student.'

'Yeah . . . at the uni,' said Hod. He took his hands out his pockets, pointed at me. 'You thinking what I think you're thinking?'

'What's that?'

'Honey trap?'

I had to laugh. What was this, espionage? 'Shit no, man. I was thinking she might be able to do a bit of groundwork, maybe sniff out the word around campus.'

Hod shook his head. 'I don't know . . .'

'What?' I was scoobied. This was a perfect opportunity to make an in, both for the case and for him.

Hod turned down his lip, showing his bottom row of teeth. 'Do you remember the state she was in last time round?'

She'd went overboard, got herself a pole-dancing gig at a strip joint in the Pubic Triangle, ended up with some cell time and a threat of prostitution charges from plod. Hod was right about one thing: we didn't want a repeat of that. But she was a smart girl; surely she'd have matured a bit in the intervening years. And this was small-time. I mean, how risky could it be for her to go shake down a few plooky students?

'That was a different matter entirely, Hod.'

He looked away. 'If you say so.'

‘What, you don’t? You think I’d put her in any danger?’

He shrugged. Set wide eyes on me. I got the message, loud and clear. Perhaps he was right – women like Amy always complicate matters. I had another idea to get to the facts, but it was a longer shot. Letting him think I was playing safe, said, ‘Okay, maybe we’ll put Amy on the bench for now.’

He seemed genuinely pleased. ‘Good, I think that’s for the best.’ Could tell he was still keen on the girl; another complication I could do without.

As I put my tab under the sole of my Doc Marten, white-van man screeched into the street at speed. It was Mac.

‘This our wheels?’ Was a Bedford Midi, white, but wearing almost as much rust. ‘Jesus Christ . . .’

Mac leaned out the window. ‘Your chariot awaits.’

We looked at him, said nowt. Took the sliding door and got in. Mac gunned it, Hod and I rolled onto our sides in the back.

‘Mac, cool the fucking beans, eh,’ shouted Hod.

‘Aye, okay, okay . . . It’s a bit jumpy in the low gears. Needs a servicing.’

‘Don’t we fucking all . . . but just keep the heid, eh.’ Hod brushed dust from his coatsleeve. ‘So, you were saying . . .’

‘What we want is an inside track.’

‘Come again?’

‘Some way of getting amongst the students and fishing out what the word is.’

'Well, we're both a bit long in the tooth for that gig. Don't think we'd even pull off the mature student act.'

Mac shouted back to us, 'What the fuck are you pair jabbering about?'

'A job.'

'What?'

'We're on a job . . . at the university.'

Mac laughed it up. 'Only job you pair of widos will find at the university will be as fucking jannies!'

Hod's eyes beamed, a smile split his face. 'I think he's onto something.'

Got my vote. Said, 'Maybe you're right.'

CHAPTER 7

Got off the bus at North Bridge. Had managed two steps before some skanky yoof with a lip piercing started to seriously agg me, walking backwards waving fliers for a comedy gig. Got to love Festival time. I tried to walk around him, went left, then right. Wasn't happening. Skinny jeans and Converse All Stars working overtime to keep up.

'What's your comedy passion, geezer?'

Did he just call me geezer? 'Comedy passion . . . Go away and find sense, lad.'

Undeterred: 'You look like a serious man. Political satire, I'm guessing?'

'What's that . . . Harpo Marx?'

Still undeterred, those matchstick legs doubled their pace. He wasn't giving up. But he was new to this patter, I had that sussed early on. Turning my stride towards the edge of the pavement, I subtly steered Student Grant at the pile of cardboard boxes outside Argos. His legs actually managed to fly in the air at the same time as he hit them. His arse thudded into the boxes like an anvil falling on Wile E. Coyote. Managed a laugh;

almost felt grateful to him for that. Not grateful enough to help him pick up the fliers that floated into the gutter though.

At the uni I had a deep sense of unease; felt ready to go off like a ten-bob rocket. Had already had enough of the type of brat who frequented this joint. Was relieved beyond words to see the place virtually empty. I fronted a tabard-wearing old girl with a mop. 'Hello, there . . .'

World-weary eyes rolled skyward. 'Aye?'

'I was wondering, who's running the show right now? Looks like the *Mary Celeste* in here.'

Didn't register. I got pointed to the stairs, 'Office is up there, might find some folk knocking about . . . Might no', mind.'

I thanked her, gave a grateful nod, went for the stairs. I could feel the alcohol oozing through my pores. There was a cold sweat rising on my brow and an icicle forming on my spine. I knew it was time for a heart-starter, blast on the Grouse to melt the frost; knew that was an unlikely shout for the foreseeable. My stomach griped, threatened to start greetin'. I clenched fists in my pockets and tried to stamp the craving out on the marble steps. At the top landing I headed for the door. The office was empty save some tweedy Morningside lady with a teapot, mid-pour. Said, 'Hello there.'

The biddy looked startled. The spout trembled; some tea escaped onto the saucer. 'Oh, dear, dear.' She started to move some papers away from the spreading spill.

I walked over, gave her a hand. She pressed out a weak smile, showing some yellowed teeth. 'Thanks.'

'I'm looking for Mr Calder.'

'Oh yes . . . he's in today.'

Playing it cool: 'He is. Grand.'

She took a box of man-size tissues from a desk drawer. 'He's been in the whole time. Pretty much gave up his vacation since the, well, y'know . . .'

I watched her mop up the tea. 'Since the . . . ?'

'Incident.' She spoke sharply, I missed all intonation. Thought: Pity – would like to have noted that.

'You mean the Ben Laird . . . incident.'

She straightened her back, eyed me full-on. 'Yes.' She walked away with the pile of wet tissues, dropped them in a bin on the other side of the desk, said, 'If you're looking for Joe, he's in his office.' A hand went onto her hip. She pointed to the door, continued, 'Down the corridor, second door on the left . . . His name's on the front.'

I smiled, thanked her. Something about her manner, about the way she dismissed Ben's death as no more than an *incident*, like it was all just an inconvenience, troubled me. I wanted to press her but I knew this wasn't the time. Probably wasn't the place either, but I'd be fucked if I was giving Joe Calder the same consideration. The man at the helm needed his buttons pressed right away. There was something about this case that reeked of cover-up – of those with the power abusing it.

Turned for the corridor; took the oak boards all the way down to the white-painted door with the brass nameplate on it. The prick had been pretentious enough to have the string of letters engraved after his name too. Cut no ice with me. Thought about knocking but it's not my style.

Strode in, took a look about. Calder was fifty-odd, but could have passed for ten years shy of that mark. He had a lot of hair, swept back over a high forehead and tucked behind his ears, sitting in tight curls above his shoulders. From a certain angle it looked like a very bad mullet, the kind that sat over a Klem top on Hibs casuals of the eighties. Didn't rate my chances of getting along with him. Maybe it was the ox-blood brogues. He sat upright, seemed to focus on my tweed, calmed some, said, 'Is there something I can help you with?'

I strolled to the bookshelves beside his desk, eyeballing the titles. Lit on some Foucault, Sartre, Derrida . . . maybe he wasn't a total arsewipe after all. I wasn't betting on that, though. He got out of his chair, started to stroll over to me. 'Excuse me, but is there something I can help you with?'

I turned, gave him the once-over, head to toe, said, 'Might just be, Joe . . . might just be.'

His brows lifted. A loose curl of dark hair unfurled from his fringe, he swept it back with a very weak wrist movement, went, 'Do I know you?'

'I don't know, Joey Boy . . . do you?'

The puzzled look turned to panic. 'Look, what the hell is this? You come into my office and—'

I raised a hand to my mouth, motioned *shush.* He stilled, stepped back, it has to be said, nervously.

I went, 'I've been speaking to . . . your new rector.'

'What . . . I mean, what do you mean?'

'Shouldn't that be a why . . . or perhaps even a when?'

He ran fingers through his hair, straining to produce a dim smile. 'Right . . . this is some kind of joke, is it? Has Gillian put you up to this?'

I moved past him, sat on the edge of his desk. Stubbed a finger into the thick layer of dust, blew it away. 'Joke . . . do you think Gillian's in the mood for jokes after her son's been murdered?'

Calder's face drained of all expression. If there was any colour left it was in his lips . . . and they were blue.

'Don't forget to breathe, Joey Boy. I hear that can seriously impair your health . . . Y'know, like a fucking noose round your neck.'

He raised his hands to his ears, splayed fingers, then shot past me, ran for the other side of the desk and picked up the phone. He bashed a few digits, said, 'Margaret, Margaret . . . is that you?'

I followed his steps slowly, faced him.

Calder said, 'Good, can you please get that security guard up here, I have—'

I reached over the desk, cut off the phone. Calder stood with the receiver in his hand, looked at it, looked back to me, said, 'I want you out of here right now . . . whoever you are, I want you off the premises right now or I'm calling the police.'

I started to chuckle; couldn't remember putting the shits up another grown man with such ease. 'Look, Joey Boy, who the fuck do you think you're kidding? We both know the last person you want round here is plod.'

He lowered the phone, placed the receiver in its cradle. As he did so the door behind me swung open. A borderline obese fifty-something with a Ray Reardon slick came puffing in and nodded breathlessly towards us. 'Everything okay here, Mr Calder?' The words came out slowly, gave us all time to think.

'Erm, no, Mick . . . actually, I mean, yes . . . everything's fine.'

I gave the security guard a tug of the forelock; he backed out the door like a trained spaniel. Knew inside of five he'd be back in his doocot scratching his balls and whistling through his teeth at the high nipple-count in the *Star*.

I waited for the footsteps to fade from the corridor, let Calder be seated, said, 'Now then, quite a sorry fucking mess we have here, eh?'

'I don't know what you're referring to at all but—'

I cut him off, slamming hands on the desk. 'Don't cunt me around, Joey Boy . . . or it might just be your scrawny neck in the noose next.'

You get guys with out-there hairstyles, there's usually a reason for it: mam did them a bowl-cut right through to their teenage years; maybe they got stuck on Bono's *Joshua Tree* look, never got over themselves, or woke up to the fact that U2, and Bono especially, were such a bunch of wank that it was actually deeply embarrassing to contemplate. Joe Calder, it suddenly struck me, was wearing his hair long for much simpler reasons – if he didn't, he'd be the spit of Louis Theroux. He had the selfsame gangly gait, the slightly lost look to the eyes, hiding behind double-glazed glasses that could do with a good wipe. He also had that stalled, almost addled, way of communicating; like a deeply self-conscious teenager who wanted desperately to stay a small child because it had worked so well for him in the wrapping-adults-round-their-little-finger stakes. He was a man-child; guessed he'd been spoon-fed through life. He'd probably came straight to academia from his own schooling and never left because he had found the perfect place to hide. I don't think I'd ever met a man more deserving of a slap around . . . Christ Almighty, disguising the look of Louis Theroux with a fucking Michael Bolton hairstyle was seriously call-the-doctor time.

'Right, Joey Boy . . . you and me are gonna have a bit of a chat here.'

He fidgeted in his chair; the castors beneath him squeaked. He held schtum. Gave him this: he had marbles, knew when to keep his trap shut. There was nothing he could come up with that was going to dig him out with me. I had him pegged as up to his nuts in Ben Laird's death and I wasn't letting up on him. The sheer look of this streak of piss was enough to have me gantin' for his scalp; fact I had him on the back foot was all a bonus.

I eased back – felt like a leopard with a gazelle – ready to cane some big-time arse. 'Yeah, make yourself comfortable, Joey . . . I'll be taking my time here.'

He got jumpy, arked up, 'Look, I have plenty to be getting on with . . . without this.'

I laughed in his face. 'Trust me, laddo, you'll have fuck all else to be getting on with for the foreseeable.' I put the bead on him. Caught his eye; my own was steel, but he blinked and looked away to the bookshelves. Thought to tell him there were no answers there for him; he could keep his learning. Way I was playing it, there was no *Dummies* guide could help him. I kept it zipped, though, let him squirm a bit, wonder what in the name of fuck I was playing at.

I strolled over to the window, stared out, removed a pack of Rothmans and sparked up. 'Quite a spot you have here,' I said. I turned head in time to see Calder shrug. Of course he had no idea how nice a spot this was, he'd known nothing else; slogging in a call centre or wheeling tyres at Kwik Fit wasn't ever on the cards for this arsewipe. I drew deep on my tab, felt a heavy craving for something a bit stronger. My throat constricted with every twinge of desire. I was suddenly in the ballpark of hallucinations; don't know where the feeling came from but it welled up in me, sent tremors through my bones. I wanted to shake myself, step outside my body, but there was nowhere to run. I was trapped. My hands started to tremble. I took a nervous glance at Calder – he was staring at his shoes, had seen nothing. The moment had passed off without incident, but I knew there was going to be a time when I wouldn't be so lucky.

I spat, 'Is this fucking office dry or what?'

'I don't . . . you mean alcohol?'

'What do you think? The middle classes not offer their guests a drop?'

He raised himself from the creaky chair, crossed the rugged boards to a little wooden cabinet. 'I actually don't drink myself.'

Great surprise indeed. 'Yeah, well, I do.'

That got me a glower. The balls on him.

The bottle of Glenfiddich was a fair age – had seen the logo updated at least once since it was last on the shelves – but it was still three-quarters full. He poured out two fingers' worth . . . Felt the frown creeping up my face. 'Jesus, wet the glass, would you!'

He poured in some more, smirked. If he thought this was the moral high ground he'd been clambering for, he was sorely mistaken. I was here to talk about a young lad's death . . . not my predilections and peccadilloes.

I grabbed the glass, said, 'Cop on, Joey . . . it's not me on trial.'

'I don't believe I am either.'

I slugged deep. 'Yeah well, not yet anyway.'

Pushing past him, I went over to the cabinet and retrieved the bottle to top up my glass. I was a bit overenthusiastic: my hand trembled as the whisky reached the brim and tipped over. I clawed it back, took a good pelt and prodded Louis Bolton back to his chair. He was far too malleable; even in my condition I could see this. There was no way I should be pushing him about so easily. It unsettled me. He was hiding something, deffo. Only the guy's social skills were so sub-*Rain Man* that he didn't know how to conceal it. He was conforming to type: the real world was out there, beyond the quadrangle . . . not somewhere Joey Boy often set foot. This was either going to be very easy, or next door to impossible. I knew if I pushed this loser too hard that he was going to cave, completely fold on me, and that would be it: no more from him.

The whisky settled my cravings, put my gut back a notch or two on the cement-mixer setting it had adopted earlier. I was functioning. Yep, that was the word, heard it all the time, I was a *functioning alcoholic*. Only, I knew it. I figured those jakeys on the street didn't have a scooby the nick they were in; I had that going for me, I had the nous to know I was fucked. F. Scott Fitzgerald described a first-rate intelligence as the ability to keep two seemingly opposed thoughts in your head at the same time; never really sussed what he meant, until now. By God, I knew there were conflicting emotions and thoughts flying around inside me:

I had the case to be getting on with, Hod to be dragged from the shit, and my insides crying to be put out of their misery, finished off . . . and, also in the pot, the deep knowledge that something wasn't right here. That there were people, people I didn't like much, covering up.

I had no pretensions to a first-rate intelligence as Fitzgerald described it – fuck, if I did, I wouldn't be in this kip – but I knew where he was coming from. I screwed the nut, tight.

'Okay, Joe, let's start in the low gears, eh?'

His eyes widened. 'I'm sorry, I don't quite understand.'

'I think the phrase is . . . take it from the top.'

'You're talking about Benjamin.'

I managed a wry smile. 'That's right, tell me about the night Ben . . . died.'

He eased himself back in the chair; the castors squealed out. The noise seemed to unsettle him, forced his palms together. He laced fingers, unlaced them, then wrung his hands out. 'I wasn't here, of course.'

'Of course . . .'

His eyes came up to meet mine. 'I mean I don't live on campus.'

I nodded, trying to appear calm, reassuring. 'Go on.'

He sighed. 'There was a call in the night, can't even remember who it was from . . . one of the security staff. They said the police were here and wanted to speak to someone.'

I kept my tone calm. 'That would be you.'

'Yes, well . . . someone had to.'

'Go on.'

'I came down and there was a phalanx . . .' he drew a line in the air, 'a wall . . .'

Was on my mind to say *I know what a bloody phalanx is*, but went with, 'The police?'

'Yes, they'd sealed off the route to the Grand Hall.'

'Why?'

'That's where they . . . found him.'

'And then . . . what?'

'Well, nothing . . . that was it, really. They told me there'd been a death, they had a name, and I identified him as one of the student body.'

Sounded very clinical, if not perfunctory. Could just be plod jumping to conclusions, looking for a quick wrap-up, but then again, none of this looked good for them . . . or the uni, the city, anyone. Lifting the carpet and sweeping it all under was never more appealing. Said, 'No one questioned you?'

Calder looked as though he'd been hit with a brick, 'Good God, no . . . Why would they . . . ? What do you mean?'

I finished my drink, reloaded, moved round to the front of the desk, eased myself down. 'A young lad was found dead . . . hanging from the rafters. You'd think questions would be asked . . . of someone.'

He got out of the chair. 'Are you implying . . . ?'

I wasn't implying anything. Wondered where the theatrics had sprung from. I pulled it back. 'Sit down, Joe . . . we're only talking here. A boy has died, smack bang in the middle of your manor. I'm guessing you'd like some answers as much as me . . . as much as his mother.'

The mention of Gillian put some steel in his spine. He found some reserves of cool. 'Yes, of course . . . it must be very difficult for the family.'

It seemed a cold thing to say, like it was the first time it had even crossed his mind. 'The woman has lost a son . . . she's finding it a bit more than difficult. She doesn't think Ben's hanging was as straightforward as the police and you want to believe . . . She wants answers.'

'Yes, I understand.'

'Do you, I mean do you really? . . . Gillian Laird is a very wealthy woman, she has influence and she has power, and that combination greases a lot of wheels in this town, Joey Boy.'

He scratched his head, turning that lank hair of his behind his ear again. 'I just don't see what I can do. I mean, I've told you all I know . . . I just work here. I'm not privy to every aspect of human interaction that takes place, I'm just a lecturer! I mean, what do you want me to say?'

He'd said plenty.

I could see Calder wasn't for caving on this first meet, but he'd said enough to let me know there was far more in the tank. He had something to say, and he'd be saying it, even if it had to be dragged out of him. I planned to stick around, keep a close eye on him. Knew he wouldn't like that, but fuck him, he wasn't the one with the hands on the levers. Said, 'Gillian tells me she sits on the recruitment board.'

He turned down his mouth. 'I think so . . . yes.'

'Say you were to appoint a new janitor . . . what would be the recruitment process?'

'A new *janitor*?'

'Well, let's skip the interview and CV and that . . . I fancy getting closer to the action – maybe we could just *pretend* I was the new janitor.'

He flustered. 'That would be irregular, to say the very least.'

I bolded it: 'And fucking murder isn't?'

Calder closed his mouth. I watched his Adam's apple rise slowly as he swallowed what looked like objections.

'How about you go hunt out one of those dust-coats for me, Joey Boy.'

CHAPTER 8

Hod had seen fit to warn me about keeping the course. Staying on track. By that he meant: off the sauce. If he thought he had any sway with me on matters of general inebriation, my daily state, he was deluded. Knew he understood that he carried no such weight at all. Hod, for all the heart in him, had a hard enough head to take reality as it comes. Which, truth told, scared the shit out of me.

I'd never seen the bloke so down on his luck; Hod was the archetypal hunter-gatherer. A survivor. Seeing his life unravel like this was a heartscald. Worse, being his only hope just turned the knife in me. This was about as close to a volte-face as you could get – Hod was usually the one bailing out my arse. If it wasn't buying the Holy Wall off me, it was subbing me the readies to take Debs down the aisle . . . and putting me up when our marriage hit the skids. Hod had pulled me through a few scrapes – it played heavy on my conscience at the best of times – but I'd never countenanced the possibility that I'd be asked to pay him back. Bastard picked his moments. There were times when I was together, stable, in the neighbourhood of happy, even. Christ, I'd had a gym membership once. But right now, at this particular point in time, I was about as lost as lost gets. If I could manage to keep myself together long enough to see the week out I'd be doing well. Felt a shiver run through me. A black crow swooped on the pavement, cawed. In a second it was off, vanished. Wondered if I'd seen it at all.

I schlepped past the Cameo, took myself into Victoria Wine and got in some essentials.

'Half Grouse, half Black Heart,' I said.

Young girl on the counter smiled; was a wry, pitying smile. Made my heart flutter, don't know why. Was well past hitting on chicks. That required far too much energy – something that was in very short supply right now.

'Anything else?' She wore an *Avengers* T-shirt, retro-style, covering quite a set too.

My mind played a trick on me, said, 'You know any good coffee shops around here?'

She blushed, thought I was gonna ask her for a date. 'Erm, well . . . there's the big Costa.' She couldn't keep eyes on me now, ran fingers through her black hair, tucked some behind her ear. God, I felt stupid . . . what was I thinking?

'Okay, cheers . . . will give it a look.'

She turned to the till. Put that sympathy smile on again.

'That'll be—'

I cut in, 'Oh, better give me forty Marlboro, too.'

'No worries.'

She bagged the lot and I hoofed it up the street, cringing.

You spend your days alone, drinking – hard-core drinking – the finer points of human interaction become lost to you. I'd jettisoned all small chat long ago. If there was ever a store of pleasantries, nodding-dog patter, or plain-old mannered chit-chat . . . I'd bumped it. What I did have was a mine of rants. Bitter? Me? Christ on the Holy Cross . . . was I ever. Funny thing was, I'd never really bothered about it before now. I dredged up a line from some fucking daytime TV agony aunt or uncle: 'Sometimes you have to hit rock bottom before you can bounce back.' Had I fallen so low? The bottom of the pit couldn't be that far away; whether I'd bounce when I hit it, though, that was the question. Way I felt right now, figured I'd just keep on falling straight through to the flames of hell.

Shook myself out of self-pity for long enough to order up a coffee in the big Costa. I saw what the chick in the offie meant, nice place indeed; but then, when you've driven every other coffee house within a country mile out of business, you can afford to be.

'What can I get you, sir?' said a lanky yoof, hefty bouffant giving off a bit of a New Romantic vibe there.

'Coffee.'

A sigh. Was that a sigh? Surely not.

'Hmm, we have latte, cappuccino, espresso—'

I held up a hand. 'Whoa-whoa . . . spare me, eh? One white coffee, call it whatever you like, Prince Charming.'

He twisted his head, stuck out his neck like a giraffe going for low leaves. 'What did you call me?'

'Look, you have to remember . . . ridicule is nothing to be scared of!'

Handed over the cash, took a seat.

Was firing up the mobi contacts when the coffee came. Got it just about thrown at me, could see there being a gob or two in there. Like I gave a shit, took a sip and topped the lot up with my half-bottle of scoosh.

Found the number I was after. Wondered would it still be in use, figured it should, it hadn't been that long since I'd spoken to Amy. With a bit of luck she'd be in the neighbourhood – her flat was around here – we needed to talk. Knew it would be the kind of conversation Hod wouldn't approve of, but then he wasn't running this show. Figured I could keep Amy's involvement under the radar for a wee while at least until she'd proved useful . . . providing I could persuade her to help out that was.

Ringing.

A tightening in my chest – what was that? Conscience? Maybe. Perhaps Hod was right about keeping her out of this – the way she attracted trouble to herself. I needed the girl's help, though. Told myself I'd keep a closer eye on her this time. Not let her get worked up with any radge ideas. That would do . . . surely.

Ringing.

'Hello?'

She'd obviously cut me out of her contacts.

Said, 'Hello, Amy.'

'Gus . . . what in the fuck?'

I smiled into the phone. 'Well, that's quite the welcome.'

Got a laugh. It was a start.

'Hey, if there's one person I didn't expect to hear from again, it's your bold self . . . How's it hanging, auld yin?'

This girl, I tell you, she had some moves.

'To the left, yeah, that'd be right . . . Yerself?'

'Just fucking peachy . . . Really good to hear from you, by the by, really good.'

Well, this was going all right . . . maybe a bit too well.

'Look, reason I'm calling, Amy, is . . . well, I was wondering if you were about today?'

'About? As in out and about?'

'Yeah, y'know . . . for a chat.'

Silence on the line. Was that cogs turning? Had our Amy grown up a bit? Learned her lesson from hanging with me? I let the quiet gap stretch out, then heard: 'A chat?'

Picked up a bit of derision in her tone; this was

good. I was happy to hand her the moral high ground if it got me what I wanted.

'Yeah, y'know, there's some stuff that I thought you might—'

She cut in, 'You asking me out, Gus? . . . That it?'

Fuck. Quandary. If I said yes, I was letting myself in for a whole heap of bother. If I said no, I risked bollixing it all up.

Played safe: 'Well, what's that mean these days, y'know . . . I mean . . . I was thinking it would be good to see you . . . to have a chat and that.' Could feel myself begin to wince. 'You still out Tollcross way?'

Another gap on the line.

Silence.

Then, a guffaw.

'Yeah, I'm still on Lothian Road,' she said.

'Grand . . . grand . . . How do you fancy me treating you to a coffee, then? . . . I'm in Costa.'

Amy sparked up, 'You treating me to a coffee . . . like, out the fucking blue, what's that all about, Dury? You after something?'

'Shit no. Y'know me, I drop off the radar now and again. Just thought it would be good to catch up, Ames.'

Day-glo-markered sarcasm: 'Yeah, yeah, yeah . . . I know you!'

I tried to batten down the conversation, went for broke. 'So, you coming or what? My shout.'

'Why not? Student life's been boring as fuck lately. Could do with some excitement, suppose!'

I laughed. 'Can't promise that.'

'You don't need to . . . trouble follows you around like bad aftershave. Get you in half an hour, Gus. I'll dress for a night in the cells, just in case!'

Knew she was only joking; well, hoped she was. My conscience was already starting to wonder about what I was getting this girl into.

Young lad with the eighties vibe hovered. Carried a whiff of Stray Cats about him now – had been at the hair with some product. I wondered about this generation, by Christ I did. Amy, though, was slightly higher on the clued-up scale; by comparison this muppet hadn't discovered fire yet.

'I got something you want, lad?'

Bristles; got that shoulder-straightening thing. 'Do you want another coffee?'

Threw him, 'That'd be just grand. Thanks so much.'

I drained my cup, making sure there was no scoosh left sticking to the base. This close to Morningside, they tend to get a bit picky about things like that. Still, I was tweeded up, like they'd fucking mess.

'Would you like anything with it? . . . We have jumbo cookies on special.'

Guess my look said that would be a no. He trotted off.

I had calls to make: was on the case, c'mon. There was never going to be a simple route to a solution, saw that coming a country mile off.

There was more going on with Gillian Laird than I could suss right now, but from the off, I had her pegged. She might be calling the shots but there'd be a bit of groundwork done there too; knew where to start as well.

Got the contacts up. Felt a slight apprehension as I hovered over the name. We'd some history . . . had we ever. I knew Fitz the Crime was not the man to go to for favours; they had a strange way of coming back with bigger price tags on them than I could afford. He was filth, there was no way around that. But even filth needed to come into the real world, at least once in a while.

Dialled.

Ringing.

Hard-ass on reception, 'Lothian and Borders Police . . .'

'I'd like Fitzsimmons, please.' If I knew his rank, I'd use it. But Fitz was flying through those stripes so fast there was no knowing where he'd be these days. Gave me some room to manoeuvre. The full-leather interior on that Lexus of his had been paid for with so much of my graft that I was entitled to a few privileges.

'Fitzsimmons.' Bit gruff. Tipping the hard-core edge in; nothing new there.

'The man himself. How's the cop trade?'

'Jaysus, Dury . . . by the cringe!'

Always the grand welcomer from this man. You'd think I wasn't one of his favourites. 'Nice to hear from you too.'

Phone shuffling, few steps taken towards seclusion, away from prying ears. 'Gus, this will never do . . . You know better than to call me here. By the holy . . . Is it my backside in a sling ye want?'

'Look, Fitz, cool the beans, eh. It's a social call.'

A loud laugh.

Huff.

Tut.

'Jaysus, Dury . . . you're a freckin' gas . . . Will be on the beg you are, as sure as there's a hole in yer arse!'

He had my number. But this wasn't going too badly; I'd seen the day when a call to Fitz was met with something closer to a curt 'get to fuck'. Phone slamming, perhaps. Could it be he was getting comfortable? Settled, maybe? There couldn't be that much competition for him at the top. He needed to watch that, though: the air up there's pretty thin, I hear.

Said, 'A man can climb to great heights but he cannot dwell there long.'

Bit of a stammer: 'What's that, a riddle? Always with the riddles ye are, Dury.'

I smiled into the phone. 'Close. A quote.'

'Y'wha'?'

'Never mind. Look, I'm sure you're not the type to forget old friends, Fitz, but in case you're thinking of coming the Big I Am—'

He put the volume up a notch, blasted, 'Hang on, Dury, we're well and truly quits, boyo. Don't start playing the old pals act with me, don't even be considering that now.'

I let the line fizz. Few seconds of static stretched out.

'Okay, Fitz . . . I hear you. Truth told, I'm messing with you.'

A laugh; forced one. 'Christ, there's a first.'

I took a deep breath, exhaled slowly. I could feel the muscles tightening in my throat. 'But . . .'

'Hah . . . I knew it. Isn't there always one of them with ye!'

I battened it down, went Zen. 'Fitz, we need to talk.'

'Oh we do, do we now?'

'I'm not fucking about here.'

'Well, that's another first.'

'I'm serious. It's Gillian Laird's son . . . I'm on the case.'

I could almost hear him hissing. 'Oh, feckin' hellfire, Dury, what in the name of Christ are ye doing there?'

'Look, Fitz, there's more to this than—'

'I have absolutely nothing to say.' He spoke through clenched teeth, I pictured him squeezing the receiver. 'I am not about to discuss official police business with you . . . not now, not ever.'

His voice was pitched for an audience. I put in the hook. 'I have something for you.'

Silence. Then, 'Like I say, I cannot discuss—'

'Meet me on the Walk . . . Thursday lunchtime in Robbie's Bar.'

'There will be no meeting. The case is an official police matter and will proceed as such, in the proper manner!'

He clicked off.

I watched the call time flash. Broke three minutes: think it was a record.

My coffee came, fired down with a free dose of derision and a roll of eyes behind thatched fringe. Didn't give him the satisfaction of acknowledgement; took up the coffee, drained a good slug and waved him along with the back of my hand. Little shitkicker was working on my last nerve. He pushed his luck any further with me, he'd be sampling one of those jumbo cookies . . . as a suppository.

Was turning the cap on my half-bottle when the door swung.

'Fucking typical!' said Amy.

'Wha'?'

'Jesus Christ . . . is it not a bit early for that?'

The only other drink I had was the Black Heart; if it was too early for the scoosh, it was definitely too early for the rum, said, 'Don't think so.'

She shook her head, ordered up a mineral water, sparkling one.

'So, you been missing me, Gus?'

She had a beam on her that wouldn't look out of place on a Seacat's searchlight. Her smile fair dazzled me. 'Yeah, something like that.' I played up to her.

Amy sat, she wore black skinny jeans with a very

high turn-up. As she crossed her legs her thigh made an arch beneath the denim. She was pretty toned. In case I doubted it she took off her jacket – top so tight I could count her ribs, and a couple of other protuberances. Jesus, she was looking fit. A warning light flashed behind my eyes; but I told myself there was no harm in looking. I could handle Amy. Sure I could.

'Actually . . . I'm mixing business with pleasure,' I said.

'Pleasure . . .' She rolled the word over her lips, pouted.

'More business, really.'

She flung back her head, laughed, clapped her hands together. 'Oh fuck, Gus, get over yourself. I'm only playing with you.'

I had a laugh at that myself. We'd broke the ice. Amy's mineral water came. She twisted the cap, then tucked her dark hair behind her ear as she sipped.

'You still at the uni?' I asked.

She rolled her eyes, kept drinking. When she removed the bottle from her lips, she took a deep breath, said, 'Uni . . . yeah, why?'

'I'm on a case.'

Her expression hardened. 'Oh, shit . . . not Bender Ben, is it?'

'Come again?'

She put the cap on her water, leaned in. 'Ben Laird . . . the actress's son.'

'You knew him?'

'Knew *of* him . . . Total cock. Sorry to speak ill of the dead and all that but he was a fucking sleaze.'

I took a blast of whisky-laced coffee, said, '*Sleaze*?'

Amy rolled her eyes again and made a wanker gesture with her hand. 'Y'know . . . spoiled little rich kid with a big fucking ego . . . thought himself the dog's bollocks. He was one of those high-visibility twats, y'know the type.'

I sure did. 'Flash arsehole?'

'Got it in one.'

Amy looked out into the street, her eyes widening a little. 'Still . . . couldn't have been happy: hanged himself, didn't he?'

I shook my head. 'Official verdict was misadventure . . . erotic asphyxiation gone wrong.'

She didn't bat a lid. 'Yeah, right . . .'

'What do you mean?'

She turned to face me. 'You buying that? He was probably out his tits and nursing the realisation that everyone thought he was a complete prick.'

I could see I'd come to the right place. Amy was just the girl I needed to do a bit of digging around.

'Ben's friends and the like . . . you know them?'

'Christ no . . . bunch of dicks. Posh twats with big ideas about themselves.'

'But, you could get to know them . . . ?'

Amy slit her eyes, crossed her legs again, towards me now, and leaned in. 'Is this going where I think it is, Gus?'

'Where's that?'

A smile, wide white teeth beneath red lipstick. Fair dos to the girl – she knew how to play up. 'Hopefully all the way.'

I coughed into my fist, suppressed a laugh.

'Let's not get too carried away, eh, Amy.'

'You're right . . . There's time enough for that, sure.'

CHAPTER 9

I watched Amy teeter up the street on vertiginous heels. As she got to the corner, she turned, winked, then took off quick-style, shaking her hips and putting out that peach of an ass. All for show. But, hey, what a show. Somewhere along the track Amy had developed some sense of self-awareness. She'd matured into the kind of chick who was secure enough in herself to laugh at what she was, take the piss, even. I had to hand it to her: she was quite the package. In a lesser mortal there'd be nothing but ego and entitlement. The kind that get tagged 'hard work'. Amy was above all that, she was all about the fun of it, laughing herself up. She had the right idea . . . But who was I to say? Christ, morose was my middle name. Lachrymose my last.

I put out for Holyrood, schlepped along by the Cameo and crossed Lothian Road. At the Art School a shower of jakies were supping on Cally Special tins. One of them had a head start, pissed himself and propped head on a lamp post. His buddies were rifling his pockets for coin and snout. Two baggy-jumper-wearing students shuffled past, eyes south, trying hard to ignore the scene. As they reached the steps they legged it, rapid-style, for the swing doors. Once safely inside they shook heads and giggled. The city streets were no more than a source of amusement for them; a wry tear welled in my eye. This would be our artists of the future then . . . the Tracey Emins and Damien Hirsts. Little middle-class careerists. What happened to conviction? I had heard the Scots genius John Byrne deriding the new wave once. He said art had always been about what was in the heart . . . but to the new crew it was all about what was in their heads. Were we all so corporate now, I wondered? Was there a vestige of soul left in this city, this world? I'd flunked college. Did it bother me? Did it fuck. This education racket was no loss to me. It was a conveyor belt, processing boardroom fodder. A nice little change of scene for the county set brats; bit of life skill polishing before the gap year in South East Asia, building up the alco-tolerance before hitting the Bundaberg rum. Jesus, wasn't life sweet. Almost felt a sense of relief for Ben Laird's passing. Lucky little fucker had managed to skip the entire Lego-bricked road that leads to full-on vacuity.

Was having real difficulty finding a note of sympathy for our Ben. Sure, he was a young lad, a life cut tragically short . . . but I couldn't see it in me to feel for him. Going on Amy's vague description, the boy was hardly one in a million; quite the opposite. He was the worst of a bad type. Yes, he was young, might have matured. But you live in Edinburgh, you watch the fuckwits dragging their knuckles to Murrayfield on match day, you start to question Darwin's theory of evolution. I could see Ben at thirty, forty even, pissing it up and getting a belt out of Immacing some prop forward's nads. I didn't have it in me to feel a shred of loss. Perhaps that was to the good. I needed to keep a level head; past cases I'd let things bottle up, get the better of me. There was a chance I might actually keep the boat steady here. And Christ, didn't I need that. Didn't Hod. And Gillian.

The Black Heart was singing in my pocket; took it out, drained a good belt. The fire of it settled my insides. I was ready for more, ready to put the bottle to bed, duck in there beside it and let the world outside go to fuck, but whilst I had one shred of conscience left in me I knew I needed to screw the nut, get on with this.

I schlepped through the Grassmarket, left out the carnage of the Royal Mile at Festival time and headed for the *Hootsman* newspaper building. There had been a time when my face was known here. There had been a time when many faces were known here, but now the place had turned into a revolving door for school leavers and work experience looking for a first rung on the ladder. They didn't realise that the first rung was also the last. The game had gone to shit. All those days I spent mourning my loss of career had been wasted; it was always coming down the pike, it seems. The game was bust.

At the chrome and glass frontage, I rocked up. Put on a bit of a swagger, not too much: spelled pisshead in here. Could remember the days when anyone who wasn't off their face at the five o'clock news conference was treated with suspicion, verging on derision, but these were changed days. The green tea drinkers had taken over.

I hit the intercom, called out to my former boss, Mr Bacon – or as I still liked to call him, Rasher.

Got a blast: 'Editorial . . .'

'Not become a by-product of Advertising yet, then.'

'Eh, what? That you, Gus?'

I played it cool – needed to get the gate buzzed for me, needed to get up to the newsroom and have a deck about in the files if poss. Gillian Laird's public fall from grace had been one of those tragic celebrity moments played out in the full glare of the TV cameras and Sunday supplements. Kind of thing I switch off to without so much as a gob in the street; well, maybe a few of those.

'Aye, aye . . . look, you got time for a catch-up?' Holy Christ, 'catch-up' – where did I pick up these sayings? The world – and me within it – was becoming way too metrosexual for my liking.

A bit of gruff: 'Well, if it's a quick one.'

Played the card: 'I'd love a quick one.'

Gate buzzed.

I took the elevator; didn't even think of calling

it the lift any more. The language was mangled. Rasher waited at the top floor. He had the same sideburns, heavy on the mutton-chop, that he'd worn since the seventies, and a shirt and tie that looked about the same vintage. There was a gut pressing hard above the belt buckle of his Farah slacks; I'd read somewhere this was a sign of optimism. Apparently wearing the belt over the gut is the opposite, a sign of pessimism.

Hand extended: 'Gus, good to see you.'

'Likewise.' I played it smooth; had some making up to do. I'd given Rasher a fair old blast at an alcoholic's intervention he'd hosted for me; could tell he hadn't forgotten either. But we had some mileage together. I'd handed Rasher more than a few scoops in my day. Washed up as I was, and as beyond help as he obviously saw me, I was still what they call in this game a 'good operator'. I could bring in the news, and say what you like about the state of play in this outfit, news was still a commodity . . . among newsmen.

We went through to Rasher's office, kicking up static from the heavy-duty carpet tiles. I took a seat as he opened the bottom drawer of a large metal filing cabinet – so old school – and brought out a bottle of Teacher's. Not my favourite drop, but it was wet.

He poured out two styrofoam cups and nodded. I took the cue. Drained a fair whack. Felt my lips cracking as the whisky punched back some of the moisture that the air-con had taken.

'So, to what do I owe the privilege?' said Rasher.

I put down the cup, crossed my legs and made a steeple of my fingers above my knee. It was a practised look: canny. Rasher failed to raise an eyebrow. Instead he clocked me head on. I said, 'I'm working a story.'

'You are?'

'Laird kid.'

He looked nonplussed, barely altered his breathing; if he did it was a sigh, 'Oh, really.'

'No interest there? You surprise me. I thought Gillian Laird was big news.'

Now an eyebrow went up. 'Aye, you're right . . . *was*.'

He was trying to say there'd been too much print given to her already, that the public can only stomach so much before it starts rebelling.

'The lezzing-off's old news, granted . . . but this isn't,' I said.

Rasher took up his cup, supped, smacked a white tongue off his lips, said, 'Folk have had enough of her coupon on the front page, Gus. You know how it is.'

What he meant was they'd given her a hard enough time of late; the lawyers had likely urged they ease off.

'Aye, sure . . . but this is a new line. I'm telling you, there's a tale in there that no one's got to yet.'

'Go on, then.'

Was that interest? Doubted it. Had seen him

more enthusiastic for the Spot the Ball solutions. Christ, they'd went overkill on Gillian's coming out, understood, but this case was worth looking at; I felt that in my gut. Did that mean I still had the stomach for this racket?

'She's convinced the kid was murdered.'

'We've ran that line.'

'Yeah, but no one's probing it, no one's looking into the facts. That's what I'm on about.'

Rasher stood up, drained his cup. He wasn't buying. He picked up the bottle of Teacher's and put it back in the filing cabinet. I watched his every move closely. Could feel my grip slipping, felt played out. Knew I'd failed to impress. He thought I'd wasted his time.

'Dury, if you have something . . . say.'

I had squat.

'Well . . .'

'Exactly. Look, it's hard to ignite public sympathy for some posh brat that got tanked up and stretched his scrawny fucking neck . . . Nobody cares. Even if you do turn something up, it's a tough sell.'

There was more to this than he was letting on. I pressed: 'Okay, what's the Hampden Roar here – you got a spoiler story?'

Rasher arked up, 'Shit no . . . Look, you'll find out soon enough, suppose. Ben Laird was no good . . . into all sorts he was.'

'Like what?'

'Trust me, everything bar a shit sandwich! He

was the campus wide boy, go-to guy for grass and brass.'

Ben was obviously more of a piece of work than I'd thought – even going on Amy's assessment. Not quite the mummy's little special, then. 'How do you know this?'

'Filth was all over him. Got some fucking record, tell you wide as a gate, that boy. No story there, though, family far too connected, nobody saying a word that doesn't come through press officers or a fucking lawyer. Trust me, it's a non-starter . . . unless.'

I knew what that 'unless' meant. I knew every permutation of 'unless' he was after. It was scandal, preferably of a sexual nature. If I could crowbar in a tug at the reins of power, maybe some corruption, or any old dirt involving some city figures, I'd be in with a shout.

'Okay, I hear you. Look, this is early days. I've only just took the job, but if you're prepared to extend me a bit of help . . .'

Rasher kicked the filing cabinet's drawer shut with the heel of his cheap plastic shoes. 'Help? . . . And what might that translate into?'

I drained my cup then stood. 'Get one of your copy boys to print me out the scoops on Gillian Laird. Do me a file of interest on Ben and—'

'Jesus, y'know how fucking short-staffed I am? That's taking someone off the job for a day or two, Dury.'

I held schtum. He sighed, a loud one. Sparked

again, 'Right, okay . . . just this once, but I'm promising nothing.'

'Except a byline.'

'You need a fucking story for that.'

'You'll have your story.' I felt a latent spark of ambition reignite. Christ, I loved this caper. 'Count on it.'

CHAPTER 10

Spent a night on the sweats. Fitful dreams, or should that be nightmares? I awoke to find myself shaking, burning up worse than a dog tied to a radiator. Mopped my brow with the sleeve of my tweed jacket – oh yeah, I'd crashed clothed. Hod's gaff, for all the uptown chic of the address, was seriously down-at-heel on the interior. Kipping on boards with nothing but scratching mice for company was a new low, even for me.

I tried to move. A familiar clatter of Cally Special tins came with me. Couldn't say they chimed, more like rattled . . . a bit like my nerves. I couldn't remember buying the beer; could remember tanning the rum but that was it. As I pushed myself up, a bottle of Bell's rolled away underfoot. The noise of it on the exposed wood sent a spike up my spine. My shoulders trembled, my head took the hit and then I scrunched eyes as the tsunami of hangover engulfed me.

There was a time when my gut would jolt at this point. I'd be crouched over a sink or a toilet bowl, dry-retching. I'd be turning myself inside out to get whatever remained of the day before's sustenance out of me. The power of those hurls still had me in fits of hurt, the fear of seeing a long dark streak of blood as the stomach lining detached itself and the white of the porcelain changed to a red warning sign in an instant. It took, I now realised, a modicum of normality to be able to chuck your guts the day after a skite. I'd gone beyond that level; probably a fair while ago now. There was nothing in me worth hacking out – felt the odds were in favour of me throwing up a badly diseased liver, probably black as tar, and being done with it. One good hurl and I was on the way . . . wherever that was.

I knew where this had came from, knew where it started. Same place it always did: in my napper. I'd lost Debs. Christ, I'd lost the dog too. She'd left me – couldn't blame her – but the way of it had stunned me. I'd known Debs for longer than I cared to tot up. We had years together. Long years, some of them. We had a history. Bleak as it may be, it was ours. Shared. Burned into us, seared sometimes, but there. No one, not even her, could deny we'd been together through thick and thin. But now, here she was, wanting to do just that: deny it.

I picked up my mobi.

My head spun, the floor looked glazed below me, the edges of the boards melding together, separating, then crossing like telegraph wires in wild winds.

I found Debs's number.

This had become a ritual now. I pressed 'call' out of sheer bloody-mindedness. I knew the routine down pat. Eight rings before voicemail. She never answered, not any more.

Six, seven, eight . . .

'Deborah, it's me . . . Gus, again. Look, I know you don't want to talk, and by Christ, who could blame you? But none of this feels right to me. I know you have your life to lead and I'm glad for you to do that . . . I seriously don't want you wasting time on me, but I need to know you're well. That's all I want from you, Debs, a few words . . . Christ, a text even, just tell me where you're at . . . in your head. I know I was a prick, I know I ballsed it all up but I'm not trying to mend it, trust me, Debs, all I want to know is that you're okay, moving on. You can give me that, can't you?'

I could hear my voice starting to croak; hung up.

This was new territory for me. In all my fights with Debs, in all our brutal and bloody battles, never once had she turned the lights out on me. She'd completely switched me off now. I didn't exist. Could I blame her? Could I even begin to comprehend what was going on in her head? Christ Al-frickin'-mighty, I'd ruined our marriage. Not just the marriage, but the attempt to patch it up. I'd let drink and arrogance and ego and misguided ambition get in the way. I'd cared more about myself and my own bloody selfish life than about her. What kind of a relationship was that?

It was over.

Sure as shit, we were done.

I knew it. Didn't question it. When we'd split the first time, I railed against the universe. Fought. Went for broke to get her back . . . but this was different. This was final. This was black-armband stuff. I had no hope in hell of getting Debs back and I accepted it fully. Truth told, I didn't want her to have anything to do with me. I was in complete agreement with her stance: shut him out. Fucking right. I'd do the same if I could. But none of that stopped me caring; wondering how on earth she was coping. I knew her too well. I knew Debs's soul. She would be shattered by the break. She would be suffering, staying in, sulking. Skipping friends and digging herself into her workday. I didn't want that for her. I didn't want her to be boxed off from reality. I wanted her to be happy. God, did I ever. I wanted that so much for her because, I knew, the cause of all her unhappiness was me.

A loud thumping started in my head. Like hammer blows. Maybe a road drill. It increased in intensity, then in volume. Thought: The fuck's this? Stroke? I should be so lucky. Something rousted me back to the land of the living. My eyes jerked open. My mouth was as dry as a pie. As I steadied myself on the bones of my arse. The hammering started again.

It came from the front door.

I tried to raise myself. Wasn't happening. Got

one foot planted on the floor, knee bent. Tried to push. The floor got the better of me.

Louder blows.

Fuck, was that an actual hammer? Was guessing a sledger.

Hod came running through. 'What's going on?'

I found some juice in my legs, raised myself. 'The door . . .'

'Some fucker's putting in my door!'

Hod legged it from the room, turned down the hallway to the front of the flat. I pegged it after him, hobbling like a jakey with one foot. My limbs ached, my heart pounded as if I was on the last hundred yards of a marathon but something kept me keeping on. When I rounded the corner the door was coming off its hinges. The only things keeping it up were some heavy-duty screws and security chain. Hod raised hands to his head, turned. He made that *Twilight Zone* face you see on the most scoobied from time to time, then balled fists.

The hammering kept up, then a chink of light came through above the chain. I didn't have enough time to process what was coming as a red-tipped axe split through the links. Then the door fell open. Wood splinters and busted bits of metal sprung into the flat.

'Holy shit!' said Hod.

I was still away with it, but the sight of Danny Gemmill and another burly pug in black leather pushing in and slamming Hod against the wall brought me round.

There's a phrase, *act first, think later*: I was making this my motto. Fired in with a haymaker right, cracked a nice bit of knuckle on bone but the effect wasn't what I'd hoped for. Gemmill raised fingers to his cheekbone, as though he was wiping off a tart's lipstick, looked at the tips then came for me.

I was quicker on my feet than I thought, dropped back a few steps, maybe managed three in total before the wall stopped me. I had less than a second to contemplate my next move. As the lump ran me, smiling, I launched my forehead at his coupon. Caught nose, got some noise from him. Thought: Result. As the hands went up to stem the blood flow, I put a thumb in his eye. This was new for me; I was going feral. Gemmill squealed. It was encouragement to me. Before I knew it I'd grabbed him round the neck – big mistake. In a flash he raised me off the floor with a swift jab, got to battering me against the wall but I hardly felt a thing. Truth told, my body was still too rubber from the sauce to register pain. As I flailed about I hoped to tire Gemmill out; caught sight of Hod getting the better of his man, raising up the axe and pinning him by the throat.

The whole scuffle was over in under five minutes.

When Gemmill dropped to his knees, Hod released his pug. The look on their faces said they couldn't comprehend this turn of events. As Hod wielded the axe like Conan the Barbarian, something told me they were gonna have to believe it whether they wanted to or not.

'Before I cut you both a new crack, better get speaking up,' said Hod.

The pair breathed heavily, and what was that, drool? Fucking drool coming from them. Bloody troglodytes.

Said, 'Liven up, lads. I've seen him take eyes out with blunter instruments.'

Gemmill, Leith as the Walk, spoke: 'You know the score . . . fucking sure you do!'

'You're Shaky's boy,' said Hod. 'But what the fuck you doing here? Just got my motor, didn't you? . . . I've got a fortnight to pay up.'

'Aye, but . . .' Gemmill spoke through his bust nose, 'Shaky's no' too pleased with that set ay wheels.'

'The fuck you on about, Gemmill?' I said. 'It's near twenty grand's worth ay motor!'

Splutters, blood. 'The alternator was gone, needed replaced, and the tyres were well tanned, had to put four new tyres on . . . And there's nae fucking tax or owt.' He was spewing, raging mad about a car that they could score the best part of twenty grand on. It didn't stack up. This was crazy mental. If I didn't know better I'd think Shaky was looking for an excuse to wipe Hod out.

'You'll be complaining I never emptied the bloody ashtrays next!' said Hod.

'Aye, well . . . aye, well . . . there wis a fag burn on the leather seat . . . passenger's side.'

Hod glowered at me.

I bit back, '*Wha'*?'

'Look, Shaky's no' fuckin' chuffed,' said the other one. Obviously not the brains of the operation – he had too much of a mouth on him. 'Says that motor's not buying you the two weeks he thought. That's you on a week to come up with the poppy or—'

I slapped his face with my right palm. 'Or fucking what, sunshine?' He watched me hover over him. Wished I had the strength to remould this guy's features round my kneecap, said, 'Here's what you tell Shaking fucking Stevens: He'll get his poppy when we're good and ready and if he doesn't like that . . .'

'Gus . . .' Hod blasted.

I flagged him down, went on: 'And if he doesn't fucking like that then he can start playing the lottery to sort out his finances.'

The mouth arked up, 'You must be off yer fucking heid, pal!'

'I am . . . pure fucking Radio Rental.' I made to grab the axe haft from Hod. It shook before the pug's face. 'Doubt me?'

The pair on the floor exchanged glances, first at each other then back to us. Hod held firm to the axe; it was a heavy job. No trouble going through a skull or two. Had I the strength, I was hyped enough to do it. I thanked Christ I hadn't . . . Dury, get a grip, I told myself.

Said, 'Now get the fuck out of here and tell that

boss of yours that he'll get his money when we have it, and if he comes for it before that then all he's getting's blood . . . and it's not gonna be fucking mine!'

They shuffled back a few feet on the floor, eased up and walked slowly to the door. Gemmill looked fit to be tied, glowering and showing teeth at me like an angry pit bull. He spoke up: 'I tell you, Dury, this is bad patter. I'm gonna kick yer cunt all over toon.'

I played hardball. 'You can try, Gemmill.'

As they left I turned back to Hod. He'd slumped against the wall, slid slowly down onto his haunches, put his head in his hands. 'Gus, what the hell have you done?'

I smiled. 'What the fuck have I done? I should be asking *you* that question.'

He looked up, eyes like a child who'd been told there was no Santa. 'What you on about?'

'I'm on about all that for a few grannies owing to Shaky. Is there something you're not telling me here, mate?'

'Gus, you know that's how Shaky's boys carry on. Fuck me, we'll be in boxes come the weekend, way you played them.'

I wasn't buying that. Either Hod was holding back or somebody else was. And it wasn't me.

'Fuck off, Hod . . . We'll talk about this later. But trust me, I know these types, they respect some balls.'

I was still flying, walked over to the wall, patted

Hod on the head. It was quite dark outside; flicked the light switch but the bulb had gone. Tried the other switch but it seemed to have gone too.

'Fused, eh?' I said.

'No . . . leccy's been cut off. Got the letter yesterday.'

'Good job we're moving on then, eh?'

Hod put his head back in his hands, sighed. 'Gus, there's nowhere far enough.'

CHAPTER 11

I'd done worse jobs; Christ I had. But at least I got paid for them. Still, jannying at the uni was gonna get me close to the action. Figured the hardest part of the job would be convincing folk I really was on the staff. I knew Calder wasn't happy about having me around, but he could hardly say no given the circumstances of his rector's son's recent demise.

I felt enormous relief to get the tweed jacket off, was like shedding a dead skin. The dustcoat seemed to be more my style; more my class of loser. Felt an atavistic pat of approval on my back – it was like getting down to honest graft, proper work, kind you got your hands dirty at. Always thought it beat desk-jockeying any day of the week.

Calder wasn't best chuffed at my snooping around the campus in the guise of a janitor. He'd threatened to 'raise the issue' with Gillian; I'd told him I didn't give two shits. A boy had been murdered on his watch and the man seemed more concerned with covering that up than finding any kind of justice. Sure, I could see why the mere fact of the matter wasn't going to attract any positive PR for him, but there was a bigger issue here: his mother was closer to the money when she'd called it murder – I became more convinced of that with every passing hour. Call it gut instinct, or a nose for bull-shit, whatever: my antennae were twitching for sure. I needed to get closer to the action, start pushing a few buttons, busting a few heads.

I looked around the doocot: lots of tin pails, heavy-duty mops, bottles of bleach in powder form and an assortment of paper handtowels and loo rolls stacked to the ceiling. There was a few gardening tools: a rake, a fork and some fencing posts sat alongside tightly wrapped bales of barbed wire. The place smelled like a heavily disinfected public urinal and had just about the same appeal. The only relief from the smell came from the odd waft of turps. I was wondering who utilised the rusty kettle and dirty cups when the door opened.

'Oh, aye . . . what's your game?' A gut-heavy twenty-something in a mustard-coloured dustcoat put wide eyes on me.

I played it safe: 'Eh, I'm Gus . . . the new help.'

'What fucking new help?' He sounded far too well bred to be a janny; I wondered what his story was.

'Mr Calder appointed me this morning.'

The bloke shook his head, took out a packet of smokes, Camel. 'Nobody tells me bloody anything in this joint . . . Sorry, not much of a welcome. Got a bit of a start to see you in here.'

I took a tab, sparked up.

'So, it's Gus . . .' he said. 'I'm Stevo.' He started

to take off the dustcoat, empty the pockets: a box of kitchen matches, packet of Rizla skins, more smokes. He transferred the lot into a scruffy Reebok rucksack hanging on the back of the door. When he put the coat up I saw there was a giant ink stain under the breast pocket and filthy smears round the hip pockets; it didn't faze him. One of the pockets had a paperback sticking out. I couldn't see the title or author's name.

'Aye . . . Gus Dury, that's me.' I stuck out a hand. 'Pleased to meet you, Stevo.'

He took a deep drag on his tab, eyeing me cautiously over thick glasses. He looked as if it hadn't been long since he'd been a student himself. A hint of acne sat on his hairline; the look of optimism hadn't yet been beaten out of him by reality. He took my hand, shook. 'Well, be interesting to see how long you last here.'

'That right?'

He laughed, then removed the paperback from his dustcoat pocket. It was Hemingway's *A Farewell to Arms*. 'Oh yes, we have what you might call a high staff turnover.'

'Tough station, is it?'

His laughter increased in intensity and pitch; he fair roared. 'It's the cushiest number going. Trust me, you'll be struggling with the boredom more than anything.' He sat down in a skanky armchair that was lodged between the sink and the table, put his feet up and delved into the book. I was already beginning to like this guy.

'Bit of a fan of Papa?'

He looked scoobied, as though he wasn't expecting any kind of intellectual stimulation within these four walls. Could hardly blame him – like I looked Mensa material.

'Erm, I'm just getting into it now . . . You read?'

Did I read?

'Big time. Hem's a favourite too. You got his best there.'

Stevo put down the book, started a long drag on his tab as he took me in. 'You've read the works, have you then?' He sounded disbelieving. I could have taken offence, but let it slide; he didn't know me from Adam.

'Every word. Even the poetry . . . and that's a push. I go for the Yanks – Hemingway, Fitzgerald, Steinbeck . . . even Salinger in his own way is a bit of a master.'

Stevo stood up, walked over to a rusting file cabinet, opened it and removed a little tin box. Inside was a block of, if I wasn't mistaken, Moroccan rock. 'Fancy a smoke?'

I smiled my widest. 'Wouldn't say no!'

He rolled out the biggest doober I'd seen in a long time; must have been a six-skinner. As we smoked I got his life story. Seemed, until last term, he'd been a student here. They'd had a raid on campus and found his stash. He'd been too fond of the Bob Hope to flush it away: big mistake. His parents were appalled, but sufficiently connected to get him suspended for one term, with a cushy little job thrown in. He even got to keep his room in the halls. The way he told it, the tale seemed nothing unusual to him. To me, it sounded like the worst kind of old-boy networking. You're either part of that gig, or apart from it – and I was well and truly the latter. The whole trip boiled my piss. Smacked of superiority – just what this joint propagated.

'This is some stuff, Stevo.' Say what you will about students, they know good gear.

'Oh yes . . . good toke, eh.'

I could see this helping me ease off the sauce. I'd tried speed once, but it had only made me even more jumpy. 'Any more where that came from?'

He seemed to lose some colour from his cheeks, got antsy: 'Erm, no . . .'

'It's okay, I'm not going to raid your stash there.'

He calmed. 'No, it's not that. Had some trouble with my dealer, that's all.'

I could feel the hit taking hold, laughed out, 'Oh, gotcha – he get turned over?'

Stevo stood up. He didn't seem to see the funny side. 'Something like that. Look, I should get off. You're the night-man, and I don't get any OT from that prick Calder.'

I waved away the hash smoke, said, 'That Calder fellow's a bit of a stuck-up old git, is he not?'

'Calder!' He spat the name out. 'Total bastard more like.'

It didn't take much to press him for more: 'Oh aye?'

'Got me kicked off the course. Could have swept

it under the carpet but wouldn't have been the thing to do for a mere pleb like me.'

It seemed to me Stevo had done okay. 'What do you mean, *mere pleb*?'

He took another heavy blast on the joint. 'Calder is part of, you might say, a cabal . . . I didn't really notice until, well, recently, but there are some people in here could get away with murder and not even get their wrist slapped.'

I kept calm, slid the word out slowly: 'Murder?'

He looked rattled, turned away and stubbed the joint. He didn't say it, but I knew he wished he could retract his last statement. 'I don't mean literally. I just mean there's a few in here more equal than others.'

This wasn't the time to press him. 'You going Orwell on me, Stevo?'

He came back to himself, laughed. 'Oh, God no . . .'

'Glad to hear it.'

I watched him put on his jacket, retrieve his rucksack from the ground. 'Right, you cool with the rounds and what have you?'

I nodded. 'Check the windows and doors . . . after *X Factor*, right?'

A smile. 'Aye, then again before you knock off.' He looked as if he was about to say something else but stopped himself.

'What is it?'

'Oh, nothing . . .'

I took a chance, played it dumb as, letting the

query sound casual, mere interest. 'That hanging . . . the actress's boy . . . were you in that night?'

He gripped the strap of his rucksack tighter, his knuckles turning white, his lower lip curling over his teeth. His eyes shifted left to right in search of some kind of answer. 'You heard about that?'

'Only what I read in the paper.'

He brought his other hand up to the strap and gripped just as tightly. 'Yeah, I was here . . . It was me that found him.'

Jackpot. I thought young Stevo might turn out to be a mine of information. He did look genuinely upset at the recollection, though, and I didn't want to press him, but knew I must. 'What did you do?'

'Nothing. I mean . . . I phoned Calder, that was it.'

'You didn't call the police?'

His lips parted. Slowly the words came: 'Oh, no . . .'

'Why?'

Stevo's face widened in a rictus smile. 'I should think that'll be obvious once you've been in here a wee while.'

I wasn't following him. Wanted to press for more answers but he was gone, out the door and off to his room with his store of information largely intact. I was left alone with the smell of turps and disinfectant. The place was eerily quiet. I didn't fancy staying until after midnight, but had no choice. I decided to take a stroll around the campus, get the fumes out of my head. I played over what I'd just witnessed – seemed to me everyone with a connection to the uni got more than a wee bit jumpy at the merest mention of Ben Laird's death. There couldn't be a conspiracy – would be way too Dan Brown – but maybe there was something at the back of it. Fear, perhaps. But who or what were they afraid of?

I was emptying some bins when I caught sight of a group of students heading for the staff block. They looked to be on a mission. I remembered their sort from my own failed attempt at academia – all piss and wind: read a few books, memorised a few quotes and thought they were Oscar Wilde. I shook my head.

'You missed one!' I turned to see a *University Challenge* escapee in a flannel shirt pointing to a bin at the far side of the square; it was overflowing. A crowd of his mates arked up beside him. They looked hyper . . . fucking rugger buggers probably just back from drinking beer out of each others' cracks.

'Excuse me?' As I watched the lad approach I got a closer look, clocked the ginger hair, the coat-hanger shoulders: it was Paul, Ben's old mate whom I'd met earlier at Gillian's place. He hadn't recognised me in janny garb.

'Isn't it your job to empty the bins? Well, you missed one.' He pointed again.

'Y'wha'?'

He looked shocked now; the watery eyes

thinned. He obviously wasn't used to back chat from the help.

Some indignation played on his quivering lips. 'I think you'll find it's your job!'

I stepped towards him. 'Now, this is a different Paul to the last time we met. This how you talk to the working classes?'

He backed off. Gave me a few glances up and down. The penny dropped; made quite a clang. 'What are you doing here?'

I let him figure that out himself for a few moments, but he looked as though he needed help, said, 'Calder appointed me.'

Paul's powdery-blue eyes widened. 'Oh, I see.' He either didn't approve, or was genuinely terrified at the prospect of what I might find. Both options got stored away.

'Is that all right with you, Paul?'

The lad stumbled, a carrier bag he'd had pressed to his hip dropped to the ground. He seemed to have a habit of dropping things when he was rattled. 'Yes, of course.' His brain-dead mates started to get antsy, grouped around him and tried to look threatening; he sent them on ahead.

'We need to have a little chat, Paul.'

He picked up the bag. 'Do we?'

'I think it might be a good idea . . . don't you?'

He straightened up, looked towards the road. His friends were a fair distance away now; he was ready to either smack me or bolt. It was pure fight-or-flight instinct. 'I have to go.'

He shrugged past me, walking at first but soon dipping into a jog. 'See you around, Paul.'

He turned, started to run, looking over his shoulder as he went.

Back in the doocot I played over what I'd just seen. Wasn't happening: I needed to let some time pass before I could look at it with any sense of detachment. I dipped into some Hemingway, *True at First Light*, that Stevo had left behind. It was a newish edition, but the book was published posthumously and had been edited by Hem's son Patrick. I had read the book once, but never was able to find the story. Perhaps it needed more editing, or should have stayed locked away in the bottom drawer. I wondered what other lost laundry lists of Papa's his family was planning to publish.

I smoked the last of Stevo's reefer; took a few pelts on a bottle of Grouse I had in my hip pocket and settled down to watch the snooker. There didn't seem to be much to this job, if you could call it that. Before long I was knocking out the Zs. I dreamt of Debs and happier times for what seemed like an age until I was woken by a loud clanging.

'The fuck's that?'

It sounded like a window banging. I got up and grabbed the flashlight. Had a thought to fashion a chib from one of the broom handles, but there was enough weight in the torch to be effective if it came to that. As I went out the door, I checked my watch. It had gone 1 a.m. The campus was desolate, not a murmur, except for that banging. I followed it, checking windows as I went.

The corridors smelled of the same disinfectant as the doocot, but much less potent. There was also a dampness creeping into the mix that no amount of scrubbing was going to dislodge. As I shone the torchlight on the floor I could see the myriad scrapes of shoe soles that had scarred and pitted the floors over the decades. Although the place felt empty, seemed empty, I got the distinct impression I wasn't alone.

When I reached the entrance to the Grand Hall I paused. This was where Ben Laird had died. I didn't want to get too close to whoever had brought him to that end, but it wasn't something I was backing away from. My hand trembled as I pushed at the door. On entry I heard scuffles but when I tried to direct the flashlight, I dropped it on the floor.

'Who the fuck's there?' I shouted.

Footfalls. Scuffles at first, then quick steps. Running.

A window slammed shut. I could still hear the shuffling of bodies nearby.

I got down on my knees and tried to locate the flashlight. It had gone out on impact with the floor. 'Fuck . . . shit.'

I tried to guess at the number of people in the hall; I couldn't count them. It was more than two or three for sure; maybe a lot more.

'Who's there? Show yourselves, y'fuckers . . .'

I flailed about for the flashlight, found it; pressed the button but it wouldn't come on again. I tapped the head of the torch in my hand, tried to get it working. Not a flicker.

I had a bad feeling as the room fell silent. Manoeuvred myself over to the wall. I kicked at the high skirting with my Docs, felt the oak panelling and slid along to the light switches. As I turned them on I was almost too scared to look. My breathing halted. In the silence of the night I could feel the cold breeze blowing from the banging window. It was nothing compared to the cold line of sweat that formed on my spine as I stared ahead.

In the centre of the stage, above a toppled stool, was Joe Calder. He was hanging by a thick rope.

'Oh, Christ . . .'

I looked about, saw the window flapping in the night air. I ran over, looked out. Saw nothing in the darkness. Whoever had been here was well and truly out of sight now. I walked back to the stage, looked up at the hanging figure.

Calder looked smaller, more pathetic than I remembered him.

His grey flannels indicated he'd vented his bowels and bladder as the rope had tightened. His face was pearl grey and contorted. He didn't look like a man who had died a happy death.

CHAPTER 12

Plod's response floored me. If I saw one flashing blue light, I saw a hundred. They swarmed on the uni, had the grounds floodlit and taped off before I could blink. A power of uniforms spread out, taking orders from a small coterie of pot-bellied detectives in the sort of coats BHS specialise in. Wife-bought, no doubt. The hall was sealed off and all the exits guarded by barrel-chested thugs in high-visibility jackets. I watched one playing with the handle on his baton; it sat in a quick-release holster; he looked primed to crack a few heads. None of the campus bods messed: a couple of stragglers in dressing gowns floated about, approached the odd WPC and got pelters for their trouble. The word had obviously went out from on high: batten this one down, fast.

'Right, eh . . . Dury?' It was a balding fifty-something with a Magnum P. I. tache and a roll-neck that had been worn to shreds by his stubbly jowls.

'Yeah, that's me.'

I didn't expect a hand to be extended, so I wasn't disappointed. 'Aye . . . you match the description.'

'*Eh*?'

A grunt; some tea-stained teeth put on show. 'You're the talk of the station.'

My rep preceded me. Was hardly surprised; a chill passed through me, though. I could recall being fitted up by these fuckers one too many times before. Three cold beads of sweat ran down my back like a cat's claw.

'Look, I gave my statement to the young lad in uniform. What is it you want from me?'

His dark eyes widened above heavy bags, stretched so much I could make out the cholesterol rings on his irises. 'I'll ask the fucking questions.' He licked the tip of a pencil, brought it down to hover above his notepad. He was still staring at me, waiting for a tell, a twitch, any excuse to lamp me one, introduce me to the slippery steps, when a Daimler pulled up. The vehicle was flagged through the cordon. Thought: Must be top brass. I watched the car roll towards the main building, then glide to a halt a few steps away from us. As the door opened, I caught sight of a star and a crown on an epaulette. Wasn't an expert on the filth but felt sure that kind of flash was reserved for the chief super.

'Oh, fuck . . .' said Magnum tache.

I looked back at him. He pressed the pencil tip into the notepad; the lead snapped.

The super made his way towards us with a purposeful stride. Silver-grey hair had been carefully parted on his head. He covered it with his cap. The badge shone in the flashing lights. Though it was the middle of the night, he was immaculately turned out; couldn't do much about the furrows on his brows, though. He looked like a man ready to bust heads under his carefully polished police-issue shoes.

'Detective.' His clipped voice sounded out of place in this century.

'Chief Super.' I half expected to see bowing and scraping, genuflexion.

The boss man started to put on brown leather gloves. They clashed with the black uniform, but I wasn't about to tell him. 'What's the SP, Detective?'

'Erm, well . . . no' much change since the briefing.' He turned to me. 'This is the bloke that found him.'

The super put steely-blue eyes on me; I felt frozen in his gaze. For a moment I thought he might speak, but he merely sussed me out, drew what he could from my appearance – by the kip of me, I dreaded to think what that might be.

The super took the notebook from the detective, flicking back a few pages. He halted on one or two points. I watched him wet his lips with a flash of grey tongue. The piercing eyes seemed to be recording every detail; he unnerved me.

'That's enough, Detective,' he said, 'back to work. I'll expect your report on my desk in the morning.'

'The morning . . . It's the middle of—'

The super lifted his head; it was enough.

'Yes, sir.'

As plod departed I was left alone with the top boy. He spoke to me for the first time: 'So, Mr Dury . . .'

Was it a conversational gambit? I didn't bite. Held schtum.

He put his hands behind his back, turned and nodded to the car park. 'Shall we take a walk?'

Couldn't say it appealed to me, but I followed on. He had a strong stride, spoke as he walked. 'You have a name I hear cropping up quite a bit these days.'

'That so?'

A piranha smirk. 'Oh, yes.' He stretched out the vowel.

'Well, better than no one talking about me, I suppose.'

We'd reached the bourne of the car park. 'I don't believe I've given you my name.' He extended his hand. 'Chief Superintendent Charles Henderson.'

I shook his hand, but it felt unnatural.

'What interest do you have in this . . . case, Mr Dury?'

I played him. 'By case, do you mean Calder's murder . . . or are you including Ben Laird's too?'

He brought a gloved hand up to his chin, rubbed the spot where most men would have stubble at this time of the night, said, 'What makes you think either were murdered?'

I let out a sigh. Most people would have taken

that as an indication that I wasn't playing the game but Henderson didn't faze. 'Well, Ben aside, for the moment, if you were properly briefed tonight you'd know that I'd heard movement in the hall before I found Calder.'

He smiled. 'It was probably just the wind. It's a draughty old hall.'

Couldn't believe I was hearing this, said, 'Are you serious?'

The smile remained. 'I'm deadly serious . . . there's no way he was murdered, Mr Dury – we found a suicide note.'

First Ben dies, put down as a gasper; then Calder's a suicide. Aye, right. I didn't button up the back.

I said, 'The note was typed, I suppose.'

'On Calder's computer.' Henderson blinked – first sign I had that he was human. 'There's no disputing it's his.'

There was no way I was buying this, arked up, 'If you think I'm stupid enough to believe—'

He raised a gloved hand, smirked. 'Mr Dury, I'm sure you're not stupid enough to challenge the official version of events.'

I eyeballed him, making sure he got my meaning. 'What you mean is . . . surely I'm not stupid enough to challenge *you*.'

He remained calm, quiet; kept that firm gaze of his on me. That earlier blink now seemed like a momentary lapse of concentration. He was back in character.

I turned, headed out of the car park. My heart was pounding so hard I thought it might pack in at any moment. I was deeper into this caper than I'd imagined; wondered if it was going to be the end of me. If filth – right at the top of the ladder – were taking an interest, it couldn't be good . . . but this turn was the worst yet. Felt as if I'd waded deep into shit creek.

On the street I turned, stared back into the dead of night. Henderson was gone, the spot on the tarmac where he'd stood now bathed in blue light flashing from a stream of exiting police cars.

CHAPTER 13

I propped myself in a Southside bar. Felt so wasted by lack of sleep and mental exhaustion I couldn't even guess at the name of the drinker. Had a vague recollection of writing a story on a shooting in there some time ago . . . Writing stories, holding down a job, was all the dim and distant past. I'd been burning my bridges for so long there was no way back for me with so many people. Call it the drink, depression, self-pity, whatever. I'd screwed over so many folk I was in danger of having no one left. Now another man had died; holy Christ, what was happening here?

Debs had said it. She'd made the prediction long ago that I'd end up alone and bitter, cursing the world, blaming everyone and everything for my mistakes. Roaring and ranting. Not even choosing my targets any more. Blasting. Just blasting. She'd seen the future, and it wasn't bright. Thing is, that was a long time ago. Funny how the past catches up with you.

Called over the barman – squat beer gut with a shaved head and a star tattooed on his neck – said, 'Pint. Chaser.'

Got a nod. All it took. Places like this, the chat's minimum, if uttered at all. Another couple of scoops and Beer Gut would be over with a nod at the pumps and we'd be away. There's a comfort in this kind of interaction, if you can even call it that; people will say these types of joints are for the lonely. They're wrong. They're for the seriously fucked off. The beyond lonely. People who are lonely crave company; people who hole up in spit-and-sawdust drinkers are after the opposite. Knew I was. I was looking for complete anonymity. If I could excoriate my skin like a snake I would, shed the lot, all identity with it. The past. The mistakes. The lost dreams. The heartache. The loss . . . Christ, I'd shed the lot.

The drinks came. Tanked them. Couldn't even look at the barman. He took the hint, said, 'Same again?'

I nodded at my empty pint glass.

My mind was all over the place. I knew where it should be: on the case. Each time I thought about it, the tweed Hod had bought me itched; I could feel those business cards weighing heavily in my breast pocket. But the straight road had long been a stranger to me. There was a place in my head, a cold spot . . . the kind that people refer to when they say *that bloke has something dark in his locker.* I did indeed. Could pinpoint it. Was the size of a football pitch, bigger maybe. Did I feel sorry for myself? Did I ever.

My mind went back, further back beyond the recent hurts . . .

I'm to be married; Debs is happy. For the first time in an age I see her start to thaw, smile again. It has been so long. She . . . *we* . . . have been through so much.

'Look at the way it sparkles.' She holds up the diamond in the engagement ring to the window. The rare blasts of Scottish sunlight – scarcer than hen's teeth, as my mam always says – alight on the diamond, the rays dissemble, spread and fill out. It's beautiful. It says happiness.

'God, it does . . . You wouldn't think something so small could shine like that.'

Debs smiles. 'It's beautiful.'

My throat tightens. I feel welled up with emotion. I want more than anything to make her happy. I put my arms around her and hold tight. We have a chance, I can sense it. The bad times are behind us now; this is a fresh start.

We collapse onto the bed, giggling.

For a long while we just lie there, looking at the diamond and smiling. I'm overwhelmed that something so simple can create so much happiness. Debs's eyes hardly blink; she's blissed out.

'I'll never take it off,' she says.

'Oh, no?'

Her face hardens. 'No . . . never. The day I take it off, it's over!'

I know she doesn't mean it, it's just one of those

things people in love say to each other, the kind of words they use to try to communicate the incommunicable. We both know there are no words for how we feel. It's written in the sky . . .

I sit up, lean in and kiss her.

Debs sits up beside me. 'Time for me to go. Got to get back to work.'

She smiles as I stand up, puts out her hand for me to raise her from the bed. I take her fingers, grip them and lean back to help her up. I've done this a million times before but something has forced me to make too dramatic a gesture this time, I heave her too suddenly. Her hand loosens within mine, seeming to shrink. She falls back onto the bed. I try to grip her fingers but they slip through my own.

As Debs lands on the bed, I feel my hand go into a fist. A small hard object is in my palm, I turn over my hand, open my fingers.

'Oh, Gus . . .' Debs's mouth widens. She touches her cheeks. The diamond engagement ring has came off in my grasp. I hold all our fallen hopes in my hand.

'I'm so sorry . . . I didn't mean to, it just . . .'

Debs's lip trembles, she starts to cry. 'Oh, Gus . . . Oh, Gus . . .' It's all she can say. She pulls herself from the bed, runs to the bathroom and locks the door behind her.

I look down at the small, shining rock.

I don't know what to do.

I walk to the bathroom door; I can hear Debs's sobs inside.

My heart flutters. There's an emptiness in the pit of my stomach that seems to be rising up into my chest, into my jaw, my head. I feel bereft.

I want to talk, to say something to her. But there're no words. Nothing can repair this. Just like there are no words to say how we truly feel, there are no words to explain this kind of message. My fist tightens around the little ring. I want to throw it into the bright sky . . . but I can't. I walk over to the dresser, place the ring in the little mauve box from the jeweller, close the lid.

My shoulders and spine tense as I pass the bathroom door, leave for the stairs, and head back to the office. I can sense the heavy hand of predestination on me as I walk along the road. I want to know what the future holds . . . but at the same time, I really don't.

'You fucking sack of shit, Dury . . .' I was drawn back into reality by the gravel tones of a short-arse pug. He was squat, but brick shithouse, jaw like a snowplough jutting in my face. My eyesight was a bit hazy after the good bucket I'd taken but I could smell Bovril on his breath, wondered who drinks that outside the footy? As my vision started to focus I saw the answer: Danny Gemmill. He had both hands on the bar, some of Elizabeth Duke's finest sovies on show. I suddenly felt a spark of life return. 'That's some manners your mother gave you, Gemmill.'

The taciturn barman arked up, got gabby for a

change: 'Look, he's been in here all afternoon, been on a right fucking sesh, but if yer up for bouncing him aff my walls ye can take that patter outside!'

Gemmill showed his bottom row of teeth, grey and craggy; two lone tombstones sat higher than the rest – made him look like a missing link between man and ape. 'Shut yer fucking yap, boss!'

Barman retreated, eyes darting left and right as he edged himself closer to the telephone.

I got off my stool, was surprised how light-headed I felt; the floor seemed to swim beneath me, or was that my legs caving? Said, 'Look, what're you about?'

Gemmill didn't seem to have an eloquent rejoinder on hand; decided he'd punch a hole in my gut instead. I folded like paper. I saw the barman pick up the phone as I fell on the floor, squirmed. It felt like my stomach was on fire; I could taste acid in my mouth. I vomited heavily. Then dark frothy blood came – a good whack of blood rose into my windpipe, spewing out of my mouth. I coughed the lot on the floor. The pug laughed.

'Look at that, fucking claret . . .'

I twisted on the ground, felt like my knackers had been cut off. The pain was beyond agony. The room started to fade on me, tables and chairs floated up to the ceiling.

Gemmill was shouting at the barman: 'Put that fucking phone down or I'll wrap it round yer fucking heid!'

The barman had plod on speed dial. 'Yes, King's Arms . . . Aye, I want polis . . . An ambulance, aye, y'better . . .'

Gemmill mounted the bar – no mean feat for such a shortarse. He grabbed the phone; I watched him slap it off the barman's brow. He dropped like a horse taking a bullet. The ripped-out phone was flung over the bar, hit an old Younger's mirror, smashed it to smithereens. Gemmill went scripto now, pulling down optics and smashing bottles. Something told him to empty the till, fill his pockets. A stack of KP nuts went for a flier as he mounted the bar. His arse skited on a Tennent's towel and cardboard mats floated to the floor.

His boots stomped towards my head, but I couldn't move. My arms held in my guts as he grabbed my collar, yanked me to my feet.

'Aff yer fucking arse, Dury. You're coming wi' me.'

I felt woozy, beyond wankered, beyond drugged. There's a phrase, *at death's door*. It seemed to fit.

'C'mon, y'cunt . . .' He shook me, squeezed my face in his mitt; a grim spark of intuition crossed his eyes as he clocked me. Said he wasn't for doing a serious stretch for my murder. He dropped me to the floor.

I curled up again; the pain in my gut was all-consuming. I felt ready to cark it. Seriously, this was the real deal. New territory. I wanted to pull the plug, anything to stop the pain. Another mouthful of blood appeared; seemed to piss off the meathead even more.

'Oh, you fucking prick . . . What's wi' the fucking blood, eh?' Gemmill looked ready to burn me but something stopped him. I couldn't see him ever taking prisoners at the footy with a Jambo at his feet. He'd either learned a few lessons or there was another reason for him holding back. But in my condition, I couldn't figure it.

I heard the sirens now. Sounded like the last bell.

I coughed again, more blood.

'You're full ay it, Dury . . . I'm having you! I've got your fucking number boyo . . . I want you out this toon or out the fucking game! You got me?'

A flashlight shone in my head: I had something on him. Managed to splutter, 'Gemmill, I don't take a scare from your like . . . suck my balls!'

That was enough for him: he stamped his boot on my stomach.

There was a second of searing agony, as though I'd split in two. Then a tractor tyre rolled over my gut and left me to writhe for a few more seconds. I was dimly aware of Gemmill putting the boot in again and again. The maniacal grimace on his face said he'd lost some control, but not all.

I held firm; held it together. The pain stopped as sharply as it had began. I never felt a thing as I watched Gemmill legging it for the door. I'd gone beyond pain. Gone beyond the beyonds, to be honest.

Everything went completely dark.

CHAPTER 14

Whiteness.

Blinding light. So much it hurt my eyes.

A slow, persistent beeping. The slight hum of footfalls, just within earshot.

I felt numb.

I couldn't feel any part of my being. There was a corporeal mass beyond the scope of my thoughts; sensed it. Just couldn't seem to focus on it, feel it, bring myself back to it.

The numbness changed, was supplanted by a buzzing in my head. I felt drowsy, thirsty – had what the Scots call a great drouth. Was like a killer hangover. Christ, I'd drank enough for that; for sure.

Remembered the ten or so pints; ten or so whisky chasers . . . doubles.

Where the fuck was I?

A flame of recognition, something stirring in my soul. Was I upstairs? The Big Fella's gaff . . . No chance. I should be so bloody lucky.

The slow beeping pulled me in, got me thinking. I let my eyes open wider, take in more of the harsh light. I could see nothing but a white mass . . . so strong it bleached everything else out. I shut my lids fast; scrunched them tight. Let them stay shut for all of fifty seconds, counted it, then tried again.

'Fucking hellfire, Gus.' My voice was a rasp, my throat hurt like hell, but I knew the score now. 'Back here!'

It was a hospital ward. Well, more of a room; had it to myself.

I scrunched my eyes again. Thoughts flooded in. I was in a hospital, yep, no mistake. I was tucked up tight in a bed. A needle in the back of my hand was attached to another drip. But this time I didn't feel savvy enough, or wise-ass enough, to try and bolt. There was a definite pain around my windpipe, a hot poker of it reaching down my oesophagus into my gut. Had a vague notion this was just the aftermath of something; like I'd been through the fucking mill.

'Blood . . .' I stuttered out the word, recalled the pub floor. Frothy vomit, then blood. Lots of it. Enough to have put the shits up Gemmill.

I was in some kip all right.

Felt the heart in me quicken; the beeping from the monitor kicked up. Had a minute or so of this, watching the needle jump with my thoughts, until the door swung open and in strode a sister.

'Oh, you're awake, then,' she said.

I spluttered, 'After a fashion.'

She approached the bed, leaned over me and squinted at the monitor before turning back. 'You must be feeling a bit groggy. Throat'll hurt, mouth a bit dry.'

I nodded.

'You've had an endoscope . . . but the drugs will take the edge off the pain. Just try to relax.'

She watched my eyes open; the look said more than any words.

'I'll get the doctor to come and have a word with you.'

This didn't exactly enthral me. Okay, I was in one piece, but I'd been probed and prodded. There was a reason for that, and the doctor's explanation, sure as shitting, wasn't going to be one I'd want to hear.

I tried to sit up on the bed.

A hand was placed on my chest. 'No! Stay still, Mr Dury. You need some rest now. Can't risk any more haemorrhaging.'

'Haemorrhaging . . .' The word came like a bullet; Vincent Price couldn't have put more fear in me.

The nurse straightened her back, turned for the door. 'The Doctor will be along in a minute or so to explain everything . . . Try to rest and please try not to worry yourself.'

Easier said than done.

I watched her close the door behind her; settled into a dark brood of thoughts. What the fuck had happened to me?

I was in bad shape – no question. But had been since Adam was a boy.

This was new school, though. This was the big league. This was the culmination of years of serious physical deterioration; my chickens coming home to roost.

I looked at my hands – pale and white, save the yellowed tips and black arcs beneath the nails. I was a wreck. I started to shake. Watched the thin sticks of bone covered in pasty white flesh twitch as if electricity was being passed through them. This was me, Gus Dury. This was what was left of me, anyway. I was down on my luck, always had been, but the way my defeat had manifested itself on my flesh was something I couldn't take in.

'What did you expect, fuckhead?' I mumbled.

I was in my bad thirties; racing towards the big four-oh. The days of tanking the sauce like a nineteen-year-old were well and truly behind me. My body was waving the white flag. I'd seen the signs for a while:

The skin like a chamois.

The mustard-coloured eyes.

The undernourished frame.

The vomiting.

The last one had been a new addition. For the longest time, I'd skipped the traditional drinker's purge. I'd managed to keep it all in. Keep the count high, and the contents on board. But somewhere along the line the rules of the game had changed. The tank still held the same amount of grog, more sometimes, but it was as though the cap leaked. Sometimes the contents made their way to the surface.

Embarrassingly, I remembered a rare guilt-ridden trip to Alcoholics Anonymous. I'd listened to a corpulent, bearded middle manager who'd clearly been to the brink and back explain how the sauce had caused his 'interior plumbing to become exterior'. He was ruddy-cheeked as he painted this picture of the dire consequences of his drinking and how it manifested itself in him having to strap a polythene bag to his ankle to catch his own piss. A chill had passed down my spinal chord; I'd put a gun to my own head before I hit that low.

'By fuck I would . . .' I'd mouthed the words before I realised I had company.

'Mr Dury . . . I'm Dr Scott.'

Couldn't say I was glad to see him, but was delighted it wasn't the no-nonsense west-coaster I'd legged it from at my last visit.

Said, 'Pleased to meet you . . . *I think*.'

Frowns, over Penfold glasses.

The doc edged over to the bed, clocked the monitor. There was a brutishness about him; hands that would have looked more at home on a boilermaker. He wasn't here to fuck around, that was a given.

He paced to the end of the bed, picked up the clipboard. He took a propelling pencil from his coat pocket, pumped it, then made some marks on the paper. His face never once changed. Held steel. He was a type I'd met before. Couldn't say I was overly enamoured with any of his lot, though they did offer a kind of reassurance: it was an image that focused on the utilitarian, the type you want to get a job done, done well even, but not the type you want to pass the time of day with. His was a fast-vanishing breed; as a race we are becoming more vacuous and lightweight every day. Things like focus and seriousness have little or no value. These days people wanted the wrapping to be bright, look the part. They want visibility, not credibility.

Dr Scott spoke: 'I suppose you'll know why you're here.'

Fuck me, was this another lecture?

Was I even biting? No way, said, 'Well, it's a lovely view . . .'

Not a flicker on him. 'Alcoholism's a progressive disease.' He returned his pencil to his pocket then the clipboard to the end of the bed. 'You'll have been aware of that, surely.' His look said, *You're not an idiot, why are you acting like one?*

I raised myself in the bed. The act was a trial: felt my chest constrict; some burn in there made me wince. The doc watched without as much as a crease appearing on his brow. I tried to use my faltering voice once more: 'Cut to the chase, eh . . .'

He stared at me for a moment, seemed to be sussing whether I was ready for the news. 'You have extremely dilated submucosal veins in your lower oesophagus.'

I rolled eyes. 'In English . . . please.'

Dr Scott took off his glasses, removed a white handkerchief from his trouser pocket and started to clean the lenses as he spoke. 'The veins in the narrow part of the tube from the oesophagus to the stomach are damaged. That's what's been causing you to vomit, Mr Dury.'

'And the blood . . . ?'

He returned his glasses to his nose, pressed the frame, 'All part of the progression. I don't want to underestimate the seriousness of this situation for you.'

I gritted my teeth. I was ready for the worst, said, 'Gimme it straight.'

'Are you a betting man, Mr Dury?'

Wasn't, but saw where this was going, said, 'Time to time.'

'Let me put it this way: your alcoholism is so advanced that you are on the final furlong.'

I felt surprisingly nonplussed, it didn't faze me. 'Heading for the home straight!'

The doc's face held steady, not a move, then, 'If you have another bleed like that it could be your last.'

'You think?'

Now emotion, deep frowns and slit eyes as he tucked his handkerchief away and raised a finger to me. 'I've seen a lot of people in your boat, son, and listen to me, if you don't get off the bottle you'll be lucky to see the year out . . . if not the month.'

The word 'son' stung. Always did. I knew the concern of his warning was genuine. I knew he was right; also knew soon as I got out of this place where I was headed.

'Thank you for your . . . assessment, Doctor.'

The impassive look returned. It screamed, *You can lead a horse to water . . .*

He went for the door, took the handle and said, 'You'll need some rest. I'm putting you on lansoprazole – don't forget to take it. I'll write out a scrip for the pharmacy, you'll need a few other things too . . . a beta blocker, propranolol, to keep your heart rate down. There's one thing you know you can never take again, but I'm sure you've heard that before, so I won't waste my breath here.' He didn't even look at me, not so much as a backward glance, as he opened the door and strode out.

I closed my eyes, dug my head back in the pillow.

Knew the forecast down pat. By this stage, there was no need to hear the words. But I also knew that as the warnings had got louder, my ability to hear them had diminished. Felt very little of the fear that I knew a man in my situation should be experiencing. My thoughts were elsewhere. They were where they always were – in the gutter.

I felt the most almighty pull to a whisky bottle.

I wanted to blot it all out. To block out the world. If it, or me, vanished for good . . . I seriously couldn't give a fuck. If I could get Hod straightened out – off the hook with Shaky – and get Gillian some peace of mind, I'd be happy. There was nothing else to hope for on the horizon. The thought goaded me like the point of a sharp knife.

CHAPTER 15

Spent a couple of days in dry dock. Only contact with the outside world was to call Hod, tell him to keep an even lower profile than I'd suggested earlier. Had a bad feeling about Shaky's sudden interest in us; figured there was more to it but couldn't get that side of the Rubik's cube to match up. Brain was still firing on half power, maybe I needed more rest . . . Yeah, like fuck: I needed a drink.

Took myself to the shower room. The place was kitted out like a caravan park, lots of black grout in the tiles and blacker mould on the bench boards. No wonder our hospitals were in such dire nick; kip of this joint, I could be adding some superbug infection to the list of troubles I had waiting to fell me.

Turned on the taps, caught sight of myself in the mirror. There were so many creases in my forehead, I made Gordon Ramsay look like an Armani model. Christ, what had happened here? I had a bad case of red-eye too. Where the whites should have been were yellowed; throw in the red and I was in the ballpark of the Stoke City away jersey. I tapped at my pale cheeks, tried to slap some colour in there – wasn't happening. I had the pallor of a corpse. Looked like Peter Cushing in the first *Star Wars* movie . . . tried to inflate my cheeks with air to see if I could fill out the hollows but the effort only made me feel light-headed.

I couldn't look any more. Turned my eyes to the sink, filled it. Was taking all my effort to drag a cold razor over my coupon when I was drawn out of myself by sheer disbelief. I clocked a twenty-year-old at the sink next to me in the midst of an act that made me despair for the future of humanity: he was applying eyeliner.

My mouth drooped.

I held the razor halfway to my chin, stared.

The lad spotted me but kept at it. How did I know what he was at? How did I identify that he had an eyeliner pencil in his mitt, applying black lines to the lids? How? I had seen my ex-wife at this caper. Spanish eyes or some shit: yes, blokes know this . . . from women. HolyChristallfuckingmighty. What had happened to the world? This feminising-the-planet lark had gone way too far. They had us carrying bags, moisturising, and now, it seemed, applying make-up. I couldn't believe it. Turned away. Knew there had to be an ad creative somewhere working on the campaign for blokes' Pretty Pollys.

The lad shrugged off; seemed quite chuffed with himself. Thought: Things you see when you don't have a gun.

I finished off shaving, felt an unbelievably macho

act to perform. Wanted more of the same: rustling cattle, maybe wrestling a steer or two. Knew I wasn't up to either; a nice facial would be more in keeping with my current capabilities.

Got back to the hospital bed, turned on my mobi. Was strictly *verboten* in here, but like I cared. Had some voicemail from Hod: 'Two things I need to chew you out about, Gus. Gillian's full-on pissed about Joe Calder. She's kicking up an awfy stink . . . wants to see us, soon as. And one word: Amy. Eh, what you playing at, Gus? You promised to leave her out. Right, bell me, eh. Sooner the better.'

He clicked off.

Said, 'Fucksake.'

Knew Hod was on bricks about this whole thing. Was seriously rattled since Shaky's pugs doorstepped us. But I'd be fucked if I was having him dictate the way I went about business. Had a flashback to his usual modus operandi: going ape, bustin' heads. Felt relieved he was being a bit more businesslike, but still, he needed some hauling back. I'd have to tell him to pull his head in. For all his involvement, help . . . this was my gig.

I checked the text situ.

One from Amy, read: *Been checking on oor Ben. No good news. You know he was connected, aye?*

That I didn't know. Had my suspicions; I mean, if Bender Ben was dealing on campus, he wasn't getting it mail order. Someone was supplying him. The other stuff, the brassers that Rasher mentioned, could all be explained away by some wido contacts, but the drugs game was all sewn up in this town, had been for years. I felt a sudden belt of fear at what Amy was getting herself into. Knew Hod wouldn't like this turn of events either.

Hit my contacts, dialled Amy.

Ringing.

More ringing.

'Shit . . . c'mon, pick up, girl!'

Went to voicemail.

Said, 'Amy . . . it's Gus. Got yer text. Look, when I got in touch I thought you might take a bit of a sniff around the uni, y'know, some of the poncy wee losers. I didn't want you going anywhere near drug dealers or anyone who might be connected to supplying Ben. You hear me? Right, that's it. Call me when you get this and for Chrissake keep out of trouble!'

Knew that kind of message would have no effect on her at all. Amy was a force of nature; she did what she did. Headstrong, that's how to describe her type of woman. I knew this because I had been married to one for so long – Amy and Debs were cut from the same cloth.

I checked the rest of my messages. Nothing special. But according to Vodafone, I'd qualified for free weekend calls. Was jumping ecstatic about that. It was Tuesday – hoped I made the weekend.

Turned on the TV. I'd been charged a Jimmy Denner for the privilege of watching telly in an NHS hospital my taxes had helped fund. Fair boiled my piss but there was worse to come on that front: Gok Wan was on *Loose Women*.

'Holy Jesus . . .'

Was there a worse combination? The hatchet-faced blonde one was keeping her trap shut, though. Probably too scared in case Gok suggested she give her face a good iron.

I couldn't watch.

Flicked to off.

Got up. I was about to start pacing when my mobi went off.

Was Amy: 'Gus boy, how's tricks?'

'Amy . . . where are you?'

'Eh . . . aye, hi there to you too, Gus.'

'Look, tell me you're not up to some shit again.' My voice was weak, rasping.

'You sound rough. Been on the piss?'

I wished. 'Amy, I mean it, I don't want a repeat of the last time . . .'

'Chill. I've only been talking to a few folk down the union bar.'

I wasn't buying that. It was the kind of weak excuse she'd always plied me with, but it felt futile arguing, went with, 'Gimme it, then.'

Amy's voice increased in pitch and velocity – she was excited. 'Well, Ben was quite the lad about town, let me tell you—'

This much I knew, said, 'Okay, cut out the preamble, eh.'

She sparked: 'Well, he was all for his Es and whizz, and one or two other things. Had a rep as being able to deliver quicker than Domino's Pizza . . . But that's not the best of it. He was pimping brassers about the party scene like you wouldn't believe. Cheesy fucker used to say they'd all been personally road tested . . . cockhead!'

Amy had only confirmed what I already knew and suspected, said, 'Who was supplying him with the drugs?' If she'd found that out, we were on to something.

A pause.

Pages flicked on a spiral-bound notebook. 'Got that somewhere . . . was some bloke called Gemmill.'

I felt a heat flash in my chest. 'Danny Gemmill?'

'Hang on . . . got it here somewhere.' She flicked through the pages, 'Right, here we go . . . Danny Gemmill, aye . . . D'you know him?'

'Could say that.' If Gemmill was mixed up in the death of Ben Laird, it made sense why he'd been playing Hod and me so hard. Sure as fuck he wouldn't want Shaky finding out; what he'd want was me off the case, pronto. At the moment, though, this was all reaching. I'd nothing to back it up. Still, it was an interesting association to have uncovered. Would take some looking into.

'Right, Amy, well done. That's a big help. You've more than earned your weight in Costa coffees. Now, get back to your studies and forget about this case.'

A huff on the line. 'Gus . . . are you brushing me off?'

She'd come good, real good – I needed to keep her sweet. 'No. No way.'

'Fucking well sounds a *lot* like it!'

I pulled it in: 'Look, Amy . . . this guy Gemmill's connected to some hard bastards. Kind that don't think twice about putting folk like me in the ground. You understand?'

'I'm not fucking dippit.' Her tone said far more than her words could.

'I know, I know . . . and that's why you'll stay clear now, Amy. Trust me, if they'll put me in the ground, they won't think twice about you. Only, way you're put together, they'll likely have some fun with you first . . . Get the picture?'

'In Technicolor.'

She hung up.

I stared at the phone, watching the backlight fade. That feeling I'd had, the unsure, hesitant feeling I'd had about contacting Amy, came back, on full heat this time. I was grateful for her help, but wondered what I had got her into. There was no way she'd be walking away from this now. I had to get moving. Dreaded to think what Amy would get up to; just hoped I'd beat her to it. She had an uncanny knack of rousing trouble, of diving in head first when she should be holding back, playing it cool.

Checked the time and date on my phone. I'd missed my meet with Fitz, but I couldn't help that. I was in hospital; he'd understand, surely.

Dialled his mobile number.

He answered fast – was driving by the sound of things – said, 'Fitzsimmons.'

'It's Dury.'

Van Morrison got turned down on the CD player. 'By the feckin' cringe . . . Dury. Thought you'd been blotted out once and for all!'

'Close . . . but no cigar.'

'What happened to ye?'

'Let's just say I . . . ran into some health issues.'

'Fucking liver packed in, has it?' He laughed that up. I didn't.

'Look, where are you? We need to meet.'

'That would be a good idea. I have some things I need to discuss with you.' This was a turn up for the books. Usually I had to claw information out of Fitz; him suggesting a meet-up was a first. He'd have an ulterior motive, no doubt. He was plod, c'mon.

'Can you get out to the infirmary . . . ?'

'*Y'wha'*?'

'You heard right. Look, I'm about to check out. Can you pick me up?'

'Jaysus feck . . . yer serious. Okay, well, gimme a few minutes. Are you fit enough for this lark, Dury? I mean, nothing I have to say to you will be a comfort in your situation.'

Comfort? What the fuck was that? 'Trust me, Fitz, I'm as good as I'm ever going to be . . . Better wear your thick skin too – don't think I'll have anything complimentary to say about your lot.

Been some serious shenanigans hereabouts. Fucking serious.'

He sighed; clicked off.

I held my breath for a moment; sighed back.

CHAPTER 16

I got dressed; in the same clothes I came in with. My shirt, a nice blue Superdry that Debs had bought for me, was covered in blood. Worse, it stank of rank puke. The front of my 501s had collected some claret on the thighs and knees, probably where I'd writhed in agony on the pub floor. I must have looked like a butcher's mate, some junior workie not long enough in the job to have gotten the overalls in. The only item of my get-up that wasn't looking the worse for wear was my Docs. Okay, they were cherry, same colour as the blood-laden barf, but those boyos were hardy; the bonny fechtirs had seen some action in the past and knew how to handle it. Wished I could still say the same about myself.

I strolled out of the ward, down the corridor to the pharmacy. I clutched at the doctor's scrip; seemed policy to get the thing filled out. I wasn't about to take any chances on a return to this place. Sure, there was as much chance of the Second Coming as me swearing off the sauce – I could feel the crave already – but screwing the nut, if not deadbolt tight, was on the cards now. Deffo.

Things were starting to look serious, not just on the health front. But the way this case was stacking – with Fitz and Hod and Amy showing an interest – I'd need to start pulling out the stops. Christ, I'd need to start pulling my weight. People were relying on me. I'd involved a shower of folk I cared about and needed to protect . . . even if it meant putting myself to the sword in the process.

The pharmacy wifey was old time, but fighting it. Had the look of one that had dragged herself up from sitting behind a counter in the Co; a chemist shop was big time for her. Could see her having once spent her nights playing dominoes down the British Legion, night at the Mecca bingo maybe. Now she'd be on the line dancing; glue-gunning sequins on her hubby's cowboy shirts and drinking bourbon and Coke. She had what Fitz, and all our Celtic cousins across the Irish Sea, call 'notions'. I didn't like her one bit, could see she was going to give me grief.

Said, 'I have this prescription from Dr Scott.'

She pretended to be busy with something, tapped a few random keys on the PC notebook in front of her, trying to look important. I was waiting for a hand to go up, a finger to the lips, maybe a 'Sshhhh'. What I got was nothing. I wasn't even worth consideration. She let me stew for a full minute, then eyed me with derision. She clocked the blood on my shirt front. I looked away, tried to close my jacket but the zip jammed. Cursed inwardly as she pinched her lips at me. I could see the deep radial lines drawing from the thin crease of her mouth out towards her nose and cheeks. Was there a face more worthy of a slap? Christ, I didn't think so, but I wasn't playing into her hands.

She spoke: 'Oh, you do?'

'Yes . . . I do.'

That needled her. If she had any more power than taking the bit of paper off me and handing it to the pharmacist, you could be sure she'd be at it. Drawing in the big guns to fire me out of the place is just the kind of crap her sort are all about. Why waste your energy helping folk out when it's far more enjoyable to piss them off . . . that's their philosophy. Christ, I wondered if there was a manual for this mob to work from.

She took the scrip, looked at it. Looked back at me. Paused. Made an O of her mouth. Closed it. Slid her lips into a semi-smile, curling up the corners. She did that looking to the top-left eye movement of the sarcastic, then turned down the corners of her mouth. It was all for show, all designed to make me think she knew what the fuck it was the doc had written down, as if it meant anything to me whether she did or not. I didn't credit her with the intelligence even to be able to read. Did she seriously think I gave a flying fuck about the few deadened sparks firing in her napper that passed for something approximating thought? She was a drone, one of a million like her, all programmed to play the same role. Folk like her are here to remind us that the good can't exist without the bad: everything in this life is a contrast, including the people you surround yourself with. I felt sorry for her family.

Got motioned to a plastic chair by the wall – was the same stamp as the ones we had in the sixth year common room. Made me think of Debs. Again. Didn't want to go there. Didn't want to think about the fact that I'd left another voicemail message on her phone that had been ignored. Didn't want to think about what she was up to. How she was coping. If she'd moved on. Found someone else. It was a heartscald to think of all Debs and I had been through, but I knew it was over now. There was no road back, the bridges had been burned. We'd tried again, and failed. I knew, in my heart, it was all down to me. I had let her down and I had to accept that. So I did. But it didn't stop me caring. Wondering if she was going to be okay. Nothing would stop that.

Lately, there'd been a part of me looking on from Debs. There'd been an awakening, a realisation that life had to go on. Whether I wanted it to or not wasn't part of the deal. It was like an animal instinct in me – a call for survival. My conscious mind was telling me I was finished, but my subconscious was working to a whole other set of rules. I was being pulled one way and then the next. I knew it: I was fighting myself. The answer, though, the only answer if I was being honest, was moving on. But what did that mean?

Starting over? Finding someone else? I knew there would never be anyone to replace Debs. I'd known once that I would never even contemplate it; but here I was doing just that, it seemed.

'Angus Dury.' The old wifey called out my name, managed to make it sound like something she'd trodden in.

I stood up, smiled at her, said, 'That's me.'

The smile cut no ice. She peered down at me with a look that said, *Don't let the door hit your arse on the way out.* I took the bag of goodies, trudged out.

In the car park the sun was shining down like it meant business. I could hardly recognise the place. The brightness bleached out the landscape; the buildings and spires shimmered into insignificance. I watched the blue cloudless sky for a few moments and felt transported. Had I really just come close to death? Had I really just left a hospital and been told I'd be lucky to see the year, maybe the month, out? Did I want that for myself? My mind didn't seem my own, I felt controlled somehow by thoughts that weren't mine. I wanted to get my shit together. I wanted to enjoy sunny days, the wonder of life. The joy of being alive. But was that really there for me? Had it ever been? Could it ever be?

My phone beeped – was a text, from Amy: *What did you mean – 'way I'm put together'? You manage to make a knock-back sound like a come-on, Gus!! Are you trying to mess with my head??*

Christ.

What had I said?

What had I done?

Had an idea what the answer to both those questions was: sent the girl mixed messages. She'd always carried a torch for me; I must have been an idiot to contact her in the first place. Dr Scott's look flashed back to me, one that said, *You're not an idiot. Why are you acting like one?*

Maybe I knew exactly what I was playing at. I tucked the phone back in my pocket. This whole business with Amy needed more thought.

A car pulled out in front of the hospital; a horn sounded.

'By the holy, ye look rough as all guts, Dury.' Fitz was on top form as ever.

I approached the passenger's door, got in. 'You all right?'

He eyed me curiously. It was a look I couldn't remember seeing on his face before, a strange mix of compassion and shock. 'Are ye feckin' all right? Jaysus, Dury, I had no idea . . .'

I played it cool: 'What you on about?'

Fitz looked away, wiped his mouth on the back of his hand. 'Are ye sure it's okay for you to be . . . y'know, gaddin' out and about? Sure, ye look a bit worse for the old wear, son.'

The concern cut me. Fitz was showing me up; I didn't know whether to be unnerved or straight-out worried. Said, 'Trust me, mate, I'm firing on *most* cylinders.' I slapped the dash. 'Just you pump the gas.'

Fitz got the motor rolling. He drove slowly, like he was driving Miss Daisy, or heading a funeral cortège. 'Have ye had a bite?'

The thought of food made me want to chuck; the thought that even Fitz wanted to look after me made me despair. 'I'm fine . . .' Though there was another craving that needed satisfied. 'Wouldn't mind a drink, though.'

Fitz pointed to the glovebox. ''Tis a wee drop in there.'

I opened it up: was a half-bottle of Talisker. I looked at it, thought about it, even felt my hand reach in, but I closed the drawer. 'Gonna keep off the hard stuff . . . for now.'

Fitz turned to me, looked stunned. 'You're off it?'

My voice croaked. 'I'm knocking the scoosh . . . but could murder a pint.' They used to give stout out in hospitals, as a builder-upper . . . and the Queen Mum thrived on it for long enough; what harm could a few pints of black do me? That was my reasoning. Well, what I told myself was reasoning. I craved alcohol – I was an alcoholic – there was no way round it. The trip to the hospital was already beginning to fade.

'Okay, so . . . I know a wee place out of town where we can talk.'

'Well, we need to do that.'

'Christ, Gus . . . don't we ever.'

'That sounds ominous.'

Fitz steadied the wheel, stared at me. 'Ominous as the devil.'

CHAPTER 17

There are few wonders in the world to behold like an Irishman on a mission. Fitz flung his filth-issue Lexus round the hospital car park as though he was auditioning for *Ashes to Ashes*. Christ on a cross, they shouldn't give high-performance motors to plod if that's the way they treat them; was a crying shame. I cringed as he crunched down the gears. Burning rubber and attendant smoke plumes appeared on cue.

I took a bit of a coughing fit on the way, felt my bones tremble. I wasn't up for this lark; should still be kipped up in the crisp white linen, turning the Sad Sam eyes on the nurses and kicking back. What was I at? This was lunacy. I was off the scale. But sure . . . when was I never?

Fitz revved the engine. I watched him spin the steering wheel.

I gripped the door handle. 'Think this is fucking Le Mans?'

He smiled, liked that. Took it as a compliment, clearly. 'In my day I was told I had a look of the Steve McQueen about me, y'know.'

I put the eye on him, 'You'd be fucking lucky to be taken for a drag queen these days.'

He found the high gears, shot along the road. Felt the back of my skull pinned to the headrest. Was in no mood for this patter, said, 'Ho, cool the beans, eh.'

'What you on about?'

'The driving . . . calm it!'

He looked at me as if I'd suggested a fruity threesome. 'Cop on man, sure, I'm a top driver.'

This was the same argument I got regularly from Hod . . . and Mac. Was there a bloke on the road didn't think he was the equal of Jenson Button? I despaired, gave up. My energy wasn't worth wasting on this lark. I settled back in the seat; as we took a corner to the main road, the bag full of Harry Hills I'd drawn from the pharmacy made a noise like a kid's rattle.

'The fuck's that? You got a snake in there?'

I laughed that up. 'One of the deadliest!'

'Ha . . . go way outta that! Sound like yer carrying a dose of chemicals there, laddo.'

I filled him in on the doc's orders. Left out some of the juicier details but could tell by the way his eyebrows dropped, the slowing of his breath, that he got the picture. There had been times in the past, long before I really knew him, that Fitz had had his own battles to fight. Some drinkers, and I've observed this from them, simply give up. They get tired of the rigmarole . . . the late starts, the brain fag, the wreckage it wreaks on your life. They crash their jet and walk away. I wasn't so lucky. Fitz was a breed apart, though. Rarely have I seen a man called that worst of misnomers – 'functioning alcoholic' – able to drop one of those tags without becoming the other: you're either an alcoholic, or you're functioning. Never both. Well, that was my experience, and most others', but Fitz had managed to cut his consumption and clean up his act. It was a dangerous path, but he kept to it. I watched him with something close to awe. What's the word? Oh aye: envy.

'I've got a few pills to get me through.'

Fitz turned his eyes from the road. 'Oh, Jaysus . . . what have they got you on – not feckin' Antabuse . . . '

'No . . . not that.' Knew I'd gone beyond the Antabuse stage – the stuff that makes you barf yer guts up at the merest whiff of an alcoholic unit. You wear too strong an aftershave, it can have the same effect. I'd read George Best had been on them; didn't do it for him. Drinkers get used to skipping the dose, going on a skite. Some just drink anyway. I remembered an episode of *Minder*, Arthur Daley had been hypnotised to stay off the cigars. Every time he had one he smelled burning rubber. Problem was, by the end of the show he'd grown to quite like the smell of burning rubber. There's very little will come between a man and his addiction; you can't save a man from himself.

'Glad to hear it . . . sounds serious, though.'

I didn't bite; knew Fitz had no more of an

interest in hearing about my problems than I had in hearing about his. There are some things you keep to yourself; if you don't, that's weakness, and I didn't do weakness.

'Look, can we get off this subject? It makes me want a fucking drink.'

Fitz's cheeks tightened, a slight smile crept onto his thin lips. 'Ah, now . . .'

'Ah, now fuck all . . . Are you my mother? Get us to a pub, eh.'

'Okay, so . . . Sure, there's no man knows what he needs better than the man himself!'

Fitz gunned it, took to the fast lane with the needle twitching. The engine purred like contentment. There was nothing to give away the extra effort save a slight lift in the bonnet. Thought: Can a car show off?

The pub was out of town, on the other side of Newtongrange, an old mining village that had been reclaimed by the tourist board for its history. I liked the place, lots of narrow streets, looked like a Hovis ad. There was a great park in the middle, full to bursting with school-holiday bairns and young mums with Maclaren buggies. I wondered if this was the patch of grass where the miners had once took the pit ponies to grab their five minutes of fresh air a day. How many of them had expired at the thought of going back into the black earth, a quarter-mile under our feet? How the place had changed; but isn't that life? Isn't it one continual change? The thought washed around in my mind. I'd been doing a lot of thinking recently; funny how a few knocks at death's door will do that to you.

The barmaid was friendly and, unusually, Scottish. I'd grown accustomed to having my order taken with a Polish or an Australian lilt these days.

Fitz ordered: 'Make mine a Jameson and for my laddo here . . .' He turned to me.

'What stout you got?'

She pinched her lips. 'Oh . . . Guinness. Might have a bottle of something else if I have a look about.'

Went for the old favourite. 'The black stuff's fine, love.'

Her face lit up as I called her love. Don't know where that came from – wasn't like me to be so familiar. There were changes afoot in this man and I didn't understand a one of them.

Fitz nodded at a secluded table in the corner. I followed behind him with my pint glass in hand.

'So,' I said, 'coming round to my way of thinking are you?'

'Y'wha'?'

I gulped my pint, felt my entire body twinge. 'Ben Laird . . .'

Fitz played coy, sipping his whiskey, 'The actress's boy.'

I was in no mood to extract teeth, said, 'If he was murdered, Fitz, I've started taking it up the Gary . . . and you and I both know that's a fucking cover story on Calder's suicide. I was there, I heard people in the hall . . . suicide note my balls, it was typed! Anyone could have written that.'

Fitz put down his glass. 'Okay, okay. I hear ye, calm it, eh.' He looked about the room. He'd never looked comfortable in a pub since the smoking ban. Never looked comfortable in public, come to think about it; certainly not with me. 'I think you could be right.'

This was a bullseye. Normally drawing information from Fitz was like getting blood from a stone. I felt wary, he was filth after all, but I pressed him. 'If you're saying that, then you know something . . . or want something.'

A nod. Fitz inflated his chest and exhaled slowly as he spoke: 'My nephew, young Colin, he's a good lad . . . cleaner than a cat's arse, I assure you. He was at the scene on the night the Laird laddo died.'

I corrected him: 'The murder scene.'

More nods. Fitz was playing into my hands, or feeding me a line; I didn't care which if it got me what I wanted to know. 'He's sharp as a tack, our Colin, no shiny-arsed careerist either. He's only after doing the best job he can . . . 'tis green as grass to be honest.'

I could see he had something more to say. 'Go on.'

'He came to me . . . couple of days ago. Christ, he was near white as a sheet, didn't know whether to sit or shit. He says there was some *irregularities* on the night they found the lad.'

I knew it: fucking filth up to their nuts in it as usual. If Fitz was telling me this then it was bad. He was Irish – and if there's one thing they don't do it's inform. More than that, though, he was filth – and they look after their own. Fitz was doubling up on the rule-breaking and it didn't sit well with me, or him . . . that was clear enough.

He went on, 'Colin was first to the campus, secured the area and called in the squad. Only, somewhere along the line it got to be known to the ranks.'

'The ranks?'

'Top of the tree, Gus.' Fitz fingered his collar. ''Tis olde worlde, the Craft.'

He was talking about the Masons. It was a fair stretch for me to get my head around the force's top brass covering up a murder with the university's big boys. For a kick-off, what was the motive? Save the bad publicity? Or perhaps there was more to this than met the eye. For sure they were all old school, all looking out for each other, but in such an obvious fashion? It was a leap I had some trouble buying into.

'Wait a minute . . . are you saying what I think you are?'

He breathed in, exhaled slowly. His face was redder than ever and seemed to sag in dreary fashion from brow to jowl. 'Look, I've seen the word given in the past: go slow, go quiet, go fucking dumb!'

'So, what? Who's to protect?'

Fitz picked up his glass, hit the goldie. 'I don't

know the whole story . . . but I'm not shitting you here.'

I watched him wipe a line of moisture from his top lip then look away. He was either putting on a very good performance or totally convinced of what he was telling me. One more thing didn't make sense. 'Why are you telling me this?'

'You think I can go poking about in it? Jesus Christ, they'd throw me to the wolves. And then . . . then there's young Colin.'

'What about him?'

'He's implicated.'

I couldn't see it, pushed: 'All he's done is speak to you. Hardly implication.'

Fitz gasped, ran fingers through his grey hair. 'Day after, he was in the office, due to put in his report . . . he got a visit from one of the Craft laddos. Handed him an envelope, said, "There's the money I owe you" . . . walked off. There was enough in there for him to clear a deposit on his first flat in Gorgie.'

That was implication. 'The daft fucker.'

Fitz shook his head. 'What's he supposed to do, Gus? Ye have no idea of the pressure . . . There are people in there you just don't piss off. This stage of his career, he'd be finished before he got started. Hasn't he a lass and a youngster to think of.'

I looked away to the window. The sun was ducking behind a rain cloud. I watched a black cat leap onto the top of a wall. I said, 'You need to tease some more information from Colin.'

'Ah, now . . . I don't know about that.'

'Just see if he's anything to add to his story.'

'Gus . . . sure, he's still very young.'

I hit my pint, put the glass down hard on the table. 'I'll need you to do some more digging as well. Colin might know more than he's let on; just check it out. It's his arse on the line as well.'

Fitz turned over a beer mat, his red-rimmed eyes moistening; I could see the concern in them. It unsettled me, made me question what the hell I was doing. Fitz nodded slowly. 'All right . . . but don't be surprised if it's me you find swinging from a rope next.'

CHAPTER 18

I tried to keep in the ballpark of some regular hours at the uni, but even with my pretence to being part-time, I felt the cover story was slipping. Had never got the hang of this working-life lark – dunno why I expected it to be any different now. Some folk just aren't cut out for the real world. Was I one of them? Oh, yeah. Me and reality don't get on. Call me a cynic, but answer me this: what the fuck's modern life got to recommend it?

I put on my dustcoat, tidied up around the doocot. Put a few dirty coffee cups in the sink; tipped out some old newspapers – nothing in them I wanted to see anyway. Stalled for as long as possible before I had to tackle some real work. Well, as near to it as you got in this job. There wasn't much to do on the rounds so I occupied myself with moving a set of ladders from one end of the campus to the other. I took off with them under my arm but was stopped in my tracks by a face I'd been keeping an eye on. Ben Laird's so-called best mate was in animated conversation with my janny colleague, Stevo. Look of it, Paul was warming up to full-on apoplexy.

I put down the ladders and tried to get close enough to hear what was being said, but it was no good. They were too far out of range; if I moved any further in I'd blow my cover. By the body language, however, it was plain enough to see they weren't discussing what to get each other for Christmas. Paul was poking Stevo in the chest with a book he held in his hand like a dagger. His face was redder than usual. Under the red hair it was quite a sight – looked like the home stand at Tannadice. Had I been any closer I might have intervened. This was a side to Paul I hadn't seen, though I'd suspected it lurked in there. Some people you just get a feeling about.

In a few moments, the tirade seemed to pass and the ginge returned to his normal pasty complexion; save a few thousand freckles. He moved away, still pointing the book at Stevo, but backing off. I watched Stevo stand thunderstruck. He looked deflated, as if he'd been punched in the guts, or maybe given a death sentence. It was the kind of look to make old women rub you on the back and offer to get you a cup of tea. I felt for the guy.

By the time I was through moving the ladders, it was time for a smoke. I schlepped through the campus, putting friendly smiles out, but all were rebuffed. I'd been trying to hit some of the few student stragglers for info on Ben, but to a one they had held schtum. Felt my luck was up. And Calder's hanging had all but put the kybosh on it.

The place was now in a state of shock. As a new face it made my task even harder; no one was risking their neck to talk to me.

A subdued Stevo was back at base when I returned.

'All right, there,' I said.

Got a nod. He had his feet up on a bale of barbed wire.

'You got a light by any chance?' he said.

'Aye . . . aye.' I handed him my Zippo, pulled out a Marlboro for myself.

Stevo produced a half-tanned reefer, let it droop from his lip, sparked up. I watched him take the smoke deep into his lungs, let it settle there, then exhale slowly. It seemed to do the trick, calmed him. His eyes rolled up behind heavy lids.

'Busy morning?' I said.

'Could say that.'

I tried to move the conversation on. 'The gents' toilets overflowing again?'

Frowns. 'I put in a new ballcock . . . Should be fine.'

'You make it sound like a doddle. Bet it's a big job.'

'Not really.'

I let him get comfortable, took a couple of blasts on the joint myself. It seemed to put him at ease; made him think he was in friendly company. I wanted him to think that. He was a good bloke. I liked his company and I knew he could be of some use to me – if I could prise some proper chat from him. It had proved next door to impossible up till now, but nothing lasts for ever.

'Stevo . . . what do you make of the Calder thing?'

He had his eyes closed as he toked away, kept them shut. I saw them twitch behind those heavy lids as he spoke. 'What do you mean?'

'Well . . . seems a bit strange, doesn't it?'

'Does it?'

He was acting coy. This from the guy who had found Ben hanging, who had no time for Calder . . . I wondered what he was up to with Paul earlier, where he fitted into all of this. 'Aye, well, I was thinking . . . y'know, with the Ben Laird hanging, then him hanging himself in such a short period of time.'

Stevo opened his eyes wide. The whites dazzled me. 'Paper said Calder felt guilty . . . it was in his note.'

'You believe that?'

He sat up straight, spoke fast: 'Maybe! He was a funny bloke.'

I finished off my tab, took out another Marlboro, offered one to Stevo. 'I hear a lot of folk never liked him. Do you think, y'know . . . ?'

Stevo's mouth twitched now. His gaze moved from me to the window. 'What, that he was done over?'

I tried to look nonplussed as he put his eyes back on me. 'Well, it happens doesn't it.'

'Oh, yeah . . . wouldn't put it past—' He cut himself off.

I leaned forward. 'You wouldn't put it past *who*?'

Stevo realised he'd said too much. He got up and went over to the tray with the kettle and the coffee cups. 'You want a coffee?' It was all a distraction.

'Go on then.' I let him think I was finished with the subject, played the game.

When he brought over my coffee I started again. 'You were saying?'

'What about?'

'About Calder. You said you wouldn't put it past someone?'

'Did I? . . . Don't think so.'

He was being infuriating now. It was on my mind to jump out of the chair and clamp a good wake-up slap on him. But I had to keep my cool. There was no point in blowing my stack with Stevo, he was too decent a bloke for that kind of treatment. He'd come good yet, I figured, soon as his conscience got the better of him.

I changed tack. 'Did you know Ben Laird?'

'Bender Ben . . . oh, yeah.'

'Bender Ben . . .' I played dumb. 'What's that all about?'

Stevo sipped his coffee: was too hot; he blew on it, said, 'That's what they called him . . . Was a bit of a party animal. Seen him out on the town a couple of times. He was always the most drunk bloke in the room . . . Had this motto, "You're a long time dead".'

'Did he really?'

Stevo seemed to be more interested in talking about Ben. A smile cut his cheeks. 'He was a good man to get a bag of puff from, if you know what I mean.'

'A dealer?'

He reached for a biscuit from a pack of ginger nuts. His heavy stomach looked as if it had been suddenly sliced in two, the top sagging like a full sack over his belt. 'In more ways than one . . . He offered to get me some serious gear, y'know. And more besides.' He giggled, a boyish gleam in his eye. 'He offered me a go at a pro they'd brought back one night!'

I kept my tone flat, feigned low interest. 'They?'

'Ben and his boys. There's a wee clique of them.'

'Would this be the ones you talked about before?'

Suddenly Stevo started to get cagey again. He sat back in his seat, clamming up. 'They're just a group.' He dunked his half-eaten ginger nut in his coffee. Filled his mouth with the biscuit like it was a gag.

I shook my head, made to laugh. 'Sounds like quite a wild wee gang.'

He sparked up, 'I never said they were a gang!'

'Okay. Okay, Stevo . . . we're only talking here. Why so defensive?'

'Look, Gus . . . there are things in here you know nothing about.' He got out of his seat. Coffee spilled from the cup in his hand. 'You don't want to mess about with that lot. I've seen them, heard them in the hall going on about being the masters and the born rulers . . . They're out of control! Out of fucking control!'

It was the first time I'd seen Stevo in this much of a state. For a doper he was seriously animated.

'Okay, mate . . . we're only talking here.' The words sounded trite.

Stevo dropped his cup. The last of the coffee spilled as the pottery shattered on the floor. I thought the lad might hyperventilate, his skin darkened and his cheeks puffed up. 'You don't know what you're doing, Gus . . . I've had them asking about you! They know you're up to something!'

I rose to face him. 'Who, Stevo? Who's been asking about me?'

He brought his chubby fingers to his lips. His hand trembled for a moment then he jerked it away. His face seemed to tighten now; his jaw drooped and his mouth contorted like Munch's *Scream*. For a second he was frozen, then he turned and bolted for the door.

I went after him but I was too slow on my pins to catch him.

'Stevo . . . Stevo . . . come back!'

He took off down the corridor at a fine clip, never looking back once. For a big biffer, he could fairly shift it.

'Stevo . . .' I yelled.

He was round the corner and out of sight before I could call him again.

CHAPTER 19

I kept my return visit to hospital from Hod. He handed me the newspaper as I walked into the car park. Calder's obituary had been written by some po-faced cadet journo who looked young enough to still be a student herself. A photo-byline on an obit as well . . . what next? She'd even failed to link it to Ben Laird's murder – went on the line of Calder being overcome with guilt at the death of a student. It was the same old pish again. Was beginning to tire of hearing it.

'Utter bullshit!' I said. Made me want to chuck.

'You really are away with the mixer now, Dury,' said Hod.

I said nowt; kept my eyes fixed on him, though. It was a well-worn look, I'd perfected it in my marriage to Debs. Let him know he could only get away with this kind of rant for so long.

Hod reloaded: 'I mean, where was your mind, man? Going to shake down Calder . . . Gillian blames you for his death, y'know.'

'Oh, really.' What did he know? Hod was baggage. I was merely carrying him along.

'Y'know . . . we still haven't signed this contract

with her. This is just the kind of thing that would put her off. Do I need to remind you—'

Enough was enough. 'Shut the fuck up, Hod.' I crushed up the newspaper, raised a finger, shook it left to right. 'If you think you're starting on that patter with me you can fucking well think again. We're mates, not family.'

Hit the right note; he drew in his head. Could almost see the shoulders recoiling as he sighed. Hod walked over to the edge of the car park, sat down on a wall. I watched him fold arms, quickly raising a paw to test the stubble on his chin. He looked lost.

I walked over, sat next to him. 'Look, mate . . . what's your game?'

'Come again?'

That had come out wrong. I rephrased it: 'I mean, you're a businessman, I'm right?'

'Suppose . . . feel like a fucking shit one right now.'

I turned out my pockets looking for a tab. Found a pack of Regal smalls that I'd been avoiding until I was desperate, sparked up. 'You're not a shit businessman, mate. You've had a rough stretch.' I knew all about rough stretches, went on, 'Way this economy is, your mob – builders – were always gonna take the worst hit . . .'

He shrugged. 'What you getting at?'

'What I'm saying is . . . this racket, investigating, it's not your game, mate. It's mine.'

That registered. He let out a slow breath, rubbed

the back of his neck. 'Okay . . . I hear you. You have the form . . . do it your way.'

'Grand.' I smiled, slapped him on the back, said, 'I ever need a conservatory building, I won't question how you put the windows in!'

A nod, huff. 'So, what's next?'

I stood up, stubbed my tab at the halfway mark; bloody rotten smoke anyway. 'We go see Herself . . . pour some oil on the waters.'

'Might take more than that.'

'Trust me, what I have uncovered so far, she needs us more than ever.'

Hod's eyes lit. 'And what would that be?'

He was firmly on a need-to-know basis, said, 'Plenty.'

'Want to keep me in the loop?'

Shook my head. 'Spare me the business speak, eh.'

He took the hint. Followed me to Mac's van. We drove out to the West End in relative silence. I could tell Hod was deep in thought. He was putting a lot of faith in me; I felt the weight of it. There was a time when I would have been stressed out, but I knew we'd scratched enough at this scab to see the blood. We were far from a solution, far from anything that could even be called a better understanding . . . but we were on to something. I sensed it. Could feel the pulse in me quickening the second I saw Fitz's face reveal the fact that the Craft was in on this. Say what you will, there's something deeply satisfying about uncovering the kind of secretive shit some people make a virtue out of hiding. Secrets. Lies. They all wither and die in the light.

'So, what did Gillian say?' I pressed Hod.

'She arked up is what she bloody did. She knew Calder. She's not chuffed he's dead. She doesn't want it on her conscience.'

I coughed to clear my throat. 'Did she expect me to dig around in her son's murder without upsetting people?'

Hod slid the wheel, shot me a glower. 'I think it was more the fact that you used her as leverage, then the second you've got the janny's job, he turns up . . . dead.'

'Well, y'know, if the two were related then Calder had more to answer for than we thought . . . Maybe I should have pushed him harder.'

Hod frowned. 'Yeah, well . . . tell her that – be interesting to see how she takes it.'

I chewed on that for a bit. Figured if Madam didn't like the way I worked she could find herself a new shitkicker. I held this thought for a moment, then remembered who I was really working for, said, 'Look, Hod, leave this to me. Don't sweat it, I'll sort it all out.'

Hod looked impassive. His face seemed to be paler than usual. For the first time I registered he'd probably not been on a sunbed for over a month – his gym membership was likely revoked. Christ on a rubber cross, the bloke must be feeling it. Said, 'I mean it . . . just chill. I must have interviewed a thousand snooty-nosed celebrities for the papers. All they need's a bit of ego-massaging and they're Cool and the Gang.'

He huffed, 'I hope you're right . . .'

'I am . . . They're the most simply packaged morons at root. Honestly, leave Gillian to me.'

He turned eyes back to the road, spoke softly: 'Just remember there's more at stake here than your rep, Gus. Or your own ego . . . We have Shaky to think about.'

He wasn't wrong. Shaky – and Danny Gemmill – were a serious consideration. No fucking kidding they were.

I settled back in my seat, watched the Festival traffic snarl up. This time of year was beyond nightmare scenarios on the roads. Crusty-laden Bedfords and skanky caravans creeping along at a snail's pace were only one part of the deal. There were the day-trippers to think about: the families from Falkirk dragging wee Tarquin and Jemima through for a taste of culture in the school-run 4x4 . . . like we didn't have enough of those on our roads already. It was chaos. Time to time a horn would blare, maybe a window would be wound down and an abusive driver give vent. I'd seen it all before. You live in Edinburgh, you get used to this annual circus; and the fact that this is a city run entirely for those who visit it, not those who live in it.

We travelled in silence the remainder of the way to the West End. Hod parked the van a street away to keep it out of Gillian's view. As he turned off the engine there wasn't so much as a glance in my direction. I could sense the heavy import he wanted to portray. It wasn't about money for Hod now; maybe it never had been. Sure, he was broke . . . but what use was money when it was your knackers on the line? He slipped out the door and closed it gently, waited for me on the kerb. I got out; I wasn't aware I was nibbling my lower lip but Hod clocked it and rolled his eyes. My heart seized. Craved a scoosh – bottle of. Swear if I'd had one on me I'd have downed it in a oner. My confidence evaporated as we turned for Gillian Laird's home.

Knew where this was going, how it would play out. I'd had my arse in a sling so many times it felt like comfort. This was my default gear: reverse. She'd kick off big time, maybe threaten to take her business elsewhere, which was a worry. Christ it was. Shit Street beckoned for Hod and me if that came to pass. My best card was the fact that I had a plan: there was a method in my madness; convincing a theatrical type of the fact might be a bit more difficult, though. Gillian was hard work, understood, but I figured I could play up to her and win her round. It was all about the vanity with celebrity types. To a one they had a deep-seated need to be praised, flattered, loved in disproportion to anything they deserved. No, it was the blonde by Gillian's side who was the main worry. Something about Tina unsettled me, and it went way beyond the fact that she didn't much like the look of my coupon.

The heavy soles of my Docs crunched on the gravel driveway as we approached. My legs felt heavy as I walked, there was a knot tightening in my stomach that I couldn't ignore. The discomfort threatened to have me chucking up but I fought it, schlepped on. The curtains twitched; my nerves joined in. Had they been hanging on our visit that much? Waiting by the window, ready to pounce.

My mind emptied of all thoughts. Felt light as air as Hod pressed the bell.

The dogs barked, kicking off behind the door. I straightened myself, tried to drop some steel in my spine. 'Here goes,' I said.

Hod held schtum; kept eyes focused front. I wondered what was going on behind those heavy brows of his but forced it out of my mind. I had enough to think about now.

As the door eased open I anticipated the same rigmarole from the butler bloke as we'd received on our earlier visit, but he was unfazed, not a sneer as he ushered us through the doorway. I was thinking this was going far too easy – as though he was on his best behaviour for some reason – and then my pulse jigged as I saw the cause of it.

Gillian was waiting in the hall, hands on hips.

The woman was ready to rumble.

I'd seen that look before. You get to my stage of life, my state of a life, with an ex-wife on the dial, you've seen just about every look of disappointment a woman's face can muster. Trust me on this, I know the territory. But that doesn't mean I know a way out of it.

Gillian removed her hands from her hips. For a second her fingers lay limply at her sides, then were quickly drawn into fists. Debs had never raised a hand to me, had known I'd had enough of that as a kid from my father, but if she had I was guessing she'd have been wearing this stance in the seconds before. I let Gillian see me looking her up and down, real slow; let her know if she was contemplating going hellcat I was well able for her.

I parted my feet on the heavy rug, squared shoulders. Gillian came for me. She had a powerful stride, good solid steps making contact with the hardwood flooring. There was no mistaking the sense of purpose in her movements. Had I been one of her movie directors, I'd have been smirking at the sheer power of her performance. This was award-winning stuff – had to admire her artistry, though I was guessing the whole bit was drawn from a deep well of personal hurt; there wasn't much acting going on here.

She stopped a pace or two from me, parted her mouth . . . words hung on her lips. I waited for the pay-off. None came. She closed her mouth, scrunched her brow. She actually looked confused – deeply rattled. A hand swept back a stray curl, tucked it behind her ear. The motion seemed to help her gather herself. She ran the backs of her fingers over her cheek and mouth, then quickly folded her arms. I'd always believed this was a defensive posture. It looked no such thing: Gillian was on the attack.

Her voice came slow and controlled, calm even: 'Mr Dury, if I was the type of woman to take offence, how do you think I'd be greeting you now?'

She had some moves – it was quite a gambit. I let her hang a moment, held back my desire to say *Shut the fuck up* went with: 'I believe I told you from the start, Gillian . . . if you want answers, I'm the man you need.'

Her eyes flared, went through the spectrum from warm intensity to fire in the hold, said, 'I never gave you licence, Mr Dury, to use my name to open doors like some handy credit card. And nor did I ask you to put my colleagues in such a state of fear that . . . Look, I have a reputation that extends further than this town.'

I turned away, rolled eyes. 'What you have is a dead son.'

That stung. Her lower lip trembled. It was almost imperceptible and the second it appeared she hauled it in. I waited for her reply but none came.

I continued, 'Gillian, we both know this was never going to be pretty.' I caught sight of Hod out of the corner of my eye. He looked nervous. I played it cool, dropped it down a notch or two.

'Is there somewhere we can talk? . . . There's a lot you need to know, a lot I've uncovered.'

Gillian's eyes flashed back to life. She nodded quickly, waving a palm towards the sitting room. Hod and I followed her. The leggy Tina eased herself from the shadows where she had been leaning on the jamb of a door. She wore an expression I'd seen a few times before: contempt. I had half a mind to say *Got a fucking problem, hen?* Went with, 'Hello again.' She sneered at me, shook her head as she followed her partner to the sitting room. As she went I spotted a tattoo sitting above the band of her tight black mini – what is referred to colloquially as a tramp-stamp. I looked at Hod, whispered, 'What's her bloody problem?'

'You don't know? Seems obvious to me – it's you!'

Gillian walked over to the drinks cabinet, poured herself out a large brandy, swirled it about in the base of the glass. Tina gently rubbed her back, put an arm around her shoulder. I saw that the bruising I'd noticed earlier had subsided. I made a mental note of that. Seemed worthwhile keeping tabs on this girl – and she *was* just a girl.

Gillian broke away from her young partner, said, 'Drink?'

I looked at the silver tray with crystal decanters on top – seemed to be all spirits. I wasn't about to risk it in my current condition . . . no matter how loud the wail. 'Have you anything with a bit less of a kick?'

She turned from me, reached for the handle of the cabinet below her. There was a mini-fridge tucked away. 'Wine? Beer?'

I eyed the contents: Polish lager would have to do. 'A beer would be grand.' I could feel my nerves shrieking for a taste of alcohol, any taste. I needed an hour inside that fridge, maybe with a few decanters of scoosh to help me out, but I fought hard. The consequences didn't bear thinking about, no matter how much my veins screamed for it.

Gillian handed over the beer, then turned to Hod and repeated the process.

We moved to the seating area, parked ourselves. Gillian looked sheepish, as though she wasn't sure if she wanted to hear what I had to say. I watched her cross and uncross her legs, then she took Tina's hand and clasped it tightly.

With the first tug on my beer, I was gantin' to get out my face. Tried to hold it off, pushed the beer back again and let my insides think it was just a matter of time before there was more to follow. I needed to stay calm, said, 'There's been some . . . developments.'

'Go on,' said Gillian.

How did I tell her Calder was most likely killed? That her only son was about as popular as a fart in a spacesuit? How did I tell her he was dealing drugs on campus, and supplying call girls? How did I tell her Ben was mixed up with the likes of Danny Gemmill? How did I tell her the Craft was engaged in a cover-up of his death with the very university she was now heading up? None of it sat easy with me, but she'd hired me to know this, so I told her.

When I was finished Gillian looked as if she'd fallen to earth without a parachute. I thought she must be too shocked to cross-examine me, or ask for the proof; or maybe she believed it all along and was just too tired to fight her conscience any more. Tina placed an arm around her again, stroked her hair with her other hand. Gillian was devastated. I had expected anger, denials, accusations, deflection, but the sight before me was of a mother bereft. Something in the telling had struck a chord; she knew her son, and it made sense. But she was his mother and forgave him all his sins; what she wanted more than anything was peace of mind. I knew the feeling.

'Gillian, I can see much of this is of little help to you . . . I told you it wouldn't be pretty.'

She shot eyes at Hod and me. 'Yes, yes of course . . .' She rose, walked to the other side of the room, pulled open a drawer and removed Hod's contract. She signed it before us, then handed it over to Hod. 'You'll need expenses, I suppose . . .' She returned to the drawer, took out a chequebook and started to scratch away with a pen. Hod looked satisfied when she handed over the cheque.

As Gillian came back to face me, Tina got up from the couch, walked towards the door, turned, put icy blue eyes on Gillian for a moment, then walked out. Her heels sounded like hammer blows as she stomped down the hall. I figured this was a move she'd perfected storming out of some chippy or other on Leith Walk after a row with a schemie boyfriend, or maybe even a pimp. It was all street trash theatrics; she was showing her true worth – in all its glory.

'I'm sorry . . . she doesn't approve of . . . this,' said Gillian.

'Oh, no?'

She shook her head. 'Thinks sleeping dogs are best left to lie. Thinks I don't have my troubles to seek.'

'And you, what do you think?'

She pressed the sides of her mouth back. It was a weak attempt at a smile of sorts, said, 'I need to know . . . I need to know the truth about what happened to Ben.'

I felt her grief; I'd lost loved ones myself, knew that nothing prepares you. Knew the need to know eclipses everything at times of pain. Gillian wouldn't rest till she had all the answers. I admired her strength, her resolve . . . I just hoped Tina wasn't right. Though something told me her motives were entirely different from what she was letting on.

I thanked Gillian, said, 'I'll be in touch.' We headed for the door.

Tina was sulking by the window in the front room. She had a cigarette in her hand; I couldn't see an ashtray. I nodded to her. She turned away, leaned against the wall, one high-heeled shoe supporting her, just like a proper brasser.

As the door closed on us, Hod pulled out the contract and kissed it. 'Oh, Gus . . . fucking nice one, mate.'

I couldn't share his enthusiasm. I was glad for him, but I knew the shit was shaping up to hit the fan. There were so many interests lining up to stick the knife in me that I felt like yon Pop-up Pirate.

CHAPTER 20

I was woken by the mobi going off next to my ear – bit of Chemical Brothers was normally a good get, but not this time of the day. Knocked over a few empty stout tins as I reached for the phone, said, 'Hello.'

'Gus, that you?'

I recognised the hardy voice at once. 'Mr Bacon . . . yeah, it's me.'

'Good, good . . . How you keeping?'

Was this a fucking social call . . . this early? '*What*?'

'Aye, small chat, eh, screw that. Just calling to let you know I looked out that stuff you were after.'

'The files?'

'Oh, aye . . . quite a few. Some good reading in there as well.'

'There is?'

'Bastardin' sure there is. That laddie was up to his neck in some muck!'

'Oh, really . . .'

Rasher's voice arked up: 'Fucking wee scumbag, so he was . . . Looking at this load on my desk,

I'd say he wasn't far off a stretch at Her Majesty's displeasure. Total wee toley so he was.'

'Sounds like interesting stuff.'

'You're no' kidding, but that's not the half of it.'

'It's not?'

'Not by a long stretch. Turned up something that I think you might be interested in having a wee look at.'

'From the files?'

A spark of enthusiasm: 'Aye, from the files . . . and let me tell you, Dury, you get a link to this wee beauty and there's a page-one splash with your name on it!'

He had my interest. 'Go on then, spill the beans.'

'Uh-uh . . . Better we meet up for this.'

'Okay, I'll come into the office later.'

He pitched his tone lower: 'Oh fuck no. Got the top brass in today. Heid bummers from down south, got to get the red carpet out.'

I didn't want to hang about on this. 'Tomorrow, then?'

A pause, rustle of papers, opening of a desk diary. 'Friday . . . can you make the afternoon?'

Would have to do. 'Aye, okay.'

I hung up.

Spent the rest of the morning on the verge of banging seven shades of shite out of my mobile phone. Had stopped sending texts for some reason – would be close to the built-in obsolescence period, no doubt. Toyed with the idea of complaining to the shop, the service provider . . . thought better of it. Had long since given up on taking on the capitalist behemoth, better chucking the phone in the bin and buying a new one: that's what they want after all; resistance is useless. The days where I saw myself wasting precious energy on the phone to Mumbai call centres and filling in customer complaints were long over, life was too short. Mine sure as hell was.

Had holed up in a spit-and-sawdust B&B in the Southside, one of those joints where they house dole moles and immigrants. An Indian bloke was running the shop. Seemed a nice enough sort, but cringing Christ, I wouldn't like his paper round. I'd been here one night only and had already started counting fights to get myself to sleep. Rough wasn't the word.

I cracked the seal on a tin of Murphy's. I'd tanned a score of those bad boys already. Was about to spark up when my mobi rang: wasn't fully on the way out, then.

Recognised the caller ID straight off. 'Amy . . . was trying to text you but—'

'Spare me, eh.'

There was a note of derision in her voice; she had the tone down cold. Had to admire that, Amy did a nice line in no-messing attitude. I said, 'No, seriously, got some techno trouble . . . Mobi isn't texting out.'

'Fucksake, Gus . . . have you checked it's not full?'

'*Y'wha'*?'

'Look at the screen. Is there a red icon or something?'

I took a deck, spotted a little red square with an 'x' in it. Hadn't seen that before. 'Yeah, there is . . . what's that about, then?'

Amy laughed. 'Christ, Gus, get with the programme! Your phone is so shite it only stores a pissy amount of texts . . . You'll have to delete some.'

Felt a total dope. Tried to snigger around it; wasn't happening. 'Yeah, right . . . I knew that. Look, to what do I owe the pleasure, Ames?'

Her voice changed, dropped an octave or two. 'Pleasure . . . I'm all about the pleasure, Gus.'

'Yeah, keep it up, see where it gets you.' Shit, I was flirting now. Where was my head?

'That a promise?'

Clawed it back: 'Yeah, whatever . . . So, you rang.'

A stall, some deep breaths taken. I could hear her juggling the phone with the cupboard doors, cups, kettle. 'I thought you might like to know that I've got a date.'

Felt a twinge in my gut – didn't know why. If I did, I wouldn't let on. 'You have?'

'Big time.' She sounded pleased.

'Amy, I'm very happy for you . . . but did you think you needed to call and let me know or is there more to this?'

A laugh, sharp exhalation followed. 'In your fucking dreams, sunshine! I'm calling to let you know I have a date with Danny Gemmill.'

My heart stilled. I let a long silence stretch out on the line. My mind seemed to reboot: was she serious? Couldn't be for real. 'Yeah, right.'

'What?'

'Gemmill . . . you're cracking on to him? . . . Sure.'

Amy slipped into shit-stopping seriousness. 'I am as well. Think I'd make that up? Like, why?'

Now my heart kicked up a notch, felt ready to blow. This was Amy I was dealing with after all: there was no telling what the fuck she would pull next. She was off-the-scale scripto at the best of times. 'Amy, are you off yer fucking dial? Do you even know who you're messing with here? . . . Jesus Christ, he's beyond the borderline psycho range. Gemmill's a full-on mentaller!'

'I can handle myself.'

I had to laugh. She didn't like it – I heard a tut. 'Look, girl, this guy's a fucking nut-job – get me? He's already put me in the hospital. Think he'll treat you any differently when he finds out what you're up to?'

'I said I can handle myself, Gus.' She was deadly serious.

I lost it: 'Handle your fucking self! You're a silly wee lassie! Bloody hell, Amy, there's no way you're seeing Gemmill . . . no fucking way! It's just not on, not on . . . you hear me?' I was ranting so strong, so loud and long, that I'd missed the fact that she'd hung up.

'Fuck!' I hit my contacts, dialled her number.

Went to voicemail. 'Amy, look, call me back, eh. We need to talk. I'm not kidding about Danny Gemmill, he's bad news . . . Don't do this, seriously, just don't do it. I know you're not a silly wee lassie, you'll see sense, so just leave this to me now. Please, huh? . . . I'll call you later, we'll go for a bite to eat or something, grab a movie, eh. Okay, Ames, we'll speak soon, eh. Right, catch you later.' What was I saying? It was all too much too late. I'd fucked right up.

I hoped she'd see sense, that she'd hear the message and see beyond my sparking up when she'd called. I knew Amy wasn't the headstrong young girl of just a few years ago – she'd matured. Surely there was no way she'd go through with this. She'd see sense. She'd realise she'd gone too far . . . least, I hoped she would. I hoped I was right with a lot of my assumptions about Amy. Felt my stomach flutter, muttered, 'Get a grip, boy.' Where was my head? What the fuck was I thinking? Amy? Never. There was way too much baggage there.

I took the tin of Murphy's up to my mouth, slugged deep, stopped for air. Not for long, though. I started to pace. I was all over the fucking shop. Needed to sort myself out. Being holed up in a tenner-a-night kip house with woodchip on the walls and baked-in barf on the carpet had a strangely hypnotic effect on me – or maybe it was the booze – made me think I'd hit my true level.

My mind spiralled, I was seriously worried.

Played out the scenario where I called Hod, listened to him blasting me on the trip out to Amy's. I knew she was a big girl now. But Danny Gemmill, Holy Christ . . . he was a nut-job. He could seriously hurt her.

I grabbed my coat, headed for the stairs.

The way Amy operated, I knew Gemmill'd have to be fucking superhuman not to spill his guts to her, and more besides. When he found out who she was he'd string her up. What he did to her after that would be prolonged, and painful. I couldn't bear to think of it.

My mobi went.

Answered: 'Amy.'

'You chilled any yet?'

'Look, I'm only thinking about . . . y'know, you.'

I heard a sigh. 'You're pissed. I can hear it in your voice.'

'I'm not fucking pissed. Amy, I'm serious . . . I don't want you to get hurt.'

'*Hurt*?'

'Aye, Gemmill's a crazy . . . you know that.'

A pause on the line, then soft tones. 'Gus, I've been hurt before . . .' she let that hang, went, 'I'm not worried about anything that loser throws at me. I can take care of myself.'

There was no holding her back – she was a force of nature. She really thought she had the guts to go through with this, to handle Gemmill. 'Amy, this is Danny Gemmill—'

She livened. 'So what? He'll be putty in my hands.'

'Somehow I doubt that!'

A laugh. 'You perv.'

I clawed it in: 'I'm not joking. How in hell did this come about?'

'I have my ways.'

She certainly did. I still remembered her hard-core declarations of undying love for me when she was a cub reporter at the *Hootsman*: cost her a job. Still, she'd sorted herself out now, moved on a lot since then. Matured.

'I know you do. But Amy, I can't let you do this . . . it's way too dangerous.'

'Gus, I don't need mothering.'

She was right about that; I knew she was of hardy stock. I just couldn't help feeling protective. 'I know, I know but . . .'

'No buts, I know what I'm doing.'

I sparked up a Marlboro as I descended the stairs, passing through to the lobby with the rotting sash windows. 'Well, I seriously doubt that.'

'Gus . . .'

I didn't like the sound of her reaction. 'No, Amy, I mean it, I want you to stay put. Cancel Gemmill.' I eased into the street, flagged down a Joe Baxi. I needed to keep her talking now.

'Okay, okay.' She sounded perfunctory; there was no conviction in her words. It unsettled me. She was suddenly taking this far too casually; putting me on.

I covered the phone, told the driver to boot it for Amy's gaff. I needed to throw her a line. 'I've got a few other irons in the fire, don't think there's any need to go overboard. Way things are shaping, you might be seeing a bit more of me than usual.'

'*Really*?'

'I've taken a job at the uni.'

'No way!'

'Yes way . . . a janitor's job. So, when you get back, when term starts again . . .'

The laughter was deafening. 'Get the fuck out of town.'

I waited for her to dry her eyes, said, 'Are you quite finished?'

'Oh, Gus, that's a laugh riot. Have you got the Brylcreem looked out? And the teeth . . . you have to get a few teeth blacked up. Fuck me, this will be a mental laugh!'

'Yeah, okay, guffaw away. I'm not doing this for a giggle, there's a serious motive here, remember? It's a boy's death we're looking into.'

Silence.

It was short-lived. 'You're so right!'

The driver blasted his horn, shouted at some skanky junkies in blankets crossing the road.

'Amy . . . you still there?'

Her voice lightened, took on a serious note: 'Yes, Gus, but I've got to go.'

'Amy . . . Amy . . .'

The dial lit. She'd clicked off.

CHAPTER 21

There's a phrase, *burn rubber*. That's where I was at with this taxi driver already.

'C'mon, man . . . give it some poke, eh,' I yelled through the perspex.

The bloke turned. 'You serious, guv?' He was London – Christ on a cross, where did we find them? What was happening to this city? We'd have our own pearly kings and queens next.

'Fucking deadly!' I put the bead on him, let that sting in my tone settle down there a bit, take a bite out of him. He played it cool but had got the message. Two-wheeled the cab onto the kerb and floored it. We didn't have far to go, but there wasn't any time to be lost. Knew Amy was probably already putting on her lip gloss. Shit. My mind ran through a thousand dodgy scenarios.

What the hell was that girl thinking? She knew the kip of Gemmill, he wasn't going to be turning up with a fucking rose in his mouth and tickets for Rachmaninov at the Usher Hall. More likely to be ten pints at some skanky drinker at the foot of the Walk . . . phial of Rohypnol thrown in if she wasn't careful. I felt the blood pumping in my neck; my jaw tightened.

'C'mon . . . c'mon . . .'

Fair fucks to the cabbie, he was pushing it.

We flew down Lothian Road in the bus lane, turned a hairpin into Amy's street. As we pulled up I could see it was almost too late.

'Shit!' I grabbed at the handle on the door. It was locked.

'That's seven quid, guv.'

I tugged at the handle again but it wouldn't budge. I looked out the windscreen at Amy in the street, walking towards a familiar motor – Hod's Beemer. Gemmill stood grinning on the pavement, opening up the passenger door and pointing her inside. He had on the same black leather that he wore to go stomping heads. I'd had a close enough look at it myself.

'Fucking hell, let me out here, mate,' I said.

'No can do . . . need paying first.'

I ranted, waved a fist at him. He smirked beyond the perspex, then picked up the handset on his radio, threatening to call plod. 'I can drive you kicking and screaming if you like.'

I dug in my pockets, yelled, 'Fucksake . . .'

I kept an eye on Amy. Could see Gemmill putting a hand on her arse. I blew up inside – wanted to feed him that wandering mitt; would make sure I broke every digit on the way in. I rummaged in my pockets further, came up with a fiver, fed it through the slot.

'Two quid shy,' said the cabbie.

I was ready to go postal. Gemmill closed the passenger door, waving to Amy as he skipped round the back of the car. He had a grin on his face as he rubbed his palms together. I knew what was on his mind.

I rummaged in all of my pockets – they were empty.

Gemmill opened up the driver's door, ducked in behind the steering wheel.

Heard him turn over the ignition.

Exhaust fumes spilled from the back pipe.

'No, fuck . . .'

He didn't drive off. He leaned over to plant a kiss on Amy's cheek. She grabbed his face, went for the mouth. What the fuck was she thinking? Was she even thinking? This was madness.

I uncovered a two-pound coin in the pocket of my jeans; threw it at the cabbie.

'Right, that's the seven then . . .'

I amped it up: 'Open the fucking door, y'cunt!'

'There's no need for any language, guv.'

I shot him daggers; got the result. He knew he couldn't push it any further with me. The door popped.

I hit the street like Usain Bolt – tanked it towards the Beemer. Could feel my heart pounding, fit to burst. I wasn't up for this lark. Not by a long stroke. My lungs started to panic, my breath shortened. The car was still sitting in the street, though, spilling blue-grey smoke.

I could see Gemmill munching the face off Amy; it was like two teenagers under the chute for the first time. Was sure I heard someone yell, 'Get a room!' I was about fifty yards off when Gemmill broke free, engaged first gear and spun the tyres.

'No way!'

I upped the pace but my legs bucked. I felt a stagger towards the flags, for a second it was like I was flying . . . I was wrong – I was dropping. I landed face first on the paving stones. My hands broke my fall – stung like a bastard. A million tiny nerve endings registered their disapproval as the flesh ripped open and painted two black-red streaks on the pavement. My face followed, smacked my mouth off the concrete. For a second it felt as though a china cup had been broken in my mouth, then my bridgework made a bid for freedom, spilled like shattered glass on the street before me. My pain centres arked up. I felt a sharp stab in my gut as my face bounced, then my forehead slapped into the ground.

I could taste warm, salty blood rise on my tongue. For a moment I coughed to clear my throat, then gave up. I sensed a frothy stream of vomit spilling from the side of my mouth as I passed out.

The times I've seen this . . .

He's been dropped from the first team. The man carries a gut Jocky Wilson would be proud of – what does he expect? I must be twelve or thirteen, everyone says it's a 'difficult age'. They don't know the half of it.

I come in from school and I'm shocked to see him so drunk. It's not four o'clock yet. This is new territory. Even for him.

'Oh, it's himself . . . little Boy Wonder.'

I brought home a report card the day before; he has it in his hand. In the other, a tin of Cally Special. There's a stack of them in the waste bin with the Spanish dancing lady painted on the front, and more yet on the carpet. He's been sat in the seat by the fire throwing empty tins to the bin. My mother is perched on the edge of the couch like a delicate little bird; her hand trembles every time she brings the Berkeley Superking to her mouth. Her spine straightens as she sees me come in. Some ash falls from the cigarette in her pale, thin hand. Her eyes flit quickly between my father and me as I stand in the doorway. I know what's coming.

'So what the fuck do you call this?' He shakes the report card at me.

I shrug.

Mam stands up, dowps her cig in the ashtray, smooths down the sides of her skirt. 'Now, now . . . come on,' she says.

The mighty Cannis Dury roars, 'And you can shut the fuck up . . . When I want to hear an opinion from you I'll fucking well tell you what to say!'

Mam curls her lower lip. I can see the heavy

make-up filling the creases at the sides of her mouth. She puts an arm around me and pats down my stray fringe. It's as if the action sparks a bolt of life in my father. He leaps from the chair and jerks her from me.

'Get away from him.' He throws my mother on the floor. She looks up at him as she lands with a clatter of bone on wooden floorboards. Her face is twisted, her mouth seems to change colour. I want to go to her but I'm frozen to the spot. My father is looming over me. He's an awesome size, drowns my pathetic child's frame into shadows. 'What the fuck is this?' He waves the report card at me. I see the line of As . . . and the single C.

I say nothing. I feel my throat freeze but an almighty anger is burning in my gut. I want to go to my mother. She speaks: 'Please, Cannis . . . leave the laddie. He's a good laddie.'

He turns to her, waving the report card again. 'But whose fucking laddie? . . . no' fucking mine!'

I can't believe I've heard the words. I know what they mean – I'm a smart laddie, everyone says so.

My mother looks away, starts to cry. My father strides over to her, grabs her hair and throws her to the wall. She lands against the bin, Cally Special tins spill out onto the floor. Her eyes close tight as she falls; there's blood on her mouth. As she lands I see the blood drip down the side of her pure white cheek. It seems so red, so out of place on that perfectly drawn face of hers.

I watch him loom over her. She doesn't move.

Even when he kicks her in the stomach and raises her whole body from the ground again and again there doesn't seem to be any movement from her. She's lifeless. All that moves is the slow trickle of blood when he steps back from her.

'He's no' ma fucking laddie . . . C for Games. No' ma fucking laddie, y'dirty hoor.'

He's still holding the report card as he turns from her. He staggers into the dresser, breathing heavily as he approaches me. I know I should move, dive out of the way, but I'm frozen to the spot. He sees me staring at him, wipes the sweat from his brow. I wonder will he speak but he doesn't seem to have any words for me, just brushes me aside.

I hear his noisy footfalls on the staircase, then his heavy frame falling into the bed. I wait for what seems like an age for my muscles to return to my control. I feel like a different person now, confused and alone. I begin to tremble, in my shoulders to begin with, then all down my spine and into my legs. My knees are buckling and I fall over.

The floor jolts me, sends a shock through my body and I come back to myself. I remember my mother, lying beaten in the corner. I try to get up to go to her but find myself walking on all fours like a dog. When I reach her I see her pale white face is now streaked with blood. I touch her but she doesn't move. Her skin feels cold as stone. For a moment, I think he's killed her.

A bolt of electricity passes through me.

I run out to the street. I don't know where I'm going. I know my sister and brother will be home from school soon; they can't see her like this. They'd have questions – what would I tell them?

I run to the red call box at the end of the street.

I know I have no money, but quickly remember emergency calls are free. I dial 999.

In no time at all the loud bells of the ambulance are in the street. Neighbours come out to see what the commotion is all about. Old women in tabards and headscarves touch their faces and look shocked as the stretcher men carry my mother away.

My father doesn't raise himself from his bed as the ambulance bells start up again and rush her to hospital.

I watched the blue flashing lights . . .

'Mr Dury . . . Mr Dury . . . can you hear me, sir?'

I said nothing. My mind was very far away.

'Mr Dury . . .'

The words didn't register. I saw people standing over me. The street seemed to have come to a standstill. It felt like I was floating. On a cloud, maybe.

'Mr Dury . . .' said the man again. 'Nope, he's away. Get him up.'

A red blanket was brought out, the paramedics raised me.

I saw the blue lights flashing brighter for a moment, then all the lights stopped.

CHAPTER 22

I was back in hospital, trying to piece things together.

For a while now my memory hadn't been what it once was, or what it should be. There were huge gaps appearing in the annals of my mind. The day-to-day stuff I could just about get away with, bluffing out the standard responses and catch-phrases everyone used to grease the wheels of life, but the more important matters were slipping from me. Short term I was a disaster: put down a set of keys or a coat and I needed a sniffer dog to find them. Long term wasn't much better; tying dates to past events was an impossibility. About the only things that I did recall with any clarity were the hard times: boyhood beatings and scoldings from my father; the wreckage of my marriage to Debs. Figured I'd replayed those so many times in morose, whisky-soaked meanderings that they were on repeat play at the back of my mind. Couldn't wash them out with a power hose. Had tried to drown them, but that was coming back to haunt me now.

I knew I needed to confront my mother. I had been to the brink replaying the times my father had beaten her senseless . . . but one memory haunted more than others.

I'd put my mother on ice for so long now, since I'd relapsed into drink and had lost any pretence to normality, there was no way I could face her without scalding her heart. She knew me too well; she'd take one look at me and suss that I was close to the grave. Still, I didn't want to go there just yet, and I sure as hell didn't want to go there without asking her the question I'd kept inside me for all these years. Why was I thinking about this now? I knew the answer: I felt as though I was running out of time to ask her the truth.

There was a jug of water at my bedside. I felt queasy just looking at it. I needed something stronger.

Someone had put a saline drip in me again; I couldn't recall any of it.

My clothes hung on a rail at the side of the bed. I was tempted to dress and depart but my head hurt too much; I wasn't functioning. Wondered had they medicated me?

As I sat up in the bed a nurse at the end of the ward stirred and approached me.

'Back in the land of the living are you?' she said.

I winced – too close to home, said, 'Doesn't feel like it.'

A frown. 'Well, I'd say this is about as good as it gets for you right now, Mr Dury.'

The thought burned. 'Oh, right . . .'

'You're in a terrible condition . . . We got hold of your records, there's no telling you, is there?'

Did that require an answer? The look on her face, I doubted it. She was wearing me down.

'How long have I been here?'

Full-on head shakes. 'You came in with the paramedics about two hours ago. The doctor's seen you once, so he won't be back until tomorrow now, unless there's an emergency.'

'Emergency?'

'You're in a terrible condition, Mr Dury . . . like I said.'

Way I felt, I didn't doubt her. 'Thanks for passing that on.'

She turned heels, left for the door.

I wasn't about to wait for her to return. My mind was resurfacing; the memory of Amy getting into the car with Danny Gemmill flashed like headlights. I needed to get moving. Christ, what had I let that girl get herself into? I knew what Gemmill was capable of: Amy was wading into some serious shit. I'd fucked up . . . falling in the street and getting carted away by an ambulance! Holy Christ, Gus, this was a new low. But it was Amy who would be paying the price of it.

I got up, grabbed my mobi from my jacket pocket.

Dialled.

'Hod, that you?'

'Aye, aye . . . where the fuck you been?'

'Never mind that. I need a pick-up.'

'Y'what?'

'Look, get hold of Mac as well . . . We'll need some back-up.'

'I don't like the sound of this, Gus.' Normally, any hint of a rumble had Hod rubbing palms together. Funny how he'd changed.

'Neither do I.'

'I'm not sure, I mean . . . Gus, I'm lying low . . . Don't want to run into Shaky.'

I could see he was going to take some persuading. 'Hod, I have to tell you something. Now, you're not going to like this . . .'

His voice dropped to the pitch above whisper: 'Go on.'

'It's Amy—'

'Amy! Fucking hell, Gus, you said you'd keep her out of this.'

'I know. I know . . . but Amy's Amy. You can't put a bloody lead on her.'

'Jesus . . . I don't like the sound of this.'

I took a sharp intake of breath, said, 'Well, you'll like the sound of this even less. I saw her taking off with Gemmill about a couple of hours ago.'

'And now you come to me!'

I could feel Hod's anger searing down the line.

'Yeah, well . . . I got waylaid; sidetracked, you might say.'

'What you on about?'

I filled him in, told him where I was. Thought it might cut me some slack; it did, kinda. Sensed Hod felt he'd two problems to take care of now.

'Gus . . . you need to haud yer steam. This is becoming a habit.'

Like I needed telling. 'Yeah, okay.'

'I'm serious, man. Next time it won't be the hospital – they'll be taking you straight to the morgue.'

It was a lovely image. 'Thanks for that, mate.'

'If I won't tell you . . . who will?'

I walked back to the clothes rail, pulled down the hanger with my tweed jacket and trousers, said, 'Right, message received and understood . . . Get your arse into gear. I'll see you and Mac out the front in five to ten.'

Swear I could see him shaking his head. Nothing was shaping up like he'd intended – wondered if he regretted getting me on the job. Christ, he probably regretted even getting the cards printed.

Made an arse of pulling out the drip again, but was relieved not to break the needle this time. Soon as I chucked it, the shakes came back to my hands. It felt like I'd been lucky to hold them off. I dressed hurriedly, struggled on the shirt buttons and belt buckle but got there. The Docs were another matter altogether, gave up on the laces, tucked them in.

An old bloke in striped flannel pyjamas, open to the waist and exposing a bony chest, raised himself up. 'You'll break yer bloody neck, son.'

My heart seared when he called to me, said, 'That's the least of my worries.'

'Ye cannae go out with yer laces flapping aboot

. . . Here, put yer boots up.' He motioned to the edge of his bed, tapping the blanket.

I felt blown away by his kindness; walked over and raised my boot. The motion nearly felled me and I had to sit on the edge of my bed to steady myself.

The old bloke said, 'You sure yer fit for this, lad?'

'Oh aye, I'm right as rain.'

He widened his eyes, looked over the bridge of his craggy nose as he tied my bootlaces. 'Well, it's no' for me to stick my oar in.'

He tapped the bed for the second boot. As I watched him, I put his age at mid-eighties. He was a rare character. Had I more time to play with, I wouldn't have minded spending it in his company, but try as I might, the thoughts of Amy and Gemmill wouldn't subside.

'Thanks very much,' I said, 'very kind of you.'

He smiled at me, a broad toothless smirk. I fired him one back. Could feel the gaps in my mouth where my bridgework had taken a flyer; thought I must look a sight.

I stumbled out the ward, and past the reception desk at the front door.

Sparked up a Regal in the car park as I waited for Hod and Mac to appear. My hands shook so hard now that I could hardly get the tab to my gob without gripping my forearm and grasping for the filter-tip as if I was dooking for apples. Sorry state indeed.

I was on the third tab, though thinking of something much stronger, when Hod and Mac appeared. Hod was driving, chucking the van into the bends and pushing the revs. The vehicle didn't look like it could handle much more of that punishment – the lean so extreme that the shocks screeched as though they'd entered their death throes.

The pair glowered at me as they pulled up. Mac leaned out the open window; his face held firm, stony. 'Fucking hell, Dury . . . you got a death wish?'

'Yeah. Yeah,' I barked back – let them know early on that I wasn't for taking any shit on this. I'd done my best to stop her. Was it my fault that she was out of control? I didn't want to know the answer to that.

Mac opened the door then slunk back beside Hod. 'I'm no' on about the hospital . . . I'm on about Gemmill. Are you off yer fucking dial mixing it with the likes of yon?'

'He has Amy.'

'Aye, so fucking what? If that daft wee sow's no' got the marbles to—'

I cut him off, 'Shut the fuck up, Mac.'

The pair of them looked at me. Hod spoke: 'Getting a bit protective, Gus? . . . Bit late in the day for that, isn't it?'

I knew where he was coming from. I also knew he still held a flame for Amy; I let the comment slide. More conflict, more complication, I could well do without. 'Where are we headed, then?' I asked.

Mac spoke, 'Drinker in Leith. Know a man who knows Gemmill.'

'Think he's gonna tell us anything?'

Mac looked at me like I'd tested him, said, 'He'll tell us.'

I'd forgotten how connected Mac was. If he said he had a man in the know, that was good enough for me. Hod pulled out. As we drove, the silence in the cab of the van was palpable. I knew the pair of them were bursting to have a go at me, a full-on swipe for getting Amy involved, for getting myself in hospital again . . . for being the usual cockhead that I'd proven myself to be time and time again. But they held schtum. I was grateful for that – fuck knows I had nothing else to be glad of.

I put my hands in my pockets and tried to draw fists to stop the trembling. Knew it was futile. Felt the tremors spreading along the seat towards Mac and Hod. I was, as they were both dying to tell me, in some shape. I let the shakes mount up, mingle with the tension, then I fired up: 'Look, I know you're both itching to cane my arse, so let's just get that out the way, eh.'

Mac looked at Hod. They both shook their heads. This was worse than I thought. They'd gone beyond that stage. They were in damage-limitation mode. I could tell by the look on them that they thought I was past help. I was at the stage where no one else could reach me. I felt their concern; it made me think of Debs. I'd seen the look on her many times before. She knew me better than anyone. Was that why she wouldn't speak to me? Was it too painful for her to see me this way? I looked at my mobi, in forlorn hope that she might have returned one of my calls . . . Nothing. I felt an almighty urge to call her again, to tell her I thought I'd sussed her out, but I fought it. Now wasn't the time. And I had more pressing matters to worry about.

I dialled Amy's number.

Ringing.

Three rings in total, then voicemail.

I left a message: 'Amy, it's Gus . . . where the hell are you, eh? Look, I saw you with Gemmill. He's fucking dangerous, I'm not kidding. Tell me where you are, eh? Get away from him and call . . . I'll come get you. Please, Amy. This isn't a game. It's serious now, call me right back.'

I put down the phone, caught Mac's eye on me. It wasn't one of his more kindly stares.

'Yeah?' I said.

'Think that'll do any good?'

'What do you mean?'

He turned on the seat, staring intently at me, pointed a finger in my chest. 'If Gemmill knows she's connected to you, Gus, she's probably already on a fucking meathook.'

I brushed him aside, yelled at Hod, 'Look, can you drive any bloody slower?'

'Don't be sparking at me, boyo.'

I wasn't taking that. 'Boyo now, is it? Well, let me fucking remind you whose idea this case was!'

'Aye, aye . . . and who told you to keep Amy out of it?'

'You'll be accusing me of playing Cilla to her and Gemmill next!'

Mac slapped the dash. 'Right, enough's enough! . . . You heard the pair of you? Like fucking four-year-olds. Cool the beans, eh. If we're going to find this lassie we need to keep the heid.'

He was right, but I wasn't admitting anything.

I turned to the window, tucked my trembling hands back in my coat pockets as Hod drove. I could see the hallucinations returning if I didn't snap out of this frame of mind. I felt myself tripping – falling out with myself again. It was never a good state at the best of times, but in the current circumstances, with Amy's life on the line, I might as well just check out.

As we hit Leith Walk the place was in chaos. Tram works in full swing, the road dug up. A tailback stretched all the way from the roundabout down London Road. Horns blared, the normal rules of the road chucked out the window. At Festival time you expect such shit, but things were worse than ever with the tram works. Every bin in the street was full, spilling rubbish onto the ground. Tourists and locals waded through the muck, shaking their heads. Don't think I'd ever wanted out more. Felt an unholy pull towards a new life. Somewhere far away; somewhere I could be someone else. I spiralled out of control . . . out of hope.

I turned to Mac. 'So, this mate of yours . . . he reliable?'

Mac's voice was low, flat. 'Well, for a start, he's no mate of mine.'

'Sounds dodgy.'

'He's a mate of Gemmill's.'

'But you know him?'

'We were in Bar-L together. Gemmill was in for a four-stretch at the time. We all crossed paths.'

'But he kept in with Gemmill?'

'Aye . . . I didn't.'

'Why not?'

'Cos the cunt's fucking radge.'

I knew that myself, remembered his face as he'd stomped on my guts in the King's Arms. He was wild. Lost it. Out of control. None of this sounded promising. 'So what makes you think he'll fill you in on where to get Gemmill?'

Mac rubbed the edge of his Chelsea smile. 'Nothing . . . just gonna play it casual, hope he's too dippit to cop on.'

'Jesus, this could backfire badly. What if he tips off Gemmill?'

Mac dropped his hand, exhaled a long breath. 'Aye, well, I thought about that myself . . . but didn't come up with an answer. You got a better idea?'

I took my eyes off him, looked to the road in front, said, 'God help us.'

Hod butted in, forcing his voice high above its natural range: 'It's Amy you should be praying for.'

CHAPTER 23

Hod and I watched Mac cross the street to the pub. I'd seen more than my fair share of Leith drinkers but this place was a total doss. Two skelky yoofs stood outside like ornamental hoodies, hanging off filter-tips, and watching a pair of Staffies in heavy leather and brass harnesses circle each other in preparation for a scrap. Three yards from the door an old man in an Andy Capp hat and dirty mac took a piss against the wall; he could hardly stand and looked likely to keel at any moment. The snoutcasts, at least half a dozen of them, looked unfazed by either of these scenes – it was just another day in paradise.

'Some fucking kip, that place,' said Hod.

'No kidding.'

At the door, Mac took a hand out of his jacket pocket and pushed his way in. I felt relieved this was his gig and not mine. There was no way I was up to taking on any of the locals if they got uppity at the sight of a strange face. Round here, a fresh coupon is likely taken as filth.

Hod spoke: 'So, the hospital again . . .'

'What about it?' I was in no mood for a lecture. Had taken more than enough of them in my day.

'Nothing.' He knew better than to have a go. Went on, but his voice changed tone again. 'I, eh, bumped into your mam.'

This was unexpected. At the best of times Hod didn't hang anywhere my mother was likely to be, and he had been lying low. He was up to something. 'You did?'

'Aye, okay . . . Look, I called her, told her you'd been in the hospital.'

I fired up, 'You did fucking what?'

'Gus, I had to . . . She asked me to . . .'

'She asked you to what?'

He scratched at the stubble on his chin. 'She asked me to let her know if you were . . . y'know, ever in a bad way again, just to let her know.'

This wasn't good. The last thing I needed was my mother piling on the grief; Jesus, I had enough of that to be worrying about as it was. 'Oh, she did, did she?'

Hod swivelled on his hip, turned to face me, his eyelids drooping heavily as his gaze fell. 'She's worried about you. She's your mother . . .'

'I know that.'

'Then don't you think you should let her know you're okay?'

I shot him a glower. 'Do I look okay, Hod?'

'All I'm saying is, I think you should give her a call . . . pay her a visit, maybe.'

It had been on my mind anyway, for altogether

different reasons. I just didn't know if I had the bottle. 'Okay, well, thanks for the advice. I'll bear it in mind.'

He turned away again, stared back at the pub. The old jakey in the mac had tried to get back inside but was being thrown out by a biffer with a towel tucked in his waistband and tats down each arm. He handled the old bloke as though he was made of straw. I half expected to see him taken by the breeze. It was a scene that was probably being played out in dozens of pubs throughout the city; though none of the trendy pubs filled to bursting with Festival-goers would see the like. Uh-uh. We keep this stuff well out of their way. No one wants to see the real Edinburgh – no one would pay a penny for that.

Said, 'Wonder how Mac'll do?'

'I'm more worried about Amy.' The statement came with a cruel look. It was another low blow, but I didn't doubt I deserved it. I didn't doubt I deserved a whole lot worse.

'Hod, you know there's no way I'd put that girl in any danger.' It was a long shot trying to make him see that I was on his side with this one, but at the very least I hoped I could make him agree that Amy was a law unto herself. We both felt far too much for the girl to see her hurt; he got that, surely.

'Yeah, and you know what she's like, Gus.'

He had me there. It was my fault she was in this situation. I'd been stupid enough to call her in – what had I been thinking? I was in no condition to be keeping an eye on her. I wondered where my mind was? Knew exactly what my intention had been, but held schtum, covered my arse. 'Yeah, sure . . . but Hod, we needed to get moving on the case.'

'You could have kept her out of it, that's all I'm saying.'

'I didn't even hint at her getting anything off Gemmill. I asked her to snoop around at the uni . . . this was a complete shock to me as well.'

He wasn't buying it. 'Gus, have you ever known Amy to do things by halves? . . . You must have had a fucking inkling she'd go off on one.'

I was getting nowhere. 'Go on, then, blame it all on me.' I was trying to do my best by him; I knew he was in deep shit and I wanted to help out. Christ, neither of us were doing great and the case was likely too much for us but we'd taken it on now and I'd be fucked if I was walking away after what we'd uncovered. I'd seen the look on Gillian Laird's face: she knew her son hadn't been a gasper. There was more to it than that. Dealing for Danny Gemmill was bad enough, but Fitz's revelations about the Craft silencing his nephew was tipping tragic. This kind of thing fired me up – I'd never been comfortable with the games the big boys played. If they kicked their ball in my direction, it was going back with a puncture – even if it took my last breath to deliver it.

Mac appeared in the doorway again. He put his

collar up and shuffled through the smokers. I tried to read his face but he wasn't giving anything away. I hoped to Christ his contact had come good; I didn't want any more on my conscience than I had already. And I certainly didn't want to lose Amy.

Hod started the engine.

Mac kept his pace casual, not wanting to draw attention to himself in case he was being watched. He fitted in perfectly among the chib-men and heavies; Christ, didn't he just. You couldn't do better with an identikit.

When he finally got in the van he said, 'Right, back to the city.'

'You got a place?'

'Corstorphine Road. Gemmill's been drinking in some hotel out there lately.'

Hod found first, pulled out. The old engine rattled a bit, coughed out some smoke. I hoped it wouldn't overheat on the way out.

'So what's the go?' I asked.

Mac shook his head. 'There's no fucking go . . . think I got chatty with the cunt? It was casual as fuck. I just asked if he'd seen Gemmill about and if he knew where he was drinking these days.'

It sounded dodge, Mac just dropping by a strange drinker, asking questions. 'Did he cotton on?'

'Don't think so.'

'You don't *think* so . . .'

That lit a fuse. Mac's eyes turned on me; I saw plenty of the whites, tinged with angry red. 'No,

I don't. But, y'know, I'm no' a fucking mind-reader and ex-cons tend to know better than to let their faces give away what they're thinking.'

Hod slapped the wheel. 'So, what you're saying is he could be on the phone to Gemmill already.'

Mac leaned past me, flattening me in my seat to roar at Hod. 'Well, we knew that was a fucking option before I went in there! . . . I don't remember you having a better plan!'

I pushed Mac back in his seat. 'Right, enough. We'll find out when we get there, eh.'

The rest of the journey passed in silence. The traffic got heavy, tram and road works competed with Festival-goers and tour buses. Getting from Leith to Corstorphine was a trial at the best of times in this city; right now it seemed like mission impossible. Hod and Mac fumed, letting out sighs at every turn. We were stopped by every set of lights – both drivers and pedestrians took blastings from the horn. As we got to Corstorphine Road the tension in the cab hung like a fever. I felt my hands start to tremble again; beads of sweat formed on my forehead. I needed a drink, desperately.

'Thank fuck there's a bar in here . . .' I said.

'Jesus Christ, Gus,' said Mac, 'you won't be doing any drinking.'

My mind was drifting all over the place. When I got like this I felt inches from unconsciousness. I started to gnaw at my exposed gums with my lower teeth. I had gone too long without topping up my units. I felt seriously drowsy, but at the same time my heart raced.

Mac pointed to the hotel; Hod pulled the van onto the driveway scree. As he parked he caught sight of his Beemer. 'Well, he's here, then. Prick's got a cheek driving my motor, eh.'

'Perks of the job,' said Mac.

Hod braked, pulled the keys out of the ignition. 'If he's hurt that lassie he'll no' be fit for any fucking job . . . He'll be on invalidity if he's fucking lucky.'

As we got out of the van I wondered if we'd suddenly changed seasons – summer to winter. I started to shiver uncontrollably. My neck froze; I felt my stomach tightening. I blamed the stress of the situation. I was worried about Amy, said, 'I really need a drink.'

'Will you shut up about drink,' said Hod, 'Do you not remember why we're here?'

'I really do need a swally . . . my insides are burning.'

Mac grabbed the front of my coat, pulled me towards him. 'Right, get this straight . . . we're not here for a session.'

Hod stood at his shoulder. The pair of them looked ready to pound me into the ground when the doors of a blue Bedford sprung open and four or five pugs poured out. A burgundy Daimler that had been parked opposite pulled up. In the front passenger seat I could see Shaky waving arms and pointing at the three of us. In the next second my arms were put up my back and my face was spun towards the side of the Bedford.

Hod and Mac followed me as we were thrown into the back of the van. As we righted ourselves, the lumps parted to let Shaky through. Gemmill and Amy came close behind him; she'd been crying, black mascara running down her cheeks. I tried to go to her but got held back.

'Gus!' Amy yelled out.

'All right . . . you've got us, you can let the lassie go, Shaky,' I yelled.

Shaky came forward, put a shoe on the edge of the van, leaned in, 'Where'd you get the balls tae tell me to do anything, ye cunt? You've got right up my fucking nose, d'ye know that?' He pointed a tanned finger at me. 'You'll be fucking lucky no' to be wearing your arse as a hat by the time I'm finished with ye, Dury!'

CHAPTER 24

It was a fair old drive. Could have guessed somewhere in the wilds of Midlothian from the time it took us, but with the windows blacked out it was a near impossibility. Hod and Mac sat in silence. Every now and again they'd make casual glances at each other, frowning. I knew my shakes were the cause of this. I tried to put my hands in the pockets of my tweed jacket but it made little difference. The tremors merely passed up my arms into my neck, made my head bob about as if I suffered St Vitus's dance. I was a sad case and I knew it. The craving in my gut for alcohol was all-consuming. I could hardly bear a thought to our fate, though that scared me enough.

Tried a conversation starter: 'Where do you think they're taking us?'

Hod barked, 'Oh, dunno . . . maybe Ikea for one of those all-day breakfasts, eh.'

Mac looked at me and curled the corner of his mouth into a cruel sneer. 'Maybe better you just shut the fuck up, Gus.'

I wasn't having that. 'Look, it's not my fault.'

'Oh, stop pissing and whining. You sound like a ten-year-old lassie.'

I took out a hand, tried to point a finger. It fluttered like a leaf on the breeze. 'Okay, I got Amy involved. I didn't ask her to go after Gemmill like that, though, you can't be putting that on me.'

The pair of them looked away, stayed quiet. I wanted to have another go, try defending myself further, but there didn't seem to be any point. Told myself, if I got out of this in one piece, I'd be happy enough.

The Bedford's wheels rattled over what felt like a cattle grid, then we were on a rough dirt track. The three of us were thrown about in the back as the road got bumpy.

'This isn't a good sign,' said Hod.

'We're out in the fucking wilds . . . be blowing the kneecaps off us,' said Mac.

I tried to rein in some sanity. 'Christ on a cross, what have we done? Followed Gemmill . . . since when was that a kneecapping offence?'

'You forget about the money I owe Shaky!' said Hod.

'Yeah . . . and he's getting that – you still have time in hand.'

Mac arked up, lobbed an arm at me, grabbed my collar. 'Are you away wi' it? Do you remember who we're dealing with here? . . . Shaky doesn't need an excuse – he'll fucking top the lot ay us for looking at Gemmill the wrong way, just to teach us a lesson!' He threw me back down.

I knew he was right.

The brakes were applied, a loud screech as the tyres dug into dry-packed earth. I felt my stomach turning over; my mouth dried as I drew deep breath.

In a moment the door was flung open. A pug with a shaved head and bad prison tats on his face motioned us out. He had a look on him that screamed, *Give me an excuse, and you're in the ground.*

The sunshine hurt my eyes as I left the van. I raised a hand to shield the rays. Caught sight of Mac and Hod squinting in the full glare. Wherever we were, running wasn't an option. Forget my current condition – there was nothing but trees and fields for miles around. The only concession to human settlement was an abandoned bothy. Shaky and Gemmill were walking towards it, Amy was being dragged behind them, teetering on high heels, by a heavy biffer in a black leather jacket.

'Get fucking moving,' Prison Tats roared at us, pointing after Shaky. We got moving. The ground was dry and hard, baked under the sunshine. My legs were weak at the knees. They buckled once or twice and I was prodded in the back by the pug. Hod and Mac kept eyes front, staring at the door of the bothy. As we got inside a storm lantern was being lit above our heads. The biffer had taken off his leather and was rolling up his shirtsleeves. I got a good look at the size of his arms: like Popeye on steroids. He had hands like clubs; probably been used for just that. I didn't want to think about what was coming next.

Gemmill pulled out a chair. It reminded me of that scene in *Reservoir Dogs*, one where Michael Madsen cuts the cop's ear off . . . I couldn't stop a hand going up to my ear in panic.

Shaky spoke: 'Get in here, y'bunch ay pricks.' I watched him walk around the chair, wondered which of us he was going to put in there, who would be first to lose an ear. And then he sat down. He unbuttoned his overcoat; underneath he wore a purple silk shirt. With the white shoes and the quiff I got the impression he was trying to emulate his namesake's appearance. Had to suppress a nervous laugh as I visualised him balancing on his toes and belting out 'Green Door' . . .

Gemmill stood at Shaky's shoulder. He held on to Amy but she struggled to free herself and eventually won out; she ran over to my side and put her arms around me.

'Oh, touching wee picture . . . eh, Danny,' said Shaky.

Gemmill looked sheepish, let out a nervous laugh. I could see he knew exactly who Shaky blamed for this turn of events.

'What the fuck you after, Shaky?' I said. The tone of my voice got the pug's goat – he loped over and planted a fist in my eye socket. I fell like a sack of spuds. Amy screamed and dropped down beside me on the floor.

'You fucking bastards,' she yelled.

I sat up, gathered myself just enough to see Shaky laughing and Gemmill attempting to join in. 'Listen tae me, Dury. I'll be asking the fucking questions, eh.' He nodded to the pug, who came and dragged me to my feet. 'Now for starters, you can tell me why you've got yer wee tart keeping tabs on Danny Boy here.'

I felt my head spinning. I touched my eye – there was no blood but I could sense a shiner forming. 'You think I'd be that fucking daft?'

Shaky looked to Gemmill, frowned. 'You saying this is news tae you?'

Mac cut in: 'Of course it was news tae us . . . why else would we be sniffing around Gemmill's drinking buddies trying to find him?'

The pug made a move for Mac, thought better of it for a moment and the pair of them stood eyeballing each other as Amy jumped in: 'Nobody told me to go chasing after him . . . I did it myself!'

'Shut it, Amy!' I said.

She flagged me down, went over to Shaky. 'You know he's been up to all kinds of shit . . .' She pointed at Gemmill. He looked ready to bolt. 'He was supplying Ben Laird with drugs behind your back!'

Shaky started to laugh. 'Nobody does fuck all in this toon behind my back, darlin'.' He stood up, walked over to Gemmill, said, 'Danny here's on my payroll and he knows a good thing when he sees it . . . unlike some.' He turned back to Amy. 'You're a braw-looking lassie, hen. Ever think ay coming to work for the likes ay me? . . . Set you up in one ay my saunas no trouble.'

Amy spat at the ground. Shaky laughed. Danny followed suit.

'Okay . . . okay . . . I'll take that as a no.'

Amy started to speak again: 'That's not all—' but I grabbed her arm, pulled her to me and clamped a hand over her mouth.

'Wise move,' said Shaky, 'that lassie's gonna get you lot into trouble . . . more trouble, that is.' He looked at Hod. 'Where's my money, y'cunt?'

Hod stepped forward, went into his pocket and withdrew a manila envelope stuffed with notes – I knew at once it was the money we'd taken from Gillian Laird, to find her son's killer. Shaky grabbed the cash. 'What's this, best part ay a grand? . . . That's no' gonna buy you much time.'

'You'll get the rest,' Hod told him.

I could sense the wheels turning in Shaky's head. He looked at Gemmill and then he looked back to us. 'I want the rest ay this, mind . . .'

'You'll get it,' said Hod.

Shaky pocketed the cash, started to button up his overcoat. 'Oh, I know I will . . .' he walked over to Amy, eyed her up and down, 'one way or another.'

My fists clenched. I was ready to lay into him, but the part of the brain that deals with self-preservation was holding me in check. The pug pushed us aside as Shaky headed for the door.

'One last thing,' he said, 'this Laird laddie . . . I

don't want to hear you've been poking about in his death again, got me?'

I looked at Gemmill; he was staring at his shoes.

'Why, what's it got to do with you?' I asked.

Gemmill suddenly came to life for the first time: 'You'll just do what yer fucking told, Dury!'

Shaky laughed, 'Don't mind him. He means well, just a wee bit sparky. He's right about one thing, though: I hear you've been poking about in the Laird boy's death again, Dury, and your girl-friend'll be walking Leith Links . . . in black.'

CHAPTER 25

A lift back to the city was way too much to expect. Shaky and his crew bailed on us without so much as a backwards glance. We all watched as the Bedford pumped blue-grey smoke into the countryside and rattled up the dirt track.

'Where the fuck are we?' said Mac.

He was looking at Hod, but didn't get an answer. I tried friendly, verging on optimistic: 'Well, we've got a nice day for a walk.'

Amy looked pensive. She scratched her elbow as she began to speak, 'There's something you should know . . .'

Now she had our attention.

'Go on.'

'When I was talking to Danny . . . before the date, he told me that Ben Laird owed him money.'

'He what?'

She dropped her arms to her side, 'I know he's shitting it that the police will find out.'

I cut in, 'He's no danger there. Plod is officially sweeping this one under the carpet.'

Hod spoke, 'Aye, but Shaky doesn't know that.'

It was the first bit of room we'd had to manoeuvre. There was no getting around Shaky's threat to stay away from the case, but now we knew what was behind his threat, we could act on it. 'He's running scared, then . . .'

'Do you think Gemmill's had something to do with the murder?' said Mac.

I didn't know the answer to that, there were far too many variables floating about, but I knew one thing. 'He looked scared enough to have.'

'Aye, but you'd be looking scared too if you had just pissed off Shaky in that fashion,' said Hod.

He had a point.

'Maybe we should start taking a closer look at Danny Gemmill,' said Mac.

'Well, somebody should . . .'

'What do you mean by that?'

I walked to the edge of the building, took out my mobi, dialled.

Ringing.

An answer: 'Fitzsimmons.'

'Are you glad to hear from me?'

'Jaysus, Dury . . .' He lowered his voice. 'What have I told you about ringin' me on the landline?'

'Never mind that. I need to meet you.'

'Out of the question. I'm up to me eyes in it here.'

'I have some very interesting information about that case . . . one your nephew is involved in.'

A gap on the line.

Long exhalation of breath.

Sighs. 'Okay, give me a place.'

'How about the Regent . . . top of Abbeymount.'

'Christ Almighty, that's a feckin' fruity bar!'

'Yeah, I know . . . Don't go changing. I thought it would be the last place we'd be expected. Say about eight tonight?'

Fitz agreed, hung up.

I motioned the others back to the dirt road, said, 'Get those thumbs out – gonna need them.'

I traipsed down the Mile, past a shower of crusty, dreadlocked fire-eaters and a unicyclist in a jester's hat. Never ceases to amaze me the characters this Festival attracts – every one a total bell-end. I turned eyes to the sky, longing for the day this annual nonsense would all be over.

There was a jakey with a paper cup full of coins sitting outside the *Hootsman* building. He smiled a toothless grin at me; I matched him with my own, dropped in a few pence.

'Thank you, sir . . . have a nice day now.'

Fuck me, it had come to something when even the beggars in this city had completed customer appreciation courses. I marched through the front door, rocked up to the wall panel that had replaced the receptionists, and buzzed for Rasher.

In the elevator I removed the can of Guinness I was carrying in my jacket pocket, took a reassuring belt on it. The smooth liquid soothed me as it went down, but I knew there was a deeper craving calling out to be settled. I couldn't give in to it, though; if I did, it might just be my last.

Sky News played in the newsroom – some twenty-one-year-old was reading the day's headlines in a cocktail dress and push-up bra. I shook my head. There was a big picture of Rupert Murdoch on one of the monitors as I passed. The place was abuzz with the announcement that he was going to start charging for web content on his newspapers' sites. 'Quality journalism doesn't come cheap . . .' was his explanation. I had to laugh: he owned the *Sun*. And he'd aged so much he now looked like Yoda's sack.

Rasher greeted me in the middle of the floor. 'Gus lad . . . good to see you.' It was all a bit forced, but welcome none the less . . . I needed all the help I could get.

I returned the bonhomie with some good Scots derision: 'What you after?'

'Nothing . . . nothing.'

He'd be telling me he was just being friendly next. Never trust a friendly hack – rule one in the manual.

We strolled through to his office. The newsroom had been decimated. Even thinner than the last time I'd been around, said, 'Where the fuck is everyone?'

'Ah, we bumped the sub-editors.'

'You what? How do you put out a paper without subs?'

I could tell he was still trying to figure that one out. 'The reporters write into boxes . . . read over each other's copy.'

I almost laughed. The idea of a reporter writing a paragraph that didn't need rewriting was a stretch. 'And what happens when the first big court action comes in because your eighteen-year-old hack missed the legal?'

Rasher frowned, looked skywards. 'Upstairs have budgeted for that.'

I immediately got it: was cheaper to fight a court action every other month than maintain the wages bill for the sub-editors. This corporate world we live in made me want to chuck. The lunatics had truly taken over the asylum.

We went into Rasher's office, sat. He produced a bottle of Johnnie Walker. It had been well hit: hardly two fingers sitting in the bottom of it. I felt like necking the lot, but waved aside the offer; he filled his coffee cup.

'So . . . you took yer time getting here,' he said.

Did I explain the hospital visit, the Amy farrago, the trip to the countryside with Boaby Stevens's crew? Uh-uh. I glossed: 'Yeah well, busy man . . .'

'You still working the same story?' He leaned over, looked more interested than I'd seen him in a long time. He had his sleeves rolled up and it added to the air of 'let's get to business' that he carried.

'Oh, aye . . .' Recycled a line: 'Quality journalism doesn't come cheap.'

He laughed. 'Very good . . . very good.'

My left hand started to tremble slightly. I knew it as a sign that the other would be following suit soon if I didn't take a drink. I removed the Guinness can once more, took a belt on it. Rasher's eyes widened, he put on a 'Christ, that's a jakey look, Gus' expression. Like I gave a fuck at this stage.

'So, you got something for me?'

Rasher dug in his drawer, removed a pale blue folder, he opened it up. Inside were a lot of photocopied cuttings. He put a finger on the top one. 'This is the Laird laddie's court coverage. All in here: bit of Bob Hope possession, some dealing, argy-bargy with a polisman . . . few others. Like I say, a charmer, real charmer he was.' I watched Rasher delve further into the files. He spoke again: 'I have to say, the lassie did a grand job going through the library . . . better than I expected.'

'Oh, yeah? . . . What did she turn up?'

A grin – wide one, kind he reserved for special occasions, said, 'Wouldn't you like to know?' He slammed the folder closed.

This was a turn in events, Rasher playing cat and mouse with me. 'What's this?'

He stood up, drained his cup, said, 'You really don't know, do you? You really have no idea?'

I watched him closely. There was a full-on smile playing on his face now. That was rare enough, but this was a smile unlike any other I'd seen on him. He seemed genuinely delighted with himself.

Said, 'Right, spill the beans, eh, Rasher.'

He went back to his desk, picked up the folder and started waving it in the air. 'I wonder how much this is worth to you.'

If he thought there was a chance of money exchanging hands, he was deluded. 'I have about five sovs in my pocket . . . bit change, and that's me.'

He laughed that up. 'I don't mean money.'

'Well, what do you mean?'

He sat down quickly, opened the folder and leafed through to the bottom of the pile. He produced a photocopy that, going by the fonts, was about twenty or thirty years old. 'See this? . . . This is big time!'

He handed over the cutting, watched me read.

The story was dated 1979 and had the eye-catching header: CITY SHOCKED BY UNIVERSITY HANGING.

I read on.

Genuinely intrigued.

The story told of a boy about the same age as Ben Laird being hanged, in an almost identical manner, some thirty years previously.

'Well, well, well . . .' I said.

'Indeed.'

'This puts quite a different complexion on things.'

'Doesn't it just . . . What a fucking story!'

I'd been a hack too long to be shocked by the crassness of Rasher's statement. 'If there's a link, you mean.'

'Oh, aye . . . of course. But if there's a link, you'll find it, eh?'

What he was saying was, *Go find the link so I can put it in the paper.*

'Why aren't you working it?'

'Ha!' Rasher leaned back in his seat, looked out to the newsroom. 'That lot out there are struggling enough with rewriting fucking press releases. There's not one of them capable of chasing this, Dury!' He snapped forward in his chair, put serious eyes on me. 'But you go digging, and bring back that story . . . it's a page-one exclusive!'

I stood up, leaned over the file, said, 'Can I take this?'

Hands went up. 'Be my guest.'

CHAPTER 26

Elvis Costello was on the radio, 'Accidents Will Happen'. Didn't seem like an appropriate track. Not in the slightest. I walked into the doocot and took off my jacket, hung it on the back of the door. The dustcoat was flung over the chair, inky stains on the sleeves and around the pockets adding a hint of authenticity. Stevo and I hadn't spoken since the bust-up. Well, if you could call it that; I'd be going with outburst. On his behalf.

I filled the kettle, took out a packet of Jammie Dodgers I'd bought, said, 'Fancy a brew, Stevo?' I was trying to break the ice; was glad I had. When he turned I saw he had a large Elastoplast above his left eye; his lip had been split too. 'Jesus . . . what happened to you?'

He mumbled a bit, cleared his throat, 'I walked into a door . . . It was on the nightshift, all the lights were out. I couldn't get the flashlight to work.'

It was borderline believable. I'd broken the flashlight when I dropped it the night I found Calder swinging from a rope in the Grand Hall. The memory of his white face, his toes pointing to the floor, made me flinch. The fact that nobody seemed overly concerned about his hanging made me furious.

'Aye, well . . . sorry about that. I dropped it the night I found Calder.'

He didn't press me. I got the impression he was a bit more approachable than the last time we had spoken. He came over to where I was standing at the sink, gave me his cup.

'I wanted to say . . . y'know, about that exchange of words we had,' said Stevo.

'Exchange of words' – it was such a poor euphemism. I knew what he meant, but tried to look innocent. 'What's that, Stevo?' Wasn't that the way to handle these things?

'You remember . . . you were asking about the hanging.'

I poured out the tea, motioned him to sit down. He was a good bloke, I could tell that. But he was stressed about something. I had a fair idea what. Sooner or later I'd have to apply some stress in Paul's direction, see which way the little shit squirmed.

'Which one?'

Stevo's lips drained of blood. 'Calder . . . Mr Calder.'

'We could have been talking about Ben of course.'

His eyes blinked a spasm. 'I suppose.'

'Or,' I amped it up, 'I could have been talking about the kid that was hanged here in the 1970s.'

Stevo took up his mug of tea. He looked as though he wanted to hide behind it. I walked over to him, offered a biscuit. 'You knew about that, didn't you?'

He nodded, started to twiddle with the handle of the cup; stirred in more sugar. 'H-how did you find out?'

There didn't seem any point in keeping my hand from him: figured he either knew already or had guessed. 'Stevo, Ben Laird's mother hired me to look into his death . . . I'm a private investigator.'

'I know that.'

I'd half guessed he did but the abrupt assertion blindsided me. 'How did you find out?'

He coughed into his fist, 'Paul . . . Paul told me.'

I put down my cup, stood up again, loomed over Stevo. 'Was that the day I saw you arguing with him?'

His voice was barely a whisper. He couldn't look me in the eye. 'I didn't know you'd seen that.'

'Well, now you do.'

Stevo stood up to face me. His breathing had stalled, his face ashen as he faltered on his words. 'Gus . . . I'm . . .'

'You're what?'

He looked away, trying to find something to distract him outside the window, 'These people, Gus . . .'

'Stevo, have they put a scare on you?'

He didn't move, stood still. Nodded. His head dropped onto his chest; he looked exhausted by it all.

'What did they say?'

'They wanted me to . . . warn you off.'

I let out a low laugh. 'Do you think that's likely?' I wasn't expecting an answer.

Stevo started to grow twitchy, like a rabbit in headlights that didn't know which way to run. He slumped back in the chair, started to skin up. I noticed his knuckles were scraped as he brought out his Rizlas.

'You've been in a stramash, Stevo.' I pointed to his hands. 'Think you should give me the low-down on this crew that's putting the shits up you.'

Stevo crumbled in some Moroccan rock. His top lip glistened with sweat as he spoke. 'They're part of an . . . order.'

'A *what*?'

His voice dipped, began to quiver. 'Ben was part of it too . . . It goes back years, decades and decades.'

I was having some trouble getting my head around this. 'Like some kind of secret club?'

'Have you heard of Skull and Bones?'

'The fucking pirate flag?'

Stevo managed a staccato laugh. He wiped his lip. 'It's an old fraternity in America . . . George W. and so on were members. It's like an on-campus old-boys' network. They have their rituals and . . . their secrets.'

It sounded far-fetched; I'd never encountered anything like it. Then it struck: of course I hadn't – I was never likely to, coming from my side of the tracks. 'And it goes on here too . . . in Scotland?'

'It started here.' Stevo fiddled nervously with a flap of skin under his chin, his voice trembled some more. 'They call themselves the Seriatim.'

'It means one after the other . . . What's that about?'

A shrug of heavy shoulders. 'I think they like to think of themselves as links in a chain.'

'How do you know about this, Stevo?'

'I don't really . . . but, well, I see things . . . hear things.'

'What do you mean, you see things?'

He sparked up the joint, inhaled deep. It seemed to calm him slightly. 'In this job . . . you see things, see the meetings at night and . . .'

I didn't know if I wanted to hear what he was saying. If Stevo had the kind of information I thought he had, then he was in some danger. Two people had died already, three if you included the kid in the seventies. I didn't like what I was hearing. I didn't want to see any more names added to the death list.

'Are you telling me you know something about these hangings?'

He picked a piece of stray tobacco from the end of the roach. He looked reluctant to speak. I prompted him again: 'Stevo . . . do you know something?'

He pressed the roach to his mouth, inhaled. He

took some time to speak again, gasped, 'The Seriatim – Ben was a member and so was Joe Calder. I'd hazard a guess that the one who died years ago was too.'

'It goes that far back?'

'Shit, yeah . . . years and years, hundreds even, I don't know how many. They pick out half a dozen overprivileged idiots on each intake and, y'know, look after them . . .'

I pressed, 'No, I don't know . . . what do you mean, "look after them"?'

Stevo's fingers tapped at the joint. 'They induct them, I suppose. I've seen some old boys who must have been past members from time to time. It's all a fucking game to them, think they're it. It's about connections and looking out for each other . . . that kind of bullshit.'

That might explain the Craft's involvement; it wasn't too much of a stretch to imagine some of the Seriatim's past members joining the force. If they knew about the first death or had some involvement with it – it made sense they'd want any more killings hushed up. It stank. I pressed: 'And Paul . . . is he part of the group?'

Stevo nodded slowly, his eyes sunk in his head. 'I think he's got some wee fiefdom. Seen him chatting to the top dogs, taking directions and that . . .' He seized up, said, 'I shouldn't be talking like this. If they knew, I'd be . . .'

'You'd be what, Stevo . . . killed?'

He held schtum.

'If you know anything about who killed Ben . . . or anyone else, you need to tell me. People have died – do you want there to be more?'

He shot out of the chair, growing frantic. There was terror in his eyes as he tugged at his hair. I'd put too much pressure on him. 'Leave me alone, Gus,' he snapped.

I saw I'd gone as far as I could for now, but I had to give him a warning. 'Stevo, if you won't talk to me, you should go to the police. I know a man.' I took out one of the cards Hod had printed up for me, wrote down Fitz's name and number. 'Seriously . . . talk to Fitz . . . if you won't talk to me. He'll help you . . . help you sort it all out, Stevo. Trust me on that.'

He took the card, tucked it into the pocket of his dustcoat. I didn't hold out much hope that he'd use it.

CHAPTER 27

I called Hod, made sure he was keeping a close check on Amy.

'She's watching *Hollyoaks* . . . quiet as a mouse.'

'Good. See she stays that way.'

'Nae danger.'

I had a few hours to kill before I met up with Fitz. I had it all straight in my head what I needed to say to him – and what I needed to hear from him. But there was something else worrying me that needed to be attended to. Call it my age, call it the advanced state of entropy I found myself in, but I'd been thinking a lot about my mortality. For some that means finding peace with God, for others it means tidying up their financial affairs. For me it meant getting to the bottom of the chaos of my childhood.

I knew my mother had put up with so much from my father; what I didn't know was why. Beyond that, what I needed to know was – where did it all come from? All the hate, all the bile. From one man towards his family. None of it had made any sense in my boyhood and it made no more sense now. I needed to know what it was all about: how did it happen? Why did we all have to bear so many scars?

As I walked towards my childhood home I felt old memories assail me; I saw my brother Michael playing in the garden. He could only have been five or six; in a few more years he would try to kill himself after suffering a violent beating from my father. Some people will tell you they find it hard to look back, hard to remember their childhood after a certain age. Not me. I found it hard *not* to remember. The beatings, the scoldings, the harsh words . . . I carried them with me everywhere. I replayed them on a daily basis.

Debs had said I should let them go, that I was keeping the pain alive in me – it wrecked our marriage for her to see me so miserable, ruined. I pulled out my mobile phone. I had no missed calls, no texts. I wanted to dial Debs's number, to tell her I was about to face my demons, but it seemed pointless now. She didn't want anything to do with me. I was coming to realise what that meant. I would no longer have Debs in my life. She was gone. Just like my father was gone. I needed to let them both go.

As I opened the gate to my old family home, my heart stilled. I spotted my mother behind the net curtains. She moved slowly; she was older now, but she was unmistakably the same woman who had battled to raise us for all those years. She caught sight of me and hurried to the door.

She had opened up before I had the chance to knock.

'Oh, Gus, oh my . . .' She raised her hand to her mouth.

'Hi, Mam.'

'Oh, come away in, son . . . You look like death warmed up.'

Did I tell her I felt that way too? . . . Let it slide. My mam needed no more hurts in her life.

Inside the place was tidy and spare; neat as ninepins, as the saying goes. My father's picture was still on the sideboard, Cannis Dury, in his World Cup shirt of 1982. It had been his final taste of glory; after that, his only audience had been under this roof. Every one of us would walk on fire to have missed that show.

My mother sat on the arm of the chair. Her hair had grown white. 'Gus, it's been so long.' She reached out, placed a hand on my shoulder. I started to cough. I could hear my lungs rattling.

I said, 'It has that . . . Sorry, I've been a bit, y'know . . .'

She pressed out a thin smile, rubbed my arm, 'I was sorry to hear about you and Deborah . . .'

I was shocked that she knew. I don't know why, it had been long enough now – surely my own mother had the right to know such things. How had we grown so far apart?

'You heard?' The words seemed feeble, pathetic even.

She nodded. 'Catherine bumped into her in the Co-op.'

It was a small city. I tended to forget that.

'Well, yes . . . it's over. Has been some time now.'

She rubbed harder at my arm. 'Maybe you'll get back together . . . again.'

I sensed the hope in her voice. She had every right to expect we'd patch things up – we had done it so many times in the past; but never again. I shook my head. 'No, not this time, Mam . . . not this time.'

She stood up. 'Well, they say time's a great healer . . . Give it time, son.' She walked towards the kitchen. 'Will I make us some coffee? I know you don't like tea.'

I nodded, and watched her turn away from me. She walked stiffly, uncomfortable with the rheumatism in her hips.

Alone in the room I couldn't bear to have my father's eyes upon me, I rose and turned over his picture. As I touched it I saw that my hand had started to tremble again. I reached into the pocket of my tweed jacket and removed a can of Guinness, took a quick belt. I chased it with a lengthier blast as my mother walked in carrying a tray with cups. I spluttered and removed the can from my mouth.

'Sorry, I'm virtually off it.' It was a lie and she knew it. She'd given up trying to stop me drinking; hadn't everyone. I put the can away and she went back through to the kitchen to wait for the kettle to boil.

My mind was racing. Whenever I came back to this place I felt a flood of memories assail me. The time I remembered most prominently now was the day my father died. He'd been up in his bed, confined indoors with a weak heart, but it hadn't stopped him roaring and shouting at my mother with every ounce of breath in him. She had taken it all too; had trotted up those stairs like the doting wife of old. Why? I wanted to know why she never left him. Surely we would have all been better without him.

She came through with the pot of coffee, placed it on the tray. I thought about pouring the cups out, but in my current condition, knew I'd spill the lot. I waited until she offered me a cup, my hand remained thankfully steady as I took it.

'So, you look well,' I said.

She smiled, knew she wanted to say, *Wish I could say the same about you*, but went with, 'Well . . . it's a quiet enough life.'

I wondered if that was a dig at me being absent for so long. Thought better of it – knew my mam didn't have it in her for digs. She was as close to the perfect human being as you could get; perhaps that's why her suffering hurt me so much.

'Mam, I've been thinking a lot . . .' I stalled, looked out the window. Could I really do this? My mind wandered off track, a long silence stretched out between us.

'Yes, son?'

I turned back, refocused. Her face looked open

and approachable. 'Mam, I've had some time to think . . . a lot of time, actually, since the split from Debs.'

Mam sipped her coffee. 'Is that so wise?'

'What? I mean, I know . . . thinking's never a good idea, is it?'

She seemed to agree but gave nothing away. Did she sense what I was here to ask her? The thought slayed me. I knew my mother had been through enough grief in her life – now she was old, she had earned her peace. Who was I to come here and disrupt that? And for what? To satisfy my ego, to let me sleep better at night? Christ on a bike, if any one of us deserved to sleep soundly it was her. I couldn't bring up the past in this house again. She deserved better.

She put down her coffee, clasped her fingers together, spoke: 'These walls have seen a lot over the years, have they not?' It was as if she knew what I was thinking, what it was I needed to know. 'At times these walls felt like a prison to me, Angus . . .'

'They did?'

'Oh, I think they felt like that for us all.'

I knew what she meant, but we had never spoken about him like this. It felt strange to be treading towards this territory. 'Mam, why?'

'Why what? Why did I stay with him? Why didn't I take you all away to safety . . . somewhere else?'

The words faltered on my lips. 'I-I guess so . . .'

My mother looked at me, but at the same time seemed to be staring straight through me. 'Where to, Angus? I had nowhere to go . . . Back to my family? Oh, I tried. They sent me back to him . . . It wasn't the done thing, then. You didn't leave a marriage, not when you had children. I had no choice.' Suddenly her eyes flickered. It was as if she sensed I wanted more. 'Angus . . . it would have made no difference, he would have found us. He would have found us wherever we went.'

She made him sound like a monster; my own mother conceded that my father's actions had harmed us all. She knew all we had suffered at his hand, she knew Catherine and I were still damaged and confused children at heart and she knew it was all because of him.

'Mam, do you remember the night I had to call the ambulance?' There had been many nights I'd had to call the ambulance, but only one like this. 'For you.'

Her face changed shape; she seemed to straighten her back. She spoke through pinched lips: 'I remember it, yes.' It was hard for her to find any words. I didn't want to make her speak. I didn't want to force her to tell me the answer to the question I had carried around with me for decades.

I stood up. 'I should go, Mam.'

She watched me rise. 'Your father had something inside him, Angus . . . a dark place that he couldn't escape. No matter what good he had in his life, the darkness was always there.'

I knew what she was trying to say.

'Mam, I have to go . . . I'm sorry to—'

She placed a hand on my face. It felt soft and cold. 'I know you have the same dark place inside of you, son . . . but you have a better heart than him. Please, son . . . try and listen to that heart of yours, and not the other place.'

CHAPTER 28

I made my way to the Regent, ordered in a pint of Guinness. Got some looks from a fruity boy at the bar in a boy band get-up, all low-cut T-shirt, tight waistcoat and skinny jeans. I gave him a smile, a good wide view of my gaping mouth. He turned tail. Couldn't say I was taken with the place, but at least it looked like a drinker and not a gay bar. Don't know what I expected – men with handlebar moustaches dancing to 'YMCA' maybe? – but this place seemed down to earth. I made a note to stop flying to all kinds of conclusions about people based on their personal make-up. I knew that now, more than ever, I needed to put the brakes on my assumptions. Ben Laird's murderer – and likely Calder's – was still out there. If I was to get to the root of these killings, I'd have to sweep aside every silver-spooned animus I harboured.

Took a seat at the front window and kept an eye out for Fitz. My mind was working overtime; surprisingly, since my visit to my mam, I felt rejuvenated. Was in a 'glass is half full' as opposed to 'half empty' mood. But I knew it wouldn't last long. I had stopped worrying about whether the man I called father had actually fathered me; but the realisation that I *was* his son didn't fill me with joy. Somewhere inside me I guess I had always hoped that I wasn't his. Even when I knew in my heart that I was.

I knew exactly what my mother had meant about the dark place. It was the Black Dog. It had leapt from him onto me and I had never been able to shake the bastard. Debs knew it was there, and that's why she had left. I knew I had no chance of a reconciliation with her, like my mother had hinted at; I knew I didn't even want that now. More and more my mind was turning to Amy. I had been worried about her at first, but now she was becoming a full-time concern. Hoped I wasn't substituting her for Debs – that would lead to no good, guaranteed.

I changed tack, kept my mind focused on the job at hand. Tried to weigh up the news Rasher had delivered. A previous killing at the university was something worth covering up for sure, for obvious reasons. The uni was big business these days, and no big business wants to attract bad publicity – presuming the weakened media could deliver some. It was the same situ with Shaky, but on a lower scale. However, as a motive for murder, it didn't sit well with me.

I knew the Craft were up to their necks in this too, but I got the impression their involvement was more crisis management – covering tracks. The reason for their intervention was still to be confirmed but I had an idea Fitz could check that out. When you weighed it all up, I was still missing the bigger part of the puzzle and I needed to get to it. And soon.

I was on my second pint when the bold Fitzsimmons strode in. His face was flushed red, the collar of his white shirt open at the neck. He ordered himself a whisky at the bar then scanned the room, made for my table. He looked over his shoulder as he walked, his gait unsteady, like he was breaking in new shoes.

'I don't like this, Dury . . . not one feckin' iota I don't.' He seemed edgy.

'It's a nasty business all right.'

'Jaysus, I'm not on about that.' He pressed his index finger into the table. 'I mean meeting in here. First crack I hear about taking it up the Gary, I will swing for ye, Dury!'

I let out a laugh. 'Yeah, well . . . I need to keep a low profile for now.'

Fitz riled, 'So what's feckin' new?'

I told him about being hoyed up by Shaky, the trip to the countryside, the threats. I stretched out all the juicy bits, made him fully aware of how seriously he should take it. After all, there were implications here that he needed to consider too. Shaky might not be the kind of criminal that he spent his days chasing after any more, but he understood how they operated, knew every one in his manor and liked to think he could keep them under control.

Fitz rubbed his fat cheek as he spoke. 'I'm not getting this. Why's Stevens so concerned with the Laird Boy?'

'Simple. The kid owed his man money. Gemmill has form for GBH and a serious record. If it was to be known that he had been helping the lad set himself up as a dealer it wouldn't look good for Shaky, would it?'

Fitz sipped his whisky, savoured the taste a little, showed his bottom row of teeth, then spoke: 'There's that, I suppose. But then, why doesn't he just cut Gemmill loose? . . . Be the answer to all his problems.'

'Gemmill's too deep into that organisation. If he went he could sink him, or worse, set up on his own, and nobody wants a bloody drugs war.'

Fitz sighed, waved a hand at me in a 'slow down' motion. 'Okay, okay . . . whatever his reasons, what we have is Stevens putting the frighteners on you to keep away from the Laird boy's murder investigation. Let's stick to those facts for now.'

'All right . . . so where does that get us?' I played wingman to Fitz; sometimes it paid to let him think he was the smartest man in the room.

'Way I see it, with the Craft involved, and the uni's boyos . . . this investigation is as dead in the water as our Laird laddie. At least, they think it is . . . if Stevens was connected to that mob, he wouldn't be shitting himself about you poking yer nose in.'

I put the tick in the box, let him see I was paying

attention: 'So he's running scared without any cause . . .'

'Correct! Or should I say . . . up to a point.'

I saw where he was going with this now. 'What you mean is, it doesn't matter to the Craft who killed Ben Laird; they just want it swept under the carpet. But if it was Gemmill who killed him, and he's trying to cover his own tracks, in fucking clumsy fashion, then he might just blow this whole thing open.'

Fitz raised his glass, slugged deep. I watched his Adam's apple move up and down. He licked his lower lip, put down the glass, 'You leave young Gemmill to me, and fucking Shaky as well . . . By Christ, I'll give the fucker a shake, so I will.'

I liked the sound of that. 'You'll keep me out of the picture?'

'Jaysus, of course. I'll be watching him closely, though. He'll know he has serious police interest and if he puts a foot wrong he'll be hauled in . . . Should free you up a bit to get down to brass tacks.'

There was certainly plenty to be getting on with. 'Well, there's some progress.' I produced the folder from Rasher, opening it at the cutting with the headline about the seventies killing. I pushed it towards Fitz.

'What's this?' His face drooped as he took in the header, and the implications.

'Read 'em and weep.'

Fitz scratched his head as he scanned the

cutting. He was a slow reader. I watched his brow crease up as he digested the piece. Once or twice he looked up from the print, shook his head a bit, then his eyes returned to the cutting. When he was finished he sat back in his chair and pinched the flabby skin under his chin, said, 'Christ Al-fucking-mighty . . . they've got form for this caper.'

'Oh, yes.'

He held up the cutting, winced. 'Where did you get this?'

I finished off my pint, said, 'The paper . . . they're all over it. I have to tell you, they're looking to go big on this, mate.' I went back to the file, produced another cutting that I'd found tucked away at the bottom of the pile. 'This makes especially interesting news. I was looking through the file and I found this.' I handed over a picture of the class of '79 that the paper had reproduced. 'I don't think the hacks have cottoned on to this, but that one I've circled . . . recognise him?'

Fitz squinted, 'No . . . who is it?'

'It's Joe Calder. He was a classmate of the boy that was hanged. This goes way back, Fitz . . . years back. If this gets blown up, there's people with lots to hide that'll be thrown into the spotlight.'

'Oh, the feckin' Craft will love this discovery.' Fitz rubbed his hands together, laughed it up. I saw him register the way this might play out – old scores settled for him; top brass shed from the force. And his nephew in the clear. It was a pretty payday ahead for him . . . if he worked it right.

I smiled, wiping the froth of Guinness from my mouth. 'Thought you might say that. You need to check out if any more of those faces are matched to names in the force . . . and especially the Craft.'

Fitz leaned forward, rested on his elbows. 'I'm all over it.'

CHAPTER 29

I hadn't seen Amy since her ordeal with Danny Gemmill and Shaky, but she didn't seem to be too worse for wear. Pacing about the flat in a pair of flared white hipsters and a flowery top that tied around the back. She was blasting Hod as she went.

'You old fart,' she yelled, 'since when were you appointed my father?' Hod looked wrecked, standing at the end of the sofa with his fist resting on his chin. 'Gus, thank fuck!' He reached for his jacket. The chair it lay on nearly went with him. 'Your turn, mate . . . you can do some babysitting for her.'

Amy stood in the doorway, one hand on her hip, the other in a single-digit salute directed at Hod.

'See some folk . . . no matter what you do for them, it's never enough,' said Hod.

'I told you, I don't need looking after,' roared Amy.

I had to laugh.

Hod said, 'Isn't that your tune, Dury?'

He had me there. I opened the front door for him, said, 'Where you off to?'

'Away . . . any-fucking-where!'

'Aye, well, watch out, eh. Remember, Shaky's still got your number and he wants paying.'

'Aye, aye, aye.'

As the door closed Amy balled fists, raised them and looked to the ceiling. 'Oh, thank fucking Christ. He won't even let me sit in my room on my own in case I shimmy down the drainpipe.'

I smiled at the image. 'Well, he's got a point.'

She picked up her foot, showing me a set of five-inch heels. 'C'mon, in these? I'm good but I'm not that good!'

I went over to the window, watched Hod head for the Scotbet on Lothian Road. Wondered where he got the money to put a line on. Let it slide. He was probably only going in to soak up the atmosphere. Anywhere would be an escape from the claustrophobia of Amy's flat.

'Had any visitors?' I asked.

'Oh, aye . . . the other one, other part of Haud It 'n' Daud It!'

'Mac?'

'Yeah, whatever you want to call him. They've been taking it in turns to mind me. I feel like a five-year-old.'

'Good – you need looking after.'

Amy sparked up again, started waving her arms around: 'You approve of this? God Almighty, Gus . . . I thought you at least—'

I put a finger on her mouth, said 'Sshhh.'

She kissed the tip of my finger, smiled.

'Amy . . .'

'What?'

'I was trying to say that . . . we were worried about you.'

She moved closer. 'We . . . only we. Not you. That's what you want to say.'

I looked away, laughed. There was sun shining on the windowpane. 'Amy.'

'Oh, shut up, Gus. You know you're crazy about me.'

I felt shocked, exposed. I stepped back. My escape route was blocked by the wall. '*Y'wha'*?'

'C'mon . . . admit it. You can't get me out of your mind – that's what you want to say.'

She was on me now, like a big cat with its prey. I had nowhere to go as she put arms either side of me and opened her mouth. I responded for a brief moment, then pushed her away. 'Amy . . .'

'Gus, shut up.'

She managed to kiss me and undress me at the same time. This girl was impressing me no end. I went along with it . . . all the way.

It had been a while since I'd woken up with a beautiful woman on my arm; maybe too long. I'd forgotten how good it felt. As I looked down at Amy's long hair spread out on the pillow I wanted to tell her how happy I was, but the thought of it seemed to immediately cancel out that plan. It was as if the mere suggestion was enough to throw happiness out the window. I had been through this so many times with Debs – the feelings of joy, then the feelings of sorrow – that I felt destined to be alone. Christ, I had felt it was what I deserved.

I'd made Debs miserable; she had said so herself. My problems, the drink, the self-destruction – they had all taken their toll. She didn't want to be dragged down with me. Could I blame her? No way. I wanted Debs to be happy more than I wanted it for myself. As I lay there with Amy, though, I couldn't help but think of Debs.

I had spent so long with Debs that she had become a part of me; when she had left it had been like losing a limb. An arm or a leg – one day you wake up and it's gone. You get by, because you have to. But your sense of the world around you has changed. Dramatically.

I had thought I couldn't go on without Debs once, then, later, when I thought about the truth of the situation I thought I could never go on with her. It was over. That was the truth of it. I no longer wanted to be with her because I knew I was no good for her. We had went on for too long trying to keep it together when the plain truth was, *it* was never meant to be.

I looked down at Amy. She was flat out.

I risked fingertips on her shoulder, traced the line of her back. She never stirred. Warmth was radiating from her. It felt unnatural. I had slept alone for so long that I'd become used to my own cold trembling bones.

Was this really happening? It didn't seem possible; but it did feel right.

Amy was right: I wanted to be with her. I'd been fighting my feelings for so long that I'd almost convinced myself otherwise, but the truth was out now. In my warped head I could only see it going awry, but I knew I was judging her by my experience with Debs. This wasn't Debs by my side. I'd need to remind myself of that every step of the way. Amy was her own woman; she deserved to be treated as such. I needed to lose my baggage.

Amy stirred. 'Hmmnn . . . how long have I been out?'

'Dunno . . . an hour, maybe.'

She drew closer to me, hugged. 'And how long have you been awake?'

'I haven't been asleep.'

'Oh, Christ . . . analysing the situation, eh?'

I laughed. 'Sort of.' The girl knew me so well. She reminded me of Debs in this regard, but she wasn't Debs. Her perceptions were her own.

She sat up. 'Got any smokes?'

I leaned out of the bed, pulled my jeans across the floor and released a packet of Marlboro red tops from the back pocket. 'Here you go.'

'Oh, man . . . these are the heavy hitters.'

'You don't like them?'

'Nah . . . they'll do.'

We both lit up. After a couple of drags, Amy turned to me. 'So, Gus Dury . . .' she tapped on my head, 'what conclusions have you come to in that mind of yours?'

'What about?'

'Us!'

'We're an *us* now are we?'

She mock-punched me. 'Too fucking right. I don't just roll in the hay with anyone, y'know.'

I fended off some more blows, stuck my cigarette in my mouth, said, 'Okay . . . okay . . . You win.'

'I should think so.'

She smiled. I felt lucky to have her here.

'One thing, though, Amy . . . you should know that I'm a bit—'

'Of a prick! . . . Yeah, I know.'

'Apart from that . . . What I was going to say was, I've just come out of a long relationship and . . .'

Amy leaned out of the bed. I watched her bare back as she grabbed an ashtray. She stubbed out her tab as she spoke. 'Look, Gus, I know all that. And I know things aren't exactly sweetness and light in your world, but so what? We have something . . . let's just see where it goes.'

It seemed a plan. How could I argue?

'Well, I want you to know that thing you did . . . when you disappeared with Gemmill. That really put the frighteners on me.'

'Really . . . Is that what I've got to do to get your attention?' She smiled, winked.

'No. And I mean that, Amy. I don't want you trying anything like that again. It's too dangerous.

The next time, we might not get away with our necks.'

She looked out of the window. The sun was going behind a cloud now. 'You know, if you lot hadn't come breenging in like that . . . I might have been okay.'

I got out of bed, pulled on my jeans. I tried to cool it, give myself enough time to find the right words but they never came. 'More than likely you'd have been killed. You don't know the kind of form Gemmill has.'

'But look at what I found out—'

'What, that Ben Laird owed money to Gemmill!' I tried to sound offhand, lying, 'That would have come up sooner or later.'

I wasn't giving her proper credit and she knew it. 'Oh yeah? . . . When exactly?'

'I dunno. All I'm saying is, it wasn't worth the risk.'

She got up, stood before me with the bed sheet wrapped around her. 'Gus, we have Gemmill and Shaky, both with form and motive, possibly in the frame for murder. That's down to me.'

I couldn't fault her, but I couldn't risk encouraging more of the same. 'Amy . . . there's more to this case than you know about. That pair are just skimming the edges. They don't even know how deep this goes . . . They're dangerous because of that, and they're scared too . . . which makes them unpredictable. You should never have gone anywhere near Gemmill.'

'Well, if you told me all the facts, maybe I'd make better decisions.'

I picked up my shirt, flung it on. This was an argument I was never going to win so I played cautious. 'The fact is, Amy, I care about you, and I don't want you hurt. Can you get your head around that?'

She nodded, moved closer and put her arms around me. 'I don't want you hurt either.'

I sighed. Way things were shaping up, that wasn't going to be an option.

CHAPTER 30

It should have been the happiest of days; I'd opened up to Amy and found myself experiencing something close to joy. Never a good state for a drinker: it means something bad is just around the corner. It's the alky's rationale. Days are meant to bring grief; it's in the contract. The minute something starts to go right, panic sets in.

I holed up in an East End drinker. I'd given up staying out of Shaky's manor. The self-destruct button had been flipped, nothing mattered to me any more. If he found out I was still working the case after he'd warned me off, so be it. Like I said, I expected grief . . . it was in the post.

The thing about getting together with Amy was that it meant dredging up more memories of Debs. I couldn't escape them, she was still a part of me. My hands trembled as I picked up my mobi. I was well on, blootered drunk. Had put away the best part of a bottle of low-flying burdie. It stung on the way down but I was past caring; I needed drink . . . I needed to be drunk. To block out the hum of thoughts circling inside my head. If it ended me, so be it.

Ringing.

I cursed her loudly. 'Fucking pick it up, Debs . . . what you doing to me?'

I wanted her to tell me she was okay, that I could move on.

Ringing.

I needed to know things were over between us for good. That all the hurt of our past was behind us. That I was free to stop worrying about her.

Ringing.

I wanted nothing from her, nothing. Why couldn't she see that? Why did I need to hear the words? My head was a mess. I knew I was in bad shape. I belched up a sliver of whisky-perfumed bile.

Voicemail.

'Oh for fucksake . . . Debs, Debs . . . it's me. Why are you doing this? Why? Why can't you just speak to me? I need to hear your voice. I'm sorry for everything . . . everything that went wrong between us. I know you don't want to hear it but it's important to me to let you know I've moved on. I just need to know you have too . . . that there's a world without Gus and Debs. Tell me, please, and I'll stop calling . . . I just need to know, Debs . . . that's all I need to know. We never spoke. We never talked about this. We just split. Please, Debs . . . tell me life goes on, eh. *Please—*'

The call timed out.

I sat the mobi on the bar.

The barman came over. 'You okay there, mate?' He was an Aussie, blond and buff – aren't they all?

'Oh, aye . . . give me another Grouse, eh.'

He looked unsure, put hands on the bar. 'I think you might have had enough, mate.'

I leaned over, grabbing his shirt front. 'Look, I'll say when I've fucking well had enough, right?'

The Aussie unhooked my fingers, motioned to the door with his eyes. 'Think you better go now.' He pointed me out to the street.

'I'm going nowhere until I get another fucking drink!'

For a moment we stared at each other in silence. I was ready to go to blows. He'd have flattened me into the floor, and knew it, but I was wankered, totally wrecked.

My phone buzzed on the bar top.

I picked it up. I had a text. From Debs.

My hand trembled as I opened the message. It read: *Life goes on Gus – Debs.*

'Mate, I think you should call it a night,' said the barman.

I looked up from the mobi. 'Yeah, yeah . . . all right.'

My head felt light as I walked out the door and into the dark night. A Festival crowd wandered past yakking about some comedian they'd just seen. They laughed as they recounted some of the gags, slapping each other on the back as they went.

'Shut yer fucking faces!' I roared. How dare they be so happy around me. They turned and laughed at me.

'Oh, aye . . . laugh it fucking up.' I was ranting.

This is what I'd come to, ranting at strangers in the street. There was a time when I picked my battles – now they picked me. More and more I was at war with the world. For what? It didn't matter.

A low screech began in my head. I could hear it, spinning around in there, mashing with the thoughts and memories. I was lost to reality. I had fallen low. I staggered down the street, feeling my way along shop fronts and walls. My legs were rubber, my feet on the end of them had no coordination, slipping and sliding all over the pavement. 'Well . . . you got what you wanted, Gus,' I told myself.

My legs suddenly buckled beneath me.

'Be careful what you fucking wish for,' I muttered.

Debs had contacted me. She'd broken her silence. I'd got what I wanted – why wasn't that enough? Why hadn't that changed everything? My thoughts mashed, all the dark imaginings subsided, but became supplanted with new, more morose musings.

'Life goes on, Gus . . . that's what she fucking said.'

I had worn her down. She wanted nothing but to be left alone and I'd forced her to give me one last out. Well, now I had it.

I'd pressed some buttons lately. My mam, who deserved to be comfortable in her retirement, had had to look at me with shame in her eyes. She'd explained herself to me as I sat before her in a state of utter deterioration. Christ, what must she have thought of me? Her son, her only remaining son, coming to her in wasted condition looking for words of comfort. I was pathetic. Truly worthy of pity.

I crossed the road at the lights and tried to straighten myself to get through the doors of what looked like the Station Bar. I couldn't be sure, because I couldn't see clearly. The sign above the door was a blur; fuck, the door was a blur. Everything was melting before me. I wanted to find oblivion, fast.

I got some looks on the way in but I didn't care. I had reached a point of drunkenness I had never experienced before. My entire mind seemed steeped in alcohol. I felt ready to blank out, but I couldn't stop the craving.

'Give me a Grouse, please.'

To my astonishment, I was served.

I put the glass to my lips and downed it.

'Get me another, please.'

The drink came. I sipped it slower. Tried to get my bearings but it soon became clear there were none. I had entered a world more surreal than *Weekend at Bernie's*. I became vaguely aware of other people in the bar; they were engaged in conversation, laughing, joking. I couldn't bring myself to join in. I felt lost in hurt and pity.

A bloke in a black leather coat approached me. 'How you doing?'

His face was a blur and I didn't recognise the voice.

Fired out, 'Well . . . well.'

I took up my glass again, drained it.

I tried to order another but I seemed to have lost the power of speech now.

'Get him oot ay here!' I heard the shout, but couldn't trace it.

I tried to move but collapsed onto a tabletop.

I heard the glasses smash and a woman scream out.

'Oh my God . . . he's bleeding.'

I tried to steady myself on the floor. I could see nothing except a red mist. My hands slipped on the wet floorboards as I made to get up. I couldn't move. I tried dragging my body to the door; but I didn't know where the door was. The place seemed to have gone quiet now, a stilled silence as the crowd stared at me – what a show I made of myself.

'For fucksake . . . get him outside before the floor's covered in blood.' It sounded like the barman again. I felt hands go under my armpits. I was lifted. My head battered on the pub doors. I felt a rush of cool air as I hit the street.

I was dropped on the flags. The doors shut behind me.

I lay face down on the cold slabs. I could feel my mouth bleeding, the salty blood seeping beyond my lips. There was, strangely, no pain. I was numb.

'Life goes on, Gus,' I said. 'Life goes on.'

I felt my hair grabbed in a bunch then the back of my head was pulled back sharply.

'You fucking think so, eh.'

It was the bloke in the leather from the pub. I recognised his voice this time: 'I know you.'

It was Shaky's pug, one who'd been rolling up his sleeves in preparation to give me a booting the last time I'd seen him. He'd looked disappointed then, but not now. He dropped my head onto the pavement. 'What are the fucking chances ay seeing you here, eh?'

I felt the bile rising in my gut. More blood flowed over my lips.

The pug raged, 'You were fucking told, Dury . . . told to leave off by Shaky and you didn't listen. How many warnings does a cunt like you need?'

I had the answer now, but it seemed pointless to let him know.

'I've had more chances than I can count already . . .'

He looked scoobied. Picked me up by the collar, dragged me towards a navy Subaru. He had the remote central locking key in his hand; the indicator lights flashed. I had no chance to protest as I was thrown in the back, a heavy fist laid on the side of my head in case I felt like checking out early.

I coughed dark blood as I fell into the back seat.

CHAPTER 31

I must have passed out. My mouth felt dry, which meant I'd stopped bringing up blood, but my lips were swollen and sore. There was a throbbing in my head, but that was nothing new. The motion of the car had my guts turning over and over, though I figured they'd have been doing all right on their own without any help. My heart battered off the insides of my ribcage where I lay, face down on the back seat. There was a pool of frothy sick, the kind the doctor had said was a sign of dire consequences to come. I knew I'd fallen off the wagon in spectacular fashion but somehow, even knocking at death's door, it seemed the least of my worries.

I turned over; groaned. Got the driver's attention. He yelled at me but I didn't register a word. My mind was fixed on the dull fizz of the street lamps that flew past the window. The world outside looked bathed in a sickly orange glow; seemed to fit.

I raised myself on an elbow. The pug was still yelling at me: 'D'ye want me to come back there and give you another slap?'

I touched my head – there was a nice cut above my left eye where his last slap had landed. I figured on there being more to come.

My senses slowly started to return to me. I had the vague notion to try and jump out of the car, make a run for it. But I knew, in my condition, that wasn't an option. Even at thirty miles an hour, I'd end up as spam the second I hit the tarmac. And as for running – there was less chance of that than me finding the winning lottery ticket on the floor.

I worked myself up to straighten my back, found I could get upright without too much effort. It surprised me . . . I had a spine, then. The pug had another yelp at me: 'You fucking better settle down or I'll be pulling over to tan yer arse for you!'

He sounded like my father; at least, his turn of phrase did.

My hands stung like a bastard. I looked down at them, saw the palms were covered in dried blood. I remembered taking a flyer in the pub, and being thrown out onto the street. It didn't matter to me which of these events had been responsible, the facts of the matter remained the same. I felt a gale of shame blow over me. I knew there would be a time when I replayed this scenario, went over every minor detail and castigated myself for it. That was the alky's way. I had wondered once if this was why I did it – if I was a shame junkie. But I'd long since stopped wondering about anything. Life had become so unmanageable now that there didn't seem any point.

I shook myself. If there was a spark of life in me, somewhere, I'd find it. I had Amy to think about and the case I was working held all Hod's hopes for getting his life back on track. I had lost Debs, I knew that, but Gillian had lost a son; there were other people out there who needed me. I couldn't let them down. The drinking, I knew now, had been a mistake . . . but I could move on from that. Or so I hoped.

'Where are you taking me?' I said.

The pug's beefy neck twitched, two fat rolls of meat quivering as he twisted round to yell at me. 'What the fuck was that? You speaking to me?'

I amped it up: 'I said . . . where the fuck are you taking me?'

He slammed on the brakes. My neck jerked backwards, then my head snapped forwards and banged off the seat in front. I took a fair dunt, but wasn't any more dazed than I had been previously.

The pug pulled off his seatbelt, got out of the driver's door and marched around the side of the car. He tugged open the back door then looked at me for a second. There was an expression on his face that said he might have been weighing up whether I was actually still alive.

'Christ al-fucking-mighty, Dury . . . you look like fucking shit.'

I managed a lame, 'Thanks . . . not looking bad yerself.'

He leaned in and clasped a mitt round my throat; I tried to loosen it but my grip was too weak. He held me for about a minute, watched me struggle for air then threw me back on the seat. As I gasped he laughed it up: 'Jesus . . . not gonna have much fun with you, y'wee sack of shit, am I?'

'Depends.'

He looked as though he'd been poked in the eye. 'What you say?'

'You taking me dancing, big boy? . . . Can fair cut a rug, y'know.'

He pulled back a fist, thought better of it. I got the impression he really wanted me in one piece.

'You'll find out soon enough where I'm taking you, ya daft cunt.'

We started out again. I watched the street lamps lining the road and my vision began to settle. My stomach felt as if someone had lit a furnace in there. I was on the verge of heaving all over the back seat, but I kept it down. Had a feeling that if I started I wouldn't stop. And that would be that.

We left the East End and headed out through Porty. The streets were quieter here – bit far out for Festival-goers – but there was still the usual after-hours carnage of blokes pissing in shop doorways, and girls in high heels and higher skirts screaming blue murder at each other through streaked make-up and lank hair. What did I ever see in this life? At night, being driven around in the back of a car, the whole city is laid bare before you. Makes you think . . . makes you want to pack up and leave. Maybe I would. If I got the chance.

I started to grow woozy, my eyes opened and closed, and I was in and out of consciousness by the time we reached Musselburgh. We seemed to be in a more residential area now; the street lamps had changed from orange to white and the roads were quieter. I rested my head on the window and caught sight of my reflection. I was beyond rough. My skin was pasty white and deep lines cut from the corners of my eyes to halfway down my cheeks. I seemed to have aged dreadfully. My mouth, minus the top row of teeth, was pinched and dour. I looked like an old jakey. I wanted to laugh, the state of me. I was so rough beyond belief that I knew the world wouldn't miss me. Who, Amy? Hod? My mam? Sure, they'd miss me . . . but would they be any worse off for not having me in their lives? I had weighed it all up and come to the conclusion that if this was the end, so be it. I wouldn't fight it. I wouldn't even contest it. It would be for the best.

The pug pulled onto a gravel driveway. Bright lights lit up as the tyres crunched into the scree. We seemed to be approaching the rear of a large baronial-style home. The car came to a halt slowly, the wheels hardly making any noise as they stilled. The pug squinted out to the back door; the lights were too bright and he made a visor of his hand above his eyes. He seemed to see what he wanted to see, smiled and made a thumbs-up. I caught sight of a bloke, a lit cigarette in his mouth, making his way down from the back steps. He was another big biffer in a white trackie.

The pug turned on me. 'Showtime!'

I had to laugh. 'Is that supposed to put the shits up me?'

His face dropped. 'I'll put the fucking shits up you, Dury.'

I managed another snort, felt less brave when I saw the corners of his mouth turning up; he looked the type who enjoys this sort of thing. It's why they got into the racket in the first place – to bust heads.

The car's back door was pulled open. I felt a cool gust of damp air and then a large hand with a heavy piece of bling on the wrist reached in and grabbed me by the collar.

In the far corner of the well-lit yard sat a one-storey building. It looked out of place, like a bunker; it seemed to have blacked-out windows. It didn't inspire confidence in me; could guess what it was used for. As we walked towards it the pug put a boot in my arse. I turned, blared, 'You can chuck that in! I'm fucking walking, amn't I?'

The pair of diddies looked at each other and laughed. Was expecting a high five, but they were beneath even that level.

When we reached the door, the trackie pug knocked a couple of times and then the door sprung open. Another shaven-headed lump opened up, nodded us down a tiled corridor. I knew why it was tiled: easier to hose down the blood. At the end of the corridor a door was ajar; I heard voices coming from inside. I was sure I recognised one of them. When I was pushed through the doorway, my worst fears were confirmed.

'Gus Dury, as I live and breathe!' said Shaky. He stood in the corner with a group of biffers. They were drinking cans of Red Stripe. 'Get you a wee tipple, Gus?'

I shook my head. That was a first. But I'd had enough for one night.

'Och, wise . . . always gets you into bother the drink, does it no'?' he said.

I walked into the middle of the room. It looked to have been a slaughterhouse at one stage. There was a rail of butcher hooks hanging from a metal bar that crossed two steel beams in the ceiling. On the ceramic floor was a gutter and grooves to let the blood drain away. If he had chosen this place for effect, it fucking well worked. I felt my throat freeze over; my heart all but stilled in my chest. All I could think of now was Amy, and how she'd feel when she heard how I went.

'Mind you, Gus . . . way things are looking for you, you might fancy a wee bevy. Sure I cannae tempt you?'

I shook my head again. Tried to speak, but couldn't manage words. Somehow I'd lost the power of speech. All language was locked away inside me, I had no access to it. As I stood there looking at the crowd of laughing idiots, all I hoped for was a quick death. I was certainly too weak to put up a fight.

'What's that, Gus? . . . Sorry, cannae hear you,' said Shaky.

The pug in the leather jacket leaned forward and slapped me across the side of the head. 'He's fucking speaking to you.'

The crowd got a laugh out of that.

'Where did you find him?' asked Shaky.

'Stoatin' about the East End . . . oot his fucking face, so he was.'

Shaky crossed the few feet between us to look me in the eye. 'What's the matter, Gus boy . . . wee barney wi' the missus?'

I found words, 'I'm not married . . . any more.'

Shaky pulled a face. 'Oh, it speaks!' He walked round behind me. 'That's right, remember hearing something about that . . . when I put my feelers out. Did you know I was taking an interest in you, Dury? Oh, aye . . . big interest, let me tell you.'

I twisted my neck, followed his pacing. 'Is that right?'

He snapped: 'I'm no' a liar! . . . In fact, anything I tell you, you can be guaranteed of it, bet the fucking farm on my word, so ye can. Now, do you remember what I told you the last time we met, son?'

I remembered, but didn't let on. Shrugged out a 'Not really.'

The crowd didn't like that, let out whoops and hisses. It was high drama for these idiots. Serious as pay-per-view sports.

Shaky felt the crowd baying for blood. 'String the cunt up.'

My hands were tugged behind my back, then a rope was tightened. One of the butcher's hooks got dragged along the rail; the shrill shriek of it set my spine on edge. I was raised up and my tied hands attached to the hook. The pain as my body's weight pulled at my shoulder blades was an agony. I wailed out in utter defeat.

The group laughed and cheered, a few banged tins of beer together. Shaky walked beneath me where I hung . . . 'Now, see that Laird laddie – he wasn't strung up like that, Dury. He had the rope round his fucking neck . . . Would you prefer that?'

I started to sweat. The pain felt as if my shoulders would explode at any moment. It's funny how, faced with your own destruction, all notions of bravery leave you. I managed some words: 'No . . . no.'

'What's that?' Shaky cupped a hand to his ear. 'Think I missed it!'

'I said no . . . No, I don't want strung up like Ben Laird.'

Jeers, some clapping. Laughter ringing off the walls.

Shaky didn't seem to like my response, though. He snapped, 'Then why the fuck are you still padding about this toon trying to rake into the cunt's death?' He grabbed my jacket collar, pulled me down closer to him. 'Eh, answer me that. Did you just choose to forget what I warned you, Dury? That it? You making a cunt oot ay me? Or are you just plain fucking stupid?'

I couldn't speak now. The pain was too much; I passed out.

When I came to, Shaky was stood over me, smoking a cigarette. He put the filter-tip in my mouth, played up to me. 'Answer me this, Dury . . . what's your fucking game here, eh? Who's working your strings? Cos either you have some serious back-up or yer on a death wish . . . which is it?'

I had nothing to lose by laying my cards on the table so I said, 'I'm not the one you need to worry about.'

'Eh? What you fucking on about?' I had his attention.

'There's worse than me you could cross.'

He arked up, grabbed my hair and pulled back my head, 'Stop pissing me about here, son. Say what you've got to say or I'll put you back up on that fucking hook, and no' by the hauns this time.'

He let go my hair, my head slumped forward. 'I know about Ben Laird and Gemmill . . . about the money he owed and that you want to see the case closed so it doesn't come back to you . . .'

'Well, if you know that, what are you fucking playing at?'

I gasped for breath. Took a gamble: 'This goes higher up than you think . . . the filth are all over this.'

'Are you on about that mad Irish bastard?'

'You've met Fitz?'

'Creeping about, rattling folks' cages . . . He's no' playing the game.'

I spat, 'And neither are you.'

Shaky's eyes burned. 'What the fuck you on about? . . . Now, spit it oot!'

I played my one and only card; it was no ace, but it was all I had. 'I know you don't want the kid's murder laid at your doorstep, so you need to let me get Gemmill out the frame . . . Trust me, if he didn't do it, I'll find out.'

'He didn't fucking do it! But you think that's gonna stop the polis hanging it on him, and my business out tae dry with him?'

I felt my breath seep out slowly. I was close to collapse again. Had little or no energy resources left to draw on. 'If I get Gemmill off . . . are we quits?'

Shaky nodded. 'Aye, oh aye . . .'

'And Hod?'

His answer came slower this time: 'You get our Danny in the clear and yourself and Hod are of no interest tae me.'

I managed a dim smile before my eyes closed on me and the room fell into blackness.

CHAPTER 32

I should have been grateful for the run back to town, but somehow the pug in the trackie wore down my enthusiasm. He played *Slowhand* on the CD, did the chords on air guitar when 'Layla' kicked in. When he got to nodding along, I thought he was a bit too used to banging his napper, didn't want to find myself on the end of it later on. As I sat beside him I could see he was carrying some meat: his gut pressed against the wheel when he turned corners and his neck shook on the cobbles. I was unnerved most of all by his bonhomie. The man was far too happy, made me think he had a surprise in store for me. Like maybe he wasn't running me back to town after all.

We flew through Musselburgh and Porty, hit Meadowbank in good time. At London Road the pug turned to me, said, 'I know a good spot.'

'A good spot? . . . Here'll do.'

That made him laugh. His meaty neck wobbled on his chest. As he smiled sharp lines cut the corners of his eyes. It was a face I could never tire of punching.

At the stadium he chucked a left, hared it past

a Skoda garage and took another left, followed the road round to a little industrial estate. He allowed himself a handbrake turn in the car park before slapping the wheel and starting to remove his watch. I got the hint; went for the door handle. It was locked.

He laughed, 'You thinking of going somewhere?'

'Are you as daft as you look, fella?'

He didn't like that. 'What the fuck did you say?'

'I said, are you as daft as you fucking look? If you're thinking of working me over . . . it's not gonna help your boss out.'

His smile returned. 'See me, I'm funny that way.' He smacked me in the mouth with a backhander, let out a 'Yee-haa!' I yelled as my head banged off the car window. After all I'd been through already, it should have been enough to call lights out, but I hung in there.

The pug walked round to my side of the car, opened the door – I fell out. As I crumpled on the tarmac he started to lay into me.

'Mouthy little cunt!' he roared out.

I watched his face contort then redden. He took his work seriously. I could tell that by the way he put his back into it. I tried fending him off for a bit – put up arms, curled into a ball – but it was only incitement to him.

'Get yer hands out the road, y'prick!' he yelled.

Like I paid any notice. It was only when he started belting my gut, and the blood came up into my mouth again, that I held off. In no time at all, I'd lost consciousness.

I woke up in hospital again. The frequency of these visits was becoming embarrassing now. Not just for me, but for the staff. A nurse loomed over me with a thermometer. She seemed to have just taken it from under my armpit.

'Oh, you're with us, are you?' she said.

I didn't have an answer for that. I didn't feel very with it. I couldn't remember too much; the lights hurt my eyes. 'What happened?'

'I believe you were found in a pool of your own . . .' she left a pause for emphasis, 'blood.'

'Makes a change from my own sick!'

She didn't see the funny side. I tried to pull myself up. A strong smell of disinfectant filled my nostrils, made me feel like chucking up again. As I settled down I noticed there was a figure at the bottom of the bed. I squinted, tried to make my eyes focus. 'Mam?'

'Hello, son.'

'What are you doing here?' I felt embarrassed for her. Heat flashed in my cheeks.

She walked around the bed, patted the nurse's arm, 'The hospital called me.'

The nurse spoke again: 'We thought we might lose you . . . it was touch and go there for a while. You know, you'd be better off playing Russian roulette, Mr Dury.'

I tried to swing my legs over the side of the bed.

'I'll bear that in mind.' My second attempt at raising a smile on her miserable coupon fell flat as well. She shook her head and went for the door. I was glad to see it close with her on the other side.

My mother came and helped me to stand. 'I didn't know what to make of it when they called.' There was a tear in her eye. 'I thought . . . well, I just thought.'

I couldn't bear to see my mother so hurt; I patted her hand. 'Mam, I'm sorry.'

'Oh, Gus.' She took a handkerchief out of the sleeve of her cardigan. 'Whatever happened to you?' I thought at first she was talking about my latest hospitalisation, but as she moved to the chair by the bed she said, 'How did it ever come to this?'

I knew what she meant. She was wondering how I had come to this level of despair. Was it the way my career went tits up? The wreckage of my marriage? My childhood? Christ, I wish I knew. I was a disaster, seemed like I always had been.

'I don't know, Mam.'

She dabbed her eyes with the handkerchief. 'I wanted so much for all of you . . . I had so many dreams and hopes. Every mother does.'

I heard the words, and I registered her hurt, but for reasons beyond me I thought of Gillian Laird. She was a mother too, she had lost a son. She needed answers, and she wasn't going to find them with me in here. I had lost too much time already. I needed to act.

'Mam, did the nurse say when they were thinking about letting me out?'

'Oh, it won't be for weeks. You need a good rest, and to heal up . . . They thought you were a goner, son . . . didn't you hear her?'

I didn't want to believe her. Jesus, how many times had I heard that in the last few weeks? I was ready to take my medicine like all the other times and move on. Figured, if I hadn't carked it yet, I was on a winning streak. And I was still standing – it couldn't be that bad, could it?

I said, 'That's not going to be possible . . . I've too much to do.'

My mother double-blinked. She dropped her handkerchief as she rose. 'But you can't go anywhere . . . there's people to see you.'

'What? . . . Who?'

She walked over to me. 'Out there . . . they wouldn't let them all in together.'

'Who's there, Mam?'

'Everyone . . . I had to call them, they said it was near the end for you . . . Was like your father all over again.'

My mind flipped out. I watched my mother go for the door. She said, 'I'll send them in . . .'

When the door opened again, the last person I expected to walk through appeared. 'Hello, Gus . . .'

'*Debs*?'

She clutched at the shoulder strap of her bag, a blush spreading on her face. I watched her eyes flit from me to the window, as if she was too embarrassed to look at me. Christ, it was a heartscald.

'Your mam called . . . when . . .'

'She said.'

Debs put down her bag, sat in the seat with her knees together and her legs turned to one side. She looked tense. 'How do you feel?'

'Like shit . . . thanks for asking.'

She laughed. 'I suppose you don't need me to tell you that's how you look!'

I smiled, 'Boom-tish!' Knew I deserved that. Worse, probably.

We looked at each other. It was great to see her again, but I felt nervous – tweaked at the hair on the back of my hand as I spoke. 'I got your text.'

'Gus, I don't want you to think that I'm re-establishing contact.'

I shot up a hand. It seemed to take more of my energy than I'd imagined it would; blood rushed to my head. 'No, Debs . . . I know.'

'That text—'

I cut in: 'Look, I just wanted to know you're okay, and now I do, so all's cool.'

She turned in the chair, fiddled with her watch strap. She searched herself for a new topic of conversation. 'I, er, met your friend, Amy.'

I flung back my head. 'Christ, is she here too?'

'She was in bits last night . . . thought she'd lost you.'

'Oh, bollocks . . . I'm sorry if you felt awkward.'

She stood up, smoothed out the creases in her jeans with the flats of her hands. 'No, Gus . . . not at all.'

'You sure?'

'She seems lovely . . . You deserve a break. I hope she makes you happy.'

'She does.'

Debs's face hardened, her eyes thinned. I wondered if she ever played over all those conversations where we'd come to the conclusion that we could never make each other happy. No matter what we said or did, or how hard we tried . . . it just wasn't in us. As I stared at Debs now, I understood we were never meant to be. We had spent so long together, but it had all been for nothing. We were never fitted as people. I hoped we could both take the lessons we had learned and move on.

'I'm glad, Gus . . .' Debs picked up her bag from the floor, slipped the strap over her shoulder. 'I'm going to go now.'

I didn't know what to say, went with, 'Okay.'

'You'll be all right now?'

It was her way of asking if we were 'good'. Had we drawn a line under things once and for all. I believed we had. It was hard to admit it, but I knew it. I'd seen her now, spoken to her, and understood where she was at in her mind. Now was time for a fresh start.

'I'll be fine . . . And you?'

She smiled. 'I'll be fine too.'

As Debs left the room it was like a part of me left with her; I no longer felt the need to go over the old times. The ground was covered. We'd parted, and we'd parted on good terms. I was happy about that. For the first time in longer than I could remember, I was happy about something.

When the door opened again, Hod, Mac and Amy came in. Amy rushed to my side and put her arms around me. Her long hair fell on my face, then she jerked back her head and stared at me. Her eyes were red and swollen but she seemed to have collected herself now. I was glad to see her.

'Oh, Gus . . . you daft prick.'

I smiled. 'Stop that . . . it only hurts when I laugh, y'know.'

'What the fuck happened to you?' said Mac. He took his hands out of his jacket pockets, weighed them in the air.

'Take a wild guess,' I said.

Hod answered: 'He got rubber and ended up in a ruck . . . Was on the pish again, after all his warnings of late.'

I sliced the air with my arm. 'Only half right, smart-arse!' I motioned Amy to sit on the bed. 'This was Shaky's doing.'

'You saw Shaky?' said Mac. 'And you're in one piece?'

'Aye, impressive, eh.'

'What's going on, Gus?' asked Hod.

I filled them in on the deal I'd struck with Shaky, on the mental pug in the trackie who was desperate to take a shot at me, and on one or two other things that I'd learned recently from Stevo and Fitz. Things were hotting up. If we didn't find Ben's killer soon, I seriously feared there would be another death. Maybe mine.

'It's fucking madness,' said Hod. 'I can hardly get my head around it.'

Amy placed a hand on her hip, butted in. 'It's this city all over. Jesus, you should see some of the brats on my course: they think they're entitled to lord it over the rest of us . . . probably always have done. It's just utter fantasy.'

Hod wasn't impressed. 'You're saying it's just deluded kids? Those wee bastards are feral.'

'Those arseholes like Ben Laird got carried away with it all,' I said. 'It's a boys' gang, silly wee boys playing silly wee games . . . but they took it too far.'

Mac was listening with his chin in his fingers. 'You're forgetting the drugs . . . they were tanning all kinds of shit. And the Laird boy was dealing . . . See, when a fair whack of poppy starts coming in, and yer off yer heid on something or other, it's easy to lose it.'

We had them sussed. But this was a group that was protected, in high places. The Craft was watching over them; and not one of them wanted to see old wounds reopened.

'There's a way forward from here,' I said. 'But we need to get moving.'

Hod laughed. 'We . . . moving. You're not including yerself in that, are you?'

'Oh aye.'

Amy slapped her hips. 'Gus, you're going nowhere. You nearly died, or have you forgotten that?'

I started to take my clothes out of the cabinet by the bed.

'Gus, did you hear the lassie?' said Mac. 'Yer no' going anywhere.'

I grabbed the bundle of neatly folded clothes. They were caked in dried claret. 'Well, I'm gonna need some new gear before I go, that's for sure.'

CHAPTER 33

I was doing okay on the wobbly pins; my knees felt loose, but then so did my ankles. Between them they seemed to work at keeping me upright. My main concern was the craving for alcohol. The hair of the dog that bit me. I needed to down some sauce soon or the shakes would be back. The hallucinations had stayed away; it would take a good few days of no intake before they kicked in. But I knew they were in the post.

I was determined to make a go of things with Amy. Christ knows why she had stood by me, but she had; I'd be an idiot to question that. In a strange sort of way, now that I had seen Debs, it was like I was given a free run at some happiness. If I had that feeling in me, life couldn't be all bad. Well, could it?

I turned down Leith Walk. Some wanky arts events had kicked off in a couple of the bars, some Student Grant types were hanging about in rugby shirts and ripped jeans. A few of them had on chunky basketball boots, and to a man they had the customary three to four inches of undercrackers on display. Throw in the foppy hairstyles and they were an accident waiting to happen down this end of the town. Hardmen with Staffies go looking for this type of action. Finding it in their own manor was like all their Christmases come at once.

I sloped passed the yaw-yawing mob, kept myself moving. Much as I despised their ilk – they got my goat, plain and simple – I'd come to feel for the parents of the brats. Ben Laird had been a piece of work, no question. He'd graduated from dabbling in drugs to dealing them, and more besides. Pimping out girls to his well-off buddies must have made him popular, but the boy had been out of control. Add that to the mix of teenage arrogance, and the hothousing of ego that went on in that moronic good old boys' group of his, and the lad was knocking on trouble's door. I had my suspicions that the very public coming out of his mother with Tina could have pushed him over the top. Dropping the 'Bender' Ben tag smacked of oversensitivity. One thing the lad needed to get straight from the off was, the world he was moving in had no place for sensitivity.

I took a turn off the Walk at Robbie's Bar, headed down to Easter Road. This part of the East End attracts some numbers on the weekend, match day, but the rest of the week it's dead at the far end.

The tenements are falling apart down here. In Edinburgh scaffolding multiplies in the summer months as roofers and the council conspire to squeeze even more out of the hard-pressed towns-folk. But round here, the roof could be in before a stick of scaffold was seen. Some yuppie flats had been stuck up by a foreign firm that didn't know the postcode was unattractive: I'd been watching the prices drop steadily on their adverts, wondering when they'd be giving them away.

As I turned for the caff I caught sight of Fitz's Lexus. I'd arranged to meet him to go over what we had turned up on the case so far. He was parking up over the road; I left him to get on with it, went in and ordered up some coffees. For the first time in months I felt like food: all my appetites seemed to be returning. I took that as a good sign – so long as the main one could be held in check.

'Could you do me a bacon roll too?' I asked.

Got some nods. Waitress shouted the order through the serving hatch.

I sat in the far corner, away from the window. It didn't do to be seen with Fitz in public. We were both agreed on that. When he came in he was sweating hard, his face was flashed red and thin wisps of grey hair stuck to his brow. He looked aggravated, ready to blow off some steam, perhaps.

'Fucking Festival . . . when's it going to be over?' he said.

'Not soon enough.'

'Annual fucking jamboree of midgets and poofs on our streets. 'Tis enough to make ye go postal.'

I stifled a laugh; the PC brigade hadn't reached this end of town yet.

The coffees arrived. They were instant. I didn't complain – meant a reprieve from the usual fifty-seven different varieties of coffee you get listed in most city caffs. You asked for a mocha in this joint, they were likely to think you were taking the piss, or ask what the fuck it was.

I tucked into my roll. Fitz turned up his shirt-sleeves; his arms were wet with sweat.

'So,' I said. 'How's Colin doing?' Didn't see any point in hanging about, or playing the slow build. We had business to do, and time was a major factor now.

Fitz creased his brows. The mention of his nephew seemed to calm him a bit. He widened his eyes and let out a slow trail of breath as he spoke: 'He's holding up . . . The lad's rattled, though.'

I didn't want to press him further. It was a sensitive issue. Fitz knew what the Craft was capable of – had seen it in action – but the young lad was new to the game, didn't know what to expect next. I wondered if that was how it had been with Ben.

'And what about you, Fitz,' I changed tack, 'did you get a look at those faces?'

He leaned forward, acted conspiratorial. I could see beads of moisture sitting in his eyebrows. None of this came easy for him. At his stage of the game, his time of life, he was looking to take things easier, not going full pelt at the top brass . . . again. 'I did, yeah.' He held back, made a pensive sigh.

I prompted, '*And*?'

Another, longer sigh. 'As we thought . . . there's some faces in that picture that found their way onto the force. Fucking fast-tracks. Two of them, Henderson and Bowman, are top dogs in the Craft . . .'

'Hang about – Charles Henderson?'

'Aye, we call him Chick . . . or Chief Super to his face.'

'We've met.'

'Y'wha'?'

I felt my mind drawn back. 'At Calder's hanging.'

'*And*?'

'He was by the book . . . firm. Never so much warned me off as advised me what might be good for my health.'

Fitz wheezed an indrawn breath, his shoulders tensing, 'I did some digging about, and yer man Calder was at the uni the same time as Chick Henderson and Bowman. The lad that got hanged back then, he was best mates with that group.'

It figured – knew it would. The scene was a little less hazy. I could see how Calder was involved, where his compulsion to cover things up had come from – but had he got fed up being leaned on? Thirty-odd years to keep a secret like that under wraps was a long time. Maybe he grew tired of it all, got spooked . . . and it cost him his life. 'Fitz, do you know about . . . the Seriatim?'

He rolled eyes, was an almost dismissive gesture. 'Bills itself as a debating chamber . . . More like posh twats' buggery and business school. They do a sideline in recruiting for the Craft.'

'How did you come by that information?'

'Ah, feck, Gus . . . you know better than to ask. All I will say is this: according to Ben Laird's file, every statement that was taken on the night of his death came from boyos in that feckin' group . . . and none of them conflicted.'

Seemed like the mob were well versed in police procedures. Of course they fucking were – they had experience of it to go on – and the filth were leading them by the hand. I felt myself drawing fists. I was surprised I had the energy to still be angered. But, by Christ, I was. 'Okay. What else can you tell me?'

'Bowman, he's away down south, some big shot at the Met, but Henderson, his career's running away with him here. Hasn't he more fucking stars than the Man U squad!'

'You think he's the one pulling the strings?'

Fitz laughed. 'I'd bet my fucking bollocks on it!'

It all fitted into place. Proving it would be another matter. But that wasn't my concern. I was after Ben Laird's murderer. What happened after I found that out wasn't for me to think about. When I found the killer, I'd light the blue touch-paper and retire. In every way, this case had just about killed me and I was in no fit shape to take on any more. I wanted to crash the rig and walk away, hopefully in one piece . . . and with Amy.

'So, what's the plan?' I said.

Fitz eased back in his seat, took up his coffee. His face was a blank sheet, impossible to read. 'I've no plan, Dury.'

I amped it up: 'You just want to see this swept under the carpet?'

A tut, then a huff. 'What would you like me to do, call in Internal Affairs?' He started to laugh. 'Christ on a fucking rubber cross, Dury, this mob run the force . . . we do things their way, or no way. What you *can* do is find yer boyo's killer and, at best, get the other cases looked at. Don't count on bringing any of this lot down – they've had too long to get their fucking act together.'

It didn't sound like the right move. My face must have gave away what I was thinking.

Fitz's voice was higher now: 'Look, if there's one thing I do know . . . when these bastards fuck up, like Calder and the Laird lad . . . their own take care of them.'

I was curious. 'What do you mean?'

He lowered his voice again. 'What I mean is . . . the Craft doesn't like having attention drawn to itself. They have ways and means of dealing with those that bring it down. They have their own kind of justice.'

'What you're saying to me is . . . if I blow this up, that'll be enough? Those that protected the killer will be punished by their own?'

Fitz nodded. 'They'll face harsher justice than any court . . . but let me give you a warning.' He put down his cup, wet his lips with his tongue.

'They will do everything they can to cover their tracks, Dury – including kill. If you push them too far, they won't give a second thought to blotting you out.'

I grinned. 'Yeah, plenty have tried before them. I'm still here.'

Fitz stopped me raising up my cup by placing a hand on my arm. 'I mean it . . . be very careful. You don't know who you're messing with here, Dury. These people are the worst sort of dangerous . . . they've lots to hide, and more to lose.'

CHAPTER 34

I had a handful of Harry Hills to take after my latest trip to the hospital. Took a scoop of them and half expected to see them again, but managed to keep the lot down. Thanked Christ for the let-off. The last twenty-four hours had been an eye-opener – in more ways than one. Couldn't say I was having difficulty coming to terms with my new status coupled off with Amy, but it did make me think about the way I'd been battering myself to bits. There was a time for drinking and despair, for raging against the world; now didn't seem like it. I kept replaying the old Lennon interview where he'd been asked if he'd found it harder to write now that he had fame, wealth and happiness. His reply had been a resounding no – that he'd found it much easier to write with cushions around him. I took his point; I'd been dining out on the wreckage of my career, marriage and life for so long that maybe it was time to let all that go. I was definitely on the mend, if not yet physically, then mentally – the clearest indicator perhaps being that I'd suddenly stopped listening to Joy Division.

Hod and I had holed up back at his gaff in Porty. He wasn't overly keen on the idea, but I gave him a guarantee that there would be no more visits from Shaky's pugs. It wasn't, strictly speaking, a promise I could keep. Well, not for certain, but I was working on it. After my chat with Fitz, I had a fair idea of what I needed to do to flush out Ben's killer. It was risky, but then, doing nothing was risky too. If I left things to progress at the pace they had done, Danny Gemmill was going to get jumpy, and I couldn't risk upsetting Shaky. Fitz too was raking up all kinds of shit with the Craft, driven by his maniacal ambition and an arrogant belief that he could protect his nephew. He wasn't bulletproof. The time when I thought of Fitz as merely filth had passed through; I didn't want to see him get any deeper in the shit than he already was.

Everything hinged on my keeping the head, staying sober, together. I needed to find Ben Laird's killer quickly. His mother had waited long enough. I got out my mobi, located Gillian's number in the contacts.

Ringing.

'Hello?'

It was Tina – know those rough tones anywhere.

'Hello, it's Gus Dury.' I let that hang there. Had an idea it niggled her, maybe more than she could afford to let on.

'Aye . . . and?' She was rough all right: this was one Leith hingoot who had come a long way. Had to give her credit for that.

'And . . . I'd like to speak to Gillian . . . if that's okay with you, Tina.'

A huff. She made the kind of tells a teenage girl did; she hadn't progressed beyond that level in many ways. Thought about telling her to watch that – it would be her undoing – but let it slide. Like I gave a fuck if she bollixed up the good wicket that she was on.

'And what if I dinnae want you to speak to her?'

I riled, clamped it down. 'Tina, I'm not looking for your approbation.'

She was thrown, sparked up, 'You think yer smart, don't you? Well, let me tell you, Gillian might no' be wise to you yet but I fucking well am.'

'Is that so?'

'Aye . . . it is.'

She played to type, but I knew how to deal with her. 'And where have you suddenly caught wisdom, Tina? Cop on, lass . . . go get your master.'

She slammed down the phone. It sounded as though it fell off the table; heard it swinging on the cord and battering off the wall again and again. Made me smile – I'd got to her. Thought: Daft sow.

A few seconds passed, then I heard high heels clacking on hard tiled flooring.

'Hello.'

'Gillian, hello . . . it's Gus.'

'What did you say to Tina?'

I winced. The girl had some plays after all. 'I, eh, you know how she is about me.'

'Look, let's get something straight, Mr Dury, I'm not paying you to upset my partner.'

I took it on the chin, although where that dippit cow Tina was concerned, it was more like a crush of the nuts. 'I think we understand each other.'

A curt, clipped, RADA-esque reply: 'Good.'

I held my impatience in check, bit on my lip before I spoke again. 'There have been some . . . developments.'

A sombre tone returned to Gillian's voice; maybe she remembered how much she needed me. 'I see . . . What kind of developments?'

I dropped in some dark tones: 'I think I should speak to you in person. Can I pay you a visit?'

Gillian inhaled sharply. 'What's happened?' She was anxious now for news.

'Nothing . . . yet.' I drew the conversation back on course. 'Can we meet today, say noon?'

She seemed to be considering the question for a few moments, or maybe her mind was blinking. Suddenly: 'Yes. Yes, of course.' I imagined her looking at Tina as she spoke, the tramp shaking her head.

'And do you think you could invite young Paul along?'

This changed her tone yet again. 'Paul? . . . What for?'

I played it cool but right down the middle. 'Paul has some questions to answer.'

'What about?'

'Gillian . . . I'm investigating a murder, this is

what I do. If I want to ask anyone questions, you can be sure they have answers I need.' I turned it up: 'Can you get Paul?'

'Of course, yes . . . I'll invite him round.'

'Good, Gillian. I'll see you about noon.'

I clicked off.

Hod had followed my side of the conversation from the kitchen doorway. Now he walked in, said, 'We on the move?'

I thought again of Tina eavesdropping. 'Your mother never tell you what happens to people who listen at open doors?'

'What's that?'

'They never hear any good of themselves.'

The bin men were holding the city to ransom again. Could always be guaranteed they'd strike when the place needed them most. They were cunning bastards. But what a union they must have – fair fucks to that lot. At Festival time, Edinburgh is submerged in a sea of styrofoam kebab boxes, Maccy D's wrappers and Starfucks cups. Add to this the greasy Home Counties crusties that can't find any kip when they're up to watch Tarquin in his first stand-up gig, and the place can look like a tip.

We drove up the Mile. Bins were piled to overflowing on the tourist thoroughfare. The scaffies had refused to take on the extra work associated with this time of year and the waste was mounting up. Foxes and seagulls had well and truly got stuck in to the muck. The cobbles were strewn with the evidence.

'This is some fucking shape to show the place off at Festival time,' I said.

Hod steered around a pile of black bags that had been kicked into the road. 'Bloody bin men . . . lazy fuckers. Can be guaranteed: any big gig in this toon and they're out on strike.'

He was right. 'Cos they get what they want. Wait till the big Hogmanay bash, world's eyes on Edinburgh – that'll be the next strike.'

Much as I was loath to admit it, we needed more like the bin men. Maybe then the ruling classes and their offspring like Ben Laird might be held a bit more in check; shake off some of their more fanciful ideas about dominating the proles. It was all a sorry state of affairs.

As we drove through the city, I scanned the *Hootsman* for any news about the case – nothing. Noticed an interesting article about foreign national brassers, mainly Brazilian and Thai, who had rocked up for the Festival and were doing a bustling trade from cheap bedsits at £35 a throw.

'Christ above . . . globalisation's got a lot to answer for.'

'Come again?'

'No never.'

When we got to Palmerston Place, Hod started to watch his driving, easing the van into Gillian's street as though he was carting nitro. When he parked up he smoothed out his shirt collar, tightened his tie in the rear-view mirror. Even managed to put a wet fingertip over his eyebrow. Would have thought he had a date.

'Quite content?' I said.

He looked me over, said, 'One of us has got to think about appearances.'

I took that on the chin, got out and made for the front door. I brushed at the shoulder of my tweed as we went – didn't seem to make much difference. I looked as crumpled as a paper bag.

We were shown through to the front room with the usual icy familiarity. Tina was already positioned by the drinks cabinet, pouring herself a large J&B. She had a cigarette burning in an ashtray which was overflowing with dowps.

'Hello, Tina,' I said.

She slit eyes at me. Thought she might swear out an insult but she held it together, merely sneered and raised a bony digit to me. Her pink fingernail had been chipped. There was no sign of Paul, but Gillian made her entrance from the French doors in her usual dramatic fashion, as if she was taking a curtain call.

'Mr Dury, glad to see you.'

That sounded like exaggeration but I was glad of the formality. It would be a help for what I had in mind. If you're going to say unconventional things, say them in conventional clothes.

'Is Paul joining us?'

'I have asked him, yes.'

Tina lit another cigarette from the tip of the one

she was smoking, sighed loudly. It was enough to call all eyes to her, momentarily.

I said, 'That's good.'

Gillian walked around the sofa, spoke, 'Are you sure it's really necessary? I mean, I don't see what he can tell us.'

I raised an eyebrow, wanted to say, *It's my case, and it's what I fucking think that matters.* Went with, 'You might be surprised.'

Tina grudgingly offered Hod and me some drinks. I took a mineral water and settled myself in the corner, back to the wall, and opposite the main sofa where Gillian sat. I wanted to have a full vantage point, didn't want to miss anything. If Her Ladyship liked theatre, she was in line for some – good-style.

We spoke for a few minutes about developments in the investigation. Gillian flustered once or twice, but held it together. I admired how buckled-up she was, under the circumstances. Tina stroked her back from time to time, making approving noises in between drags on her cigarette. It was all very touching; if you're touched by that kind of thing. Hod looked fit to hurl. I knew I'd have to listen to a commentary on his views about lezzing off all the way home, jokes about Sandi Toksvig being on the Number 73 bus . . . stuff like that.

Gillian had a few things she wanted to get off her chest, 'Why did you ask me to bring Paul here? . . . He was Ben's friend, you realise, there was nothing nefarious in their relationship.'

Had she been listening to me? What about all the times I'd reported to her about Ben's drug dealing, the brasser parties? And here she was, still playing the 'my Ben was an angel' tune. I rolled eyes. 'Look, Gillian, I hate to be the one to break it to you, but Ben and his friends were far from run-of-the-mill boyos. The whole crew had ideas above their station that got out of control.'

She looked stunned, as if I'd slapped her. 'That's not so.'

I battered that down: 'Trust me . . . I know it.'

Tina clawed at Gillian's hand, motioning her to be calm. 'I don't want to believe it.'

Hardly a breakthrough, but getting somewhere. I played the hard card. 'I need to see Paul because he was mixed up in this mess . . . and I don't want to see him get in any deeper.'

She turned to Tina, her voice faltering. 'Go and get Paul.'

Tina let her heavily mascaraed eyelashes lock shut – for a second or two we were treated to her china blue lids in all their glory – then she shook her head and noisily stropped off to the door. I waited until she was out of the room before restarting my questioning. 'How did you and Tina meet?'

Gillian fumbled her words: 'I-I . . .' She looked for an excuse not to answer, but nothing queued up behind her eyes. 'Tina was a guest at a house party we threw.'

'*We*?'

'Ben and I . . . it was after my marriage broke down.'

'Did Ben arrange this party?' I pressed her.

She turned away from me, lied, 'No. It was all my idea.'

When Tina came back with Paul he had slipped into his unctuous preppy-on-the-make persona, striding over to Gillian and grabbing her in a falsely convivial hug. I felt ready to chuck: one luvvie in the room was enough. If he thought Her Ladyship was going to protect him, he was deluded . . . more than I thought.

'Hello, Paul,' I said, tones flat.

He put those powdery-blue eyes on me, then Hod. The pair sized each other up over the rug for a moment or two, Paul dropped his gaze first. He was just a boy after all.

'I didn't expect to see you here today, Mr Dury,' he said.

I couldn't suppress a smirk. 'Oh, I bet you didn't.'

The ginge sat down between Tina and Gillian; Tina took his hand, held it firmly. I got the impression m'laddo had been waiting to be questioned for some time. That he was primed.

I got stuck right in: 'Tell me about the Seriatim.'

He smiled, touched the side of his nose. 'It's a debating group . . . a few of the boys on campus are involved. I didn't start it.'

Gillian seemed pleased with the answer; rubbed Paul's thigh.

'You didn't start the fire, eh.' They looked perplexed. I went on: 'It was always burning . . . right?'

Paul shuffled in his seat, shrugged shoulders. 'Erm, it's an old group, started in the eighteenth century by prominent city luminaries who wanted to help out the coming generations . . . It's tradition. There's not much I can say about it.'

'Sworn to secrecy?'

Paul's chest inflated. He sighed. 'It's not that kind of group,' he snapped now, getting jerky. 'It's a social thing more than anything.'

It might have started out that way, as a nice way of getting the up-and-coming brats more than their fair share of the pie, showing them the lie of the land, but this crew had got carried away. Ben had led the way with drug taking and wild parties; forays into the city's seamier side; it had all got out of control. Maybe it always had been, though. I gave him that.

'When did you and Ben start doing drugs?'

He turned to Gillian. She gave an approving look, nodded as if to say, *Go on.*

Paul said, 'I . . . we started in first year . . . There was a lot of stuff about.'

I held firm, pressed on with low tones: 'And when did Ben start dealing?'

Another long pause, then a slightly cocky smile. 'He was always the man to go to for a bit of puff.'

Paul thought he was almost in the clear, that I was going to blame Ben for everything. I upped the ante. 'And the serious stuff . . . when did he get involved with Danny Gemmill?'

Paul crossed his legs away from Gillian, 'I don't know exactly. Maybe sometime last year . . . Mr Dury, I didn't have anything to do with that side of Ben's life.'

I watched Tina light a cigarette; took my own pack out, sparked up. I walked closer to Paul. His eyes looked watery, rimmed in red. 'And what about the prostitutes . . . did you have more to do with that?'

Tina stood up. 'This is getting sick!'

Gillian flagged her down. 'Tina . . . Tina.'

'No, fuck this . . . Do we have to listen to this?' She held her cigarette like a dart. Gillian waved me on. Tina stomped for the door, jerked it violently and stormed through. A cloud of dust evacuated along the skirting as the door slammed shut.

'I'm sorry about that. Go on,' said Gillian. She moved further down the sofa, surveyed Paul's reactions as I started to question him again.

'On the day Joe Calder was hanged, Paul . . . where were you?'

He answered quickly; too quickly. 'It was in the night. I was tucked up in bed. Why are you asking me that? The police seem perfectly satisfied that it was a suicide.'

I took a deep drag on my tab. 'I'm not the police.'

Paul leaned forward, put his elbows on his knees and made a steeple of his fingers. The pose looked uncomfortable and he broke free of it, slouching backwards in the sofa. He said, 'Look, why are you asking me all of this? . . . I haven't done anything wrong.'

I put a hand in my pocket, drew a fist. I would dearly have loved to put several jabs in his smart puss. The kid was covering his arse and being cocky about it. He felt protected. I stood over him. 'Maybe your idea of right and wrong is different from mine.'

He stood, took a step towards me and inflated his chest. 'I don't much care what you think.' He was in no position to be so bold.

'Really?' I heard Hod manoeuvre himself to stand at my back. 'Is that how Stevo got the sore face? Lose that temper of yours, Paul?'

He bared teeth, near spat, then shoved past me. I caught his shoulder as it connected with my own. It spun me. He roared out, 'I'm not fucking listening to this crap!'

He got a total of two steps to the door before Hod grabbed him by the shirt collar, said, 'Think again, bonny lad.'

Paul squirmed, trying to claw at Hod's hand in his collar. His face was turning red. I fronted up to him, got right in his coupon and roared, 'What you afraid of, Paul?'

He barked back, 'Fuck you!'

Gillian rose, came running to my side. 'Mr Dury!'

I dropped my cigarette, put hands on the streak

of piss, grabbed his collar. He struggled harder in Hod's grip. 'Still playing the Big I Am, Paul? . . . You've got plenty to be scared about. Two people have died.'

Gillian shrieked, yelled at me, 'Let him go! . . . Let him go!' She tugged at my hands, I felt her nails dig deep. 'Mr Dury . . . let the boy go!'

I loosened my grip.

Paul bent like a hinge for a moment, then turned for the door. He stumbled at first, but soon found his stride. In the hall he turned back, pointed a finger at me. He tried to speak but his voice deserted him.

I imagined what he might have wanted to say; didn't scare me.

CHAPTER 35

Gillian went after the boy, tears streaming down her face. Her feet splayed out in that erratic girlie manner as she ran. It wounded me to see her abandon her composure like that. I felt for the poor woman: she had been through a lot – she was as much a victim as Ben. And I doubted she'd had the right kind of support from Tina; who had done a grand job of making a fool of her. The daft scrubber didn't know when she was well off.

I nodded to Hod. He went after Gillian, caught her up and put an arm around her. She took a few seconds to register what was happening, then she turned and sobbed into his chest. For a moment or two she beat him with fists, but she soon ran out of energy, folded like a woman beaten, defeated. Hod had to hold her up as she lost control of her legs.

'C'mon . . . it'll be okay,' he said.

Gillian started to mumble. Her words were indecipherable at first, choked deep in her throat. She broke off from Hod, pushed him away and screamed out, 'No, it won't be okay! . . . Don't you understand? It'll never be okay again!'

She dropped her arms to her sides, her knees collapsed and she fell to the floor. I watched her swoon. It seemed affected, like a stage fall, and then I heard her head connect soundly with the tiled floor and I realised that she wasn't acting. She was sparked out cold.

'Fucksake!' said Hod.

'Pick her up.' We took her back through to the front room, gently slapped the life back into her cheeks. She came round; looked woozy, lost. Like a woman on the edge; like someone who'd lost the world.

'Would you like something to drink?' I asked.

She touched her dry lips, spoke softly: 'Tina . . . where's Tina?'

'Don't worry about Tina . . . Hod, get her a brandy.'

Hod went to the sideboard, picked up a decanter, poured. When he returned, Gillian's hands were shaking as she took the glass. 'My head hurts.'

'I'm not surprised . . . that was quite a clatter you gave yourself.'

'I want Tina.'

I nodded, rose. 'I'll go get her.'

As I went for the door, I called Hod. He put a hand on Gillian's shoulder for a brief instant, then followed me out.

'Aren't you going to call Tina?' he said.

I tutted, 'That slag's the fucking last thing she needs.'

* * *

In the van we headed back to Amy's flat. The city was awash with fly-posters for the Festival. Every available wall, phone box and empty shopfront had been slapped with an ad for comedians I'd never heard of. I recognised one or two of the faces on show, with their T4 haircuts and overconfident manner shining out. They were all about the same age, all middle class and, as always, the humour would be the same: shite. I'd seen a Jerry Sadowitz show at the Festival once – pure working-class bile, and hilarious. He had commented that the only time he'd make it big was when he died and some Oxbridge student decided to recreate his show as a tribute. The sad thing was, he was fucking all too right.

This town has always been a schizophrenic schism of haves and have-nots, but more and more now it looked like those at the top were getting away from the rest. The game was fixed. A bolt of anger turned in my gut when I thought of Paul and Ben and the rest of their pathetic little crew running around the city as though they owned it. In their own way, they did.

Was I bitter, jealous? I didn't think so. I didn't aspire to their level. It was the injustice that fired me. Always had. Even though Ben hadn't been the kind of character I'd go for a bevvy with, he'd deserved better than a short drop. He got over-ambitious and got in the way – the system shut him down. His mother was broken, and I had seen enough families destroyed to know the territory.

The way Fitz had spoken about the Craft and how the case had been swept under the carpet, the more something like ambition fired in me. I wanted to blow this case wide open. I wanted to be the fly in the ointment. I wanted to do this one thing, because I could, and because I could do nothing about the rest of it. This life was a fixed game, but I had a chance to show everyone at the table for what they were, even if it was just this once.

My only problem was, I was no further forward after talking to Paul. I had hoped he would expose something important, let slip something I could use; but he had been ready for me. Had I been on better form, not losing my mind to alcohol, I might have seen the angles more clearly. Nothing was stacking up, I'd need to rely on a break. But I had a few more moves left to play. I wasn't out yet.

When we got back to the flat, Amy arked up. 'So, what's the go?' she said.

'No go,' said Hod.

Amy turned her jaw to her shoulder, putting a bead on me. 'You didn't bust Paul?'

I shook my head, removed my tweed – it felt like a straitjacket – and went to sit by the window, staring out at the skyline. The traffic was buzzing in the street below.

Amy came to sit down beside me. Hod went through to the kitchen, shouted as he ferreted in the fridge, 'So, what now?'

I kept staring out the window. My mind was

awash with possibilities . . . each one of them turning onto a dead end.

'Gus, what now?' echoed Amy.

We were at a brick wall. 'Look, what did you both expect, that the kid would just spill his guts? He was too smart for that.'

Amy crossed her legs, leaned forward; stray curls from her fringe fell over her eye, 'Okay, so how does it work, Gus?'

I drew my gaze away from her, turning back to the grey sky. 'The kid's rattled . . . trust me.'

'He is,' said Hod. 'We both saw that.' He'd brought through a can of McEwan's, cracked it open. 'You think he's rattled enough, though?'

I rose, followed Hod's cue, got myself a can, fired in. It tasted like an old dream, I wanted to fire into a lorryload of them, but fought it. My thoughts were on other matters and that helped. Said, 'My worry is that he's *too* rattled.'

'Come again?' said Hod.

I took another belt then lowered the can. 'If he's too scared, he'll kick off and that could be dangerous . . . Unless.'

Amy and Hod looked at each other. I could tell they were weighing up my words. Hod spoke: 'You mean, unless Gillian talks him round?'

'Bullseye.'

'You think that's likely?' said Amy. 'The woman hired you to—'

'She's right. Gillian's only interested in finding out who killed her son, Gus.'

I wanted to agree with them both, but something told me Gillian was none too pleased with anything the investigation had turned up so far. She'd seen the kind of life Ben had led – the drugs, the prostitutes, the company he'd kept. None of it could have been a comfort to a grieving mother. After the confrontation with Paul, I wondered if she might think better of digging any deeper. Gillian was, for all her bluster and histrionics, a sensitive soul. I knew she was hurting, and she didn't want any more hurt.

Amy cut in, 'But if that cow Tina gets her way . . . this case is over.'

'Not necessarily,' I said. I moved to the chair I'd flung my tweed on, leaned over and retrieved my mobi from the inside pocket. It had been switched off; I had two missed calls. I checked the details: one was from Gillian, she had called about twenty minutes after I'd left her home. The other was a first – it rattled me.

'Wonder what he wanted? . . . Got a call from Stevo.'

'Janny guy at the uni?' said Amy.

'Aye . . . he's never rung me before.' The thought stung and the possibilities raced before me. 'Wonder what he's after.'

'Call him back.'

'Yeah . . . in a minute,' I said. 'I have a call from Gillian too.'

'Gillian!' said Hod. 'We just left her.'

'Yeah, I know . . .' I checked my inbox. 'She's left a voicemail.'

As I listened to her message, Hod and Amy sat wide-eyed. There was nothing that they'd wanted to hear in that voicemail.

I lowered the phone.

'That's it, then.'

'What?'

I relayed the message: 'She's pulling the plug . . . wants us off the case.'

'What the fuck . . . why?' said Hod. He was on his feet.

I flagged him down. 'The woman's had enough . . . but you don't need to worry, she's paying full whack.'

Hod brightened. 'She is?'

Amy amped it up: 'For fucksake, is that all you're interested in?'

Hod fired back, 'Well, actually . . . it's a consideration, aye. I have Shaky on my back, or have you forgotten that?'

She tutted and looked away. 'Ben had a similar problem, I seem to remember.'

'Aye, and look how he ended up.'

I had dialled Stevo's number, waved at the others to shut the fuck up. 'Hello, Stevo, it's Gus.'

He seemed to be whispering, timid. 'Oh, you got my message.'

'Yes . . . sorry, my phone was switched off. Just got to it. What's up?'

There was a pause on the line. It unsettled me.

'Gus . . . I-I, er, saw Paul.'

I didn't like the sound of this already – what the fuck was Paul doing racing from Gillian's gaff to see Stevo? 'Oh, yes?'

'He seems to think that . . .' I heard a noise, a clatter of tins.

'What was that?'

Stevo held schtum. 'I don't know.'

'Is everything okay there?'

His voice dropped even lower. 'I think there might be someone outside.'

'Stevo . . . what did Paul say?'

'He asked me what I had told you . . . and some other stuff. He was very . . . animated.' He sounded pensive, on edge. His voice was choked with emotion.

'I bet he was.' This wasn't good. 'Stevo, get the fuck out of there . . . You hear me? Go home – now!'

His voice trembled; I could hear the fear in it. 'I think you might be right.'

'Look, Stevo, if you get any bother, call me right away, okay.'

Silence.

I'd missed the line going dead.

'Shit!'

I tried to call him back but it went straight to voicemail.

'Fucking hellfire!' I yelled. I grabbed up my jacket. 'C'mon . . . move yer arse. Things are kicking off.'

‘*Y’wha’*?’

‘Don’t fucking ask. We need to get to Stevo.’

I made for the door with Hod following. In the stairwell I heard Amy’s heels clacking on the stairs. ‘Where do you think you’re going?’ I asked.

‘With you.’

‘That’ll be shining bright.’ I pointed back to the door. ‘Get up those stairs.’

She made a moue of her mouth, pushed past me. ‘Fucking watch me.’

Hod shrugged. ‘No telling her.’

I knew he was right. We fired down the stairs. My heart was pounding already. A hundred scenarios flashed in my mind, none of them good. Stevo was the last person I wanted to get mixed up in this. Thing was, I knew he had more information than he had let on. He had done a good job of keeping it to himself . . . so far; I hoped he kept it that way. Dreaded to think how Paul and his mates would react to finding themselves up against someone else at this point.

For the first time, I wished I hadn’t pressed so hard on Paul. The lad was unstable. There was no predicting how he would react to the threats I had put on him. I had the dread feeling I’d fucked up. Badly.

CHAPTER 36

Hod put the pedal to the metal. For the first time in living memory Amy didn't fiddle with the CD player. We all sat, eyes front, cursing the traffic.

'This is fucked,' said Amy.

I looked at her. She was pumped, raring to go. This was the last thing I wanted. She shouldn't have been with us at all – it was no place for her. I didn't want to see her get hurt. I leaned forward. 'Hod, you need to go and see Gillian.'

'Y'wha'? . . . Thought we were going to this Stevo guy.'

'No. Drop me off, I'll sort Stevo . . . you and Amy go and see Gillian.'

Amy pointed a painted fingernail at me. 'Now hold on a minute . . .'

I put my hand around hers, clasped it. 'Look, Amy, you need to go there and suss what has changed her mind. I can't be in two places at once.'

She wasn't buying it; she was an action junkie like Hod. 'Can't we do that after?'

I shook my head, knew she'd need some persuasion. 'No. I need to know now . . . what's changed her mind in the last hour? Press her hard, push all her buttons and watch that fucking Tina one . . . she's up to her china blue lids in this shite!'

That seemed to appeal more to Amy. Thought maybe she saw herself slapping Tina about. She said, 'I can do that.'

Hod spun the wheel, looked focused as he burned up the road. 'What you thinking, Gus?'

I played it cautious: 'I don't know . . .'

A Punto driver blasted a horn at us; Hod gave him the finger. 'You must have some idea.'

I stuck to what he needed to know. 'Well, Gillian's either found out something she doesn't want to know . . . and wants to keep it from us, and plod . . . or Tina's found some leverage.'

Hod looked thoughtful. It didn't affect his driving though – that was still shit. He swerved left to right, near took out a lamp post. The traffic lights turned red but Hod fired through them. A wail of protest went up as we sped over the box junction; a VW skidded into the kerb. Some lanky crusty in a beanie found himself sprinting out of our way, raised a fist as we passed. We made it into top gear, powered up the street. All the while my mind focused on Stevo; I didn't have a good feeling about his situation. I replayed our phone call again: he'd sounded nervous, frightened. Jesus above . . . he had good cause to. The thought slayed me.

The van mounted the kerb, two wheels on the

flags as we skidded into view of the uni. 'Just out there . . . that's fine,' I said, banging the dashboard.

I let Hod pull up. As the brakes screeched Amy grabbed my arm. 'You sure this is okay?'

'Yeah, deffo. Go with Hod . . . you know what to do.'

Amy crossed her brows, sucked in her cheeks. I saw she wasn't sure about what I was suggesting; I needed to seal the deal. I found the energy to move fast, got out of the van, slammed the door behind me. Amy stared at me through the window. I raised a hand and waved them on. Hod didn't hang about, lifted the revs and sped off.

The uni was dead. Precious few students had hung about over the summer months, save the really keen ones and the ones with nothing better to do. The old buildings looked abandoned, only one or two lights burning as black clouds brewed up a storm. I crossed under the main archway into the courtyard. The front door seemed to be locked up for the day. I checked the handle to be sure – no give in it. The bolt was in place – would need a mortar launcher to budge it.

I schlepped round to the side entrance and let myself in with the janny's keys. There were no lights on here and the corridor lay in semi-darkness. I listened out for anyone, but the place was quiet as the grave. Stevo usually put the lights on when he knocked off. Seemed, if not strange, irregular. I closed the door behind me and paced towards the doocot. Something stopped me halfway there – instinct or whatever – and I made a detour to the main hall.

The sound of my footfalls on the old boards unnerved me; they echoed off the walls and the high ceiling and repeated like I was being followed. It was all just nerves, I knew it, my imagination was running away with itself. I hauled it in, gave myself a shake.

'Get yer shit together, Gus,' I told myself.

As I got to the hall, I creaked open the door and flicked the light switches – nothing.

'*Shit!*'

It was just like the night I'd found Calder; the thought jarred me. A cold bar of sweat formed between my shoulder blades, ran the length of my spine in one slow trail.

I edged back through the noisy door, made my way into the corridor and headed for the doocot. The usual disinfectant smell was strong in my nostrils, mixing with the musty, damp odour of aged buildings. There was another smell I couldn't quite put my finger on, seemed familiar enough, though. I sniffed the air a bit more and then I sussed it – Stevo's ganja. The boy had obviously been having a fair old toke. He usually kept that kind of thing in the doocot, though, didn't seem like him to be smoking out in the main corridor. Maybe he'd left the door open by mistake, I thought. But that didn't sound like Stevo either. My palate started to dry over. I pressed my tongue into the roof of my mouth, felt the gap in my teeth where the bridgework had been destroyed. My nerves were playing up – they were getting out of control.

As the doocot came into sight, my pulse quickened. There was no sign of life. The place was in darkness and the door closed. I kept my eye on the handle of the door as I walked, thoughts mashing with every step. I don't know what I expected to see: Stevo, armed with a crowbar, cowering inside . . . maybe a tale of more threats taken from Paul and his crew. He was a smart lad, Stevo, maybe he'd legged it at the first whiff of trouble. Then again, maybe he hadn't been able to . . . maybe they did get to him. Paul had been fairly ropeable when I'd seen him at Gillian's earlier; there was no telling what he would do. He was clearly off the scale; he'd some form for fronting up to Stevo – I just hoped that our recent chat hadn't prompted him to go any further.

I reached the door and I grasped the handle. It felt cold. I turned it anticlockwise. It clicked hard; The door was locked. I went back to my keychain – the red-topped key for the door was an easy find – and slipped it in the lock, turned once. The door opened up to a quarter of a foot from the jamb, then seemed to stick. Something was blocking the entrance, pressing against the other side. I pushed harder and it gave a little, but not enough. I pushed again, gained another few inches, which revealed a pool of dark liquid spilled on the floor. I reached for the light switch – this one worked. As I lowered my gaze to the floor again, I saw the liquid was red and sticky. I was standing in what looked like blood. Lots of it.

'Stevo . . . Stevo . . .' I yelled.

There was no reply.

I put my shoulder to the door, pushed harder. The blockage eased some; the more of the floor I brought into view, though, the greater the amount of blood I saw.

'Stevo . . . fucking hell . . . You in there?'

I pushed enough of a gap for me to squeeze through. My Docs slipped on the blood as I wedged myself between the jamb and the door. I had no purchase and skidded onto my arse. As I did so, the door jerked out of my hand and the pressure of the weight pushing against it forced it to slam shut.

For a moment I lay with my back on the blood-covered floor. I felt the freshness of it, it was still warm on my fingertips. I jerked up my hands, wiped them rapidly on my jeans.

'Christ! . . . Holy Jesus.' I was covered in the stuff. 'Fucking hell!'

I got up quickly and looked about the room; saw a bale of barbed wire pushed against the door. It had been untangled: a solitary, jagged strand had been fed up to the rafters and wrapped around one of the beams. As my eyes followed the line of the wire my hand shot up to my mouth. My stomach heaved as I caught the smell of blood again. But the real shock was the sight of Stevo, a barbed-wire noose around his neck, dangling from the roof beams.

I looked away. 'Oh, no . . . Stevo, Christ, no.'

The barbed wire had dug deep into the flesh around his neck. When he had been hoisted up the points had cut in, ripping open his jugular. Both front and back of his dustcoat were soaked in blood; it dripped from his chest to the tips of his shoes, where it fell with minute splashes into the pool beneath him. I turned away, but felt compelled to look back at him. Stevo's eyes were dark and ruptured. His tongue, black and bloated to twice its normal size, hung from his mouth.

I felt my insides settle – the fear and shock were replaced by anger. I looked about the small room. The place was in disarray. Paint cans had been knocked over, chairs pushed to the floor. Even the coffee cups Stevo and I had drank from were smashed. I tried to find focus, think what I needed to do, but all my thoughts ran into finding Paul and tearing him limb from limb.

'You fucker . . .' I yelled. I fired my fist into the wall. It stung like a bastard but seemed to calm me a bit. I turned back to Stevo. His face was a horrific mess: he'd been soundly beaten before they'd hanged him. I needed to get the police, but I didn't know how to play it.

'Think, Gus . . . think!'

Surely there could be no way of covering this up; the Craft couldn't get away with calling this suicide. Fitz would know how to handle it; I prayed he would, he was my only hope. I dialled his number.

'Hello, this is DI Fitzsimmons, I can't take your call right now but if you . . .'

'Oh, fucking voicemail.' I let the preamble end, ranted, 'Fitz, Fitz, there's been another death . . . another fucking murder. It's Stevo . . . he's swinging from the roof beams and dripping fucking claret—'

I didn't get any further – the phone was snatched from behind me. I hadn't heard anyone come into the doocot. They must have moved stealthily; didn't want to give themselves away. As I turned to see the mobi being casually switched off by a stooped figure, a hand grabbed at my arm, then another latched onto my wrist, turned it up my back. I was immobile, fully bound up as the figure raised its head.

'I don't think you'll be needing this,' said Paul.

At the sight of his watery eyes and his pale, freckled skin, I wanted to kill him. I lunged for him, but was held back by arms stronger than mine. I tried again, aiming my head at his face, but I couldn't reach. 'You fucking piece of shit,' I yelled.

He stepped back, put the phone in his pocket as he watched me struggling before him like a fitting lunatic, said, 'I don't think anyone's coming to save you, Mr Dury.'

I spat out – didn't faze him. Knew he was right,

though: I hadn't given Fitz my location before he'd taken the phone off me. I was dead meat now. I looked up, caught sight of Stevo, bloated and beaten, his wounds still bleeding onto the floor. I knew I was next. The thought brought a vivid image of Amy in tears once more and it felled me. 'You'll get yours, y'cunt,' I yelled out. 'Fucking sure you will.'

Paul leaned in, grabbed me by the hair, twisted it like a deadbolt. 'You really haven't a clue, have you? . . . You've no idea about any of this. You're just lurching from one disastrous gamble to the next, and you still think that somehow it'll all come right.'

I kept the bead on him, said, 'It'll be you swinging soon, Paul.'

His face tightened along the jawline; moisture glistened on his brow. One of the lads at my back spoke up: 'Come on . . . let's get going to the hall.'

Paul stepped aside. He dabbed at his face with the cuff of his shirt as I was forced past him. 'We'll see who's swinging next.'

CHAPTER 37

There were about five of them, forcing me down the corridor, towards the hall where Ben and Calder had been killed. Images of Stevo's blood followed me with every step. The thick darkness spreading over the floor, oozing from his ripped jugular. His face, beaten and bruised, returned too. Those black eyes of his, staring out from the unknown, they had seen more than he dare tell of; now he never would.

I was walking too slowly, got a shove in the back, a 'Hurry the fuck up'. I felt like a condemned man taking his final steps. Chances were that I was. Had I ballsed up? Oh, yeah. Ben had lost his life, for what I didn't know, or much care if truth be told. If this was the class of company he kept, they could all swing. Sure, his mother would go without answers, and I felt for her. But Stevo, he was different. He had just been caught in the crossfire. It burned me to know that I'd been part of that.

What had I done? I thought of Amy and my mother, all those who knew me, Hod, Mac . . . by Christ, I'd let them all down. Always had. But this kind of pain, the kind I'd be bringing them, was too much. None of them deserved it – I'd put them through too much already. *Fucking hell, Dury . . . going out in some style, eh?*

'Get going, janny man.' Another prod in the back, a kick. Got me moving.

'You in a hurry?' I snapped.

Paul spun; flecks of white spittle came as he spoke: 'We should have done you first.'

'Would that have saved Stevo?'

The fucker actually smiled at that. 'Who's to say?'

I pulled back from my restraints, tried to front up to him, but got tugged back, snapped, 'You really get something out of this . . . playing God.'

Paul ran white fingers through his mop of red hair, then quickly slapped a hand on my shoulder. 'I said, get going.'

He pushed the back of my head forward as I passed him. I collected another jab between the shoulder blades. Near dropped me on the floor – my knees caved, I coughed my guts up. There was some blood in there; I watched it drool down my front. I'd seen too much blood lately. The image of Stevo soaked head to toe in his own claret wasn't ever going to leave me. But something told me I wasn't going to have too long to be haunted by the image. The pack of boys was growing excited, they sensed another kill; they paced harder, faster.

Paul grabbed me again as we walked down the corridor to the main hall.

'You have no idea, Dury . . . no clue what we're about.' He sounded as though he wanted to explain, to defend himself. Like I gave a shit what was contained in his messed-up head.

I spat more blood, trying to rile him. 'You hear that, lads? . . . He's trying to implicate you all.'

Got nothing but laughs. They were all well gone, high on themselves. To a one they felt protected, beyond censure. They had got away with too much already; no wonder they felt invincible. I wanted to know how those in the Craft might respond to this latest turn of events – there was only so much the filth could sweep under the carpet. Another two deaths in similar fashion to the others, and on the same night, were going to set some big alarm bells ringing. I watched as two of them ran to the door – pushed it open and stood there flagging us through. They looked enthusiastic, eager even. I remembered an old movie, *Lord of the Flies*, one about the boys stranded on an island, slowly turning into savages. I felt like the lad they called Piggy, the one who'd managed to get on the wrong side of everyone.

'Nice try,' said Paul, 'but you're not going to save your sorry arse, Dury.' His face was flushed red, I could see the veins in his neck standing out like tensed rods: he was pumped for this. This sick freak was getting high on his own power to kill; it made me want to spit. As I looked at his face I knew I was staring into the last pair of eyes Stevo ever saw. I felt a heavy urge to gouge them out, stamp on them. I wanted to see Paul buried, and to dance on his grave.

An image of Ben hanging on a rope flashed before me. He had been Paul's best friend, for Chrissake – what kind of human being could kill so coldly someone they knew, and for what? For nothing, it seemed. Another life wasted for nothing. To satisfy the ego of some twisted fuck. I didn't want to count the lives this guy had wrecked; the Gillians of this world would be walking wounded for the rest of their days. He'd as well as killed them too.

It burned me to think of the people I'd be leaving behind . . . Amy especially would be felled. We'd only just got it together; I'd only just got over Debs. Things had looked so bright for us; for me, even. I know when that happens to expect the worst – but was there more than this?

'That what you told your friend, is it?' I blasted him. 'That what you said to Ben?'

Paul spun, pulled back his coat-hanger shoulders and stuck his face in mine. 'Ben chose his own way to go.'

I used what strength I had left to struggle, blared at him, 'What the fuck's that supposed to mean? . . . Chose to fucking hang himself, did he?'

'He chose to face up to his own mistakes!' Paul's voice rose to a level I hadn't thought him capable of. The red of his cheeks darkened, made his pale eyes sink deeper in his head.

'And what was that, Paul . . . getting on the wrong side of you?'

'Shut the fuck up, Dury.'

'He pissed you off, your best mate, so you killed him.'

We'd reached the hall. Paul beat the heel of his hand off his forehead. 'You don't know what you're talking about. You don't know a fucking thing, Dury.'

'I know you're off your fucking head . . . I know a sicko when I see one, a fucking mentaller, that's what you are . . . You need help, you need locked up. You're a fucking lunatic, Paul . . . do you know that?'

The two lads at the door held it open, flagged us to hurry. I could see that the lights were on inside. A heavy punt struck at my back. It hurt like hell but as I got dragged in I realised I wasn't going to have too much time to dwell on things like pain. The crowd of lads ran for the stage; two blocked the doors with a broom handle then made for the centre where a noose hung over a three-legged stool. The group arranged themselves in a semicircle facing the floor. They seemed calm, as if they'd been down this road before. I wanted to slap them back to life; they stood there like Stepford Wives in some kind of trance. They looked as though they had no idea what they were about to do. They were about to commit murder, and it seemed like it was their entitlement. My mind jarred, spun . . . but I couldn't take my eyes off the thick rope. I knew it had my name on it.

'Wake up, you fucking idiots . . . think you'll get away with this?' I roared out.

They were impassive. Lost in some *Boy's Own* adventure.

I felt my arms tugged. The pain shot through my shoulders.

'Accept your fate, Dury.' Paul pointed to the noose and my captors sprang.

My Docs scraped noisily along the floorboards as I was hauled towards the stage. Figured they'd leave a few streaks; make for some interesting evidence. Was no way I was letting them think this was a suicide . . . or that I was into tugging myself with a rope round my neck. I was going out kicking and screaming. Wondered if anyone would pay attention to the evidence this time. Doubted it.

My mind ran with the faces of the people I loved, had loved. I knew it was said that at the point of death your whole life flashes before you. I'd dismissed it as a cliché, but now I knew it wasn't. I saw my brother Michael, my father stood by him. I felt confused, lost. I knew my heartbeat couldn't sustain this rate for much longer; the pulse in my temples seemed to be squeezing my vision. I felt fragile, close to the end. Did I accept it, like Paul told me to? Did I give in, shake off this mortal coil? What the fuck had it ever done for me? Who's to say there wasn't better to come?

Fucksake, Dury . . . knowing your luck, it would be the other place, the shithole.

I felt a last surge of fire in my belly, yelled, 'This the way Ben went . . . loud and proud? That the way you killed your best mate, Paul . . . is it?'

For a young bloke, he held it together well. I expected more of a kick-off, more sparks. But he'd made that mistake once already, he wasn't about to show himself up again. He knew he needed to keep it together. Paul had some idea of himself that didn't tally with the facts, though. The lad was living up to the image of someone with more experience, years on the dial, import. But he was just a boy – who was he modelling himself on? There was no way he'd come this far without serious back-up, without protection.

'Who's pulling your strings, Paul?' I blurted.

His thin lips trembled above his weak chin as he pointed to the stage. 'Get him up there.'

'Well, who is it? . . . I know the Seriatim are hooked up with the Craft, Paul. I know the filth are wiping your fucking arse.'

He turned. His eyes were moist, watery. I watched his thin lips part, almost imperceptibly. He seemed to take a deep breath, calmed himself, then took three steps towards me and grabbed at my collar.

'Move it!' he said.

Hands bundled me onto the stage. I kicked out, tried to free my arms, but I had no energy, no strength. My hands were tied behind my back and

I was lifted onto the stool with little effort. As I stood I felt my legs tremble beneath me; my feet swayed on the stool as the noose went over my head. I stood silently for a second or two and then I felt the noose tightening round my neck. My whole body swayed in circles under the noose. The rope dug into my neck, pressed hard on my throat and arteries. The skin beneath the rope burned, I could feel the bite of it mixing with the salt of my sweat: it stung like a lash. I tried to block out the pain, to steady myself on the stool, but it was next door to impossible for me. With every movement the rope tightened on my neck. I saw my brother and my father again, they'd been joined by Stevo . . . I could taste blood, death.

Paul spoke: 'You don't understand a thing, Dury . . . not one thing.' I tried to control my eyes, focus my gaze on him. He had his hands to his head. It was difficult to follow his movements as he paced.

'I understand you killed Ben Laird,' I spat. I still had some blood rising in me; my voice was a low rasp.

Paul stopped still when he heard me. 'No . . . you're wrong!' He jerked suddenly where he stood. A shudder seemed to pass through him and he ran to my side. His hands grew animated as he spoke: 'You see . . . Ben was the one that was off his head, mad at his mother for running off with that whore . . . Did you know Tina was a whore? Bender Ben couldn't live with the shame, so he devised a little plan to get rid of Tina.' Paul walked to my side, poked at my chest with his forefinger as he continued, 'He slipped some GHB into her drink one night and introduced her to some of the lads that didn't know her, said she was just another one of his whores.' I saw where he was going with this. He didn't seem to need any encouragement either, his hands shot into the air, painting the scene for me. 'They all had her, every one of them. She was a fucking whore . . . Ben told them so.'

He turned away from me. His face reddened again and contorted with anger, sweat pooled beneath his eyes and nose, he gripped his fringe in his fingers. The knowledge of what he'd done was bursting out of him. I couldn't tell if he was proud or worried – he was certainly hyped.

I spoke, 'But Tina wasn't on the game by then—'

'No. No, she fucking wasn't *then* . . . she was with Ben's mother by then.' He slapped his hip, drew fists. 'Fucking Ben wanted rid of her . . . Ben brought this about. Put us all in danger, he fucking put us all in it . . . He didn't think about anyone other than himself!'

I felt the rope cutting into my neck again, tightening harder this time. My head grew hot under the lights. My knees were buckling. 'So you fucking hanged him for it.'

Paul flapped his arms, then hooked them around himself, shaking. 'No. You don't understand. That's not how it was . . . that's not how it was.'

I bit my lip; I could taste more blood. 'Then tell me, Paul . . . how the fuck was it?'

He scrunched his brows. His words trembled: 'When a member brings the Seriatim into disrepute, there's only one way to deal with it . . . There always has been.' He stepped back, motioned a hand to the floor. 'They're put on the stool with a noose round their neck. If they survive the night, then they're home free.'

'And if they don't?'

Paul sparked, 'Then they got what they deserved.'

I couldn't believe what I was hearing. It sounded like the kind of boys' club horseshit that you only read about in silly novels by public school ponces. Did this kind of thing really go on? Did silly wee boys think they had the right to do this? My head spun.

'So Ben never made it through the night?'

Paul shook his head. He let his chin touch his chest for a second. As he did so, there began a pounding on the door to the hall. I saw the broom jump in the handles. The pounding grew louder; some splinters fell from the hinges. I felt my feet slipping as my Docs lost their purchase on the smooth surface of the stool. I tap-danced for a few seconds, watching as the broom cracked and split. The pounding grew louder still, like a battering ram was being used, but the doors started to blur on me as the noose seemed to cut off my vision.

CHAPTER 38

My ankles turned numb, my shins ached. My calves and thighs burned up. I knew I couldn't hold on much longer. The rope dug tighter and tighter. It was hard to breathe. I started to feel my shoulders grow heavy. My mind was all over the place – awash with strange sensations. Lights, flashes. At any moment, I knew, I could slip into unconsciousness. Paul paced before me: he spoke as though he was giving a lecture, but most of it missed me. I tried to tune in, caught odd words, phrases, but everything was blurring on me. He stopped still, leaned in and stared at the stool, 'You won't last the night, Dury . . . you're just about done as it is.'

I heard more thuds on the door; they seemed to grow even louder and louder, but the broom handle held.

'Get that fucking door,' yelled Paul.

A couple of the group split off, ran for the front of the hall.

'Hurry up,' shouted Paul.

The lads got to the door, put hands on it; the banging continued. I could hear voices now, hysterical women's voices. I didn't know where they came from – my head, probably. Nothing seemed real to me any more; the noose cut deeper, blocked off my circulation. I choked, my breath thinned. I felt light-headed, drowsy. I wanted to drop into deep sleep. The women continued to wail, they called my name now, 'Gus . . . Gus . . . Gus . . .'

Christ on a cross, where was I? I felt enormous pain in my back, at the base of my neck, where my skull joined my spine. It felt like an electric drill had started boring into me. I wanted to yell in agony but I had no strength left.

Michael loomed before me, shaking his head. He was younger than I remembered, a mere boy. He admonished me, started to speak, but his words were drowned out by the women, 'Gus . . . Gus . . . Gus.'

Bright lights flashed in my eyes. Flashing like strobes. I saw two pinpoints at the end of long roads. They shone so hard I wanted to vomit.

A loud crash came. I heard scuffles, but I couldn't see a thing now. I tried to open my eyes, but the effort was too much for me. I felt a pounding in my chest, my heart started to skip beats, raced and raced. Now a tightening in my chest: if the noose didn't do for me, I knew I was minutes from cardiac arrest.

'You fuck, Dury.' It was Paul. He grabbed me, I spun on the stool. I found strength to open my eyes, my vision returned. It was blurred but I could see Paul's red fringe shaking before me. 'You did this . . . you fucking . . .'

He went on, but his voice was drowned out by the wails from the other end of the hall.

'Gus . . . Gus . . .'

I recognised the voice.

Paul looked on, open-mouthed, as the doors burst open, a blur of bodies ran into the hall. He couldn't seem to comprehend the turn of events – it just wasn't on his radar. He had the whole game sussed, so he'd thought.

'Gus . . .' the voice shrieked out, shriller than before. It was Amy. She tried to run to me but was restrained by Paul's mob. Hod was throwing wild punches, cracking heads. The grand arc of his hook dropped lads on the floor with each clean punch. He moved fast, near laughed off all attempts to land a glove on him. The man was on fire. Busting out of his skin.

Behind him Tina came running. Gillian followed, but made her way more slowly. There was a scuffle as Paul's crew ran to hold them back, but they wide-berthed them, shook them off as they ran for the stage behind Amy.

'Get off me,' roared Tina. Gillian raised her hands to her mouth as she caught sight of me, tied up on the stage, a noose round my neck. Tina yelled out again, 'Don't do it . . . don't.'

Paul jumped down from the stage to front Tina. He grabbed her arms in his hands. She struggled violently as he yelled, 'You can't tell me what to do!'

Gillian ran for Paul, pulled Tina from his clutches. 'Leave her alone, leave her . . .' She hit out, slapped at him with the flats of her hands. I felt the whole room start to spin, then fade out as the yelling continued.

'You don't understand,' said Paul.

'*You* don't fucking understand,' roared Tina. She was hysterical, screaming, tears streaming down her face: 'I saw him on the stool . . . I came here, I saw Ben on the stool.'

Hod broke away from the mob, ran to Tina. His face was bloodied, his hair wet to his brow. He was short of breath, exhausted as he shouted, 'The police are coming . . .'

I tried to call to him, but my tongue was swollen, immovable in my mouth.

Hod seemed to sense me, roared out, 'Fitz called. I told him where you were . . . he's coming.'

Paul spun off from Gillian and Tina, fronted Hod: 'You fucking moron.' He lashed out, caught Hod with a lucky punch; it floored him. I felt all hope leave me. The rope bit tighter but I couldn't feel a thing now. Paul looked maddened as he ran to the window, peered out and raised hands to his head. Blue lights were flashing on the panes; I could hear sirens.

Paul turned back to Tina. 'You saw him here?'

Gillian held on to her. 'Let me go,' said Tina. She hit out with her hands, scratching with her nails as she tried to push the actress away. She screamed out, 'I saw him on the stool . . . he wanted me to cut him down. I couldn't . . . I couldn't, Gillian . . . He raped me.'

Gillian threw arms around her again, held her tight. The pair blurred into one amorphous mass in my tired vision, 'No. No. Don't . . .' Gillian cried.

'I kicked the stool away,' said Tina. 'He raped me. They all did. I wanted him dead . . . He raped me.'

The doors to the hall swung open again. Suddenly a flood of uniforms ran in. They spread out like ants, surrounding the group of lads wherever they ran, clasping mitts on them, cuffing them up. The first figure through the door I recognised was Fitz. He stared at me, wide-eyed, his fleshy cheeks drooping with the gape of his mouth. He seemed frozen, rooted to the floor until a dark-uniformed figure swept past him, catching his arm. It was Henderson. His face had lost its hard edge. His teeth showed as he ran towards Paul, grabbed him from one of the PCs.

'You stupid little cunt!' bellowed Henderson.

He shook the lad by the collar, his face inches from Paul's as he spat, 'I fucking told you . . . but you wouldn't fucking listen!'

Fitz seemed spellbound, unmoving. He looked to be trapped where he stood, nailed to the floor. Then, as if a light had been flicked on, he turned, yelled, 'Chick . . . leave him.'

The super was unmoved, landed a leather-gloved fist in Paul's gut. 'I fucking warned you!' The lad fell to the ground. A crowd of stunned uniforms stood helpless, not knowing whether to intervene or leave well alone.

'Chick . . . Chick,' yelled Fitz. He moved now, ran at him. His prominent gut stuck out in front of him; coat-tails flapped at his back.

Henderson's cap went flying as he dropped to the ground, kneeled on Paul's chest and battered into his face with fists. He called out but the words were lost to me. As the blood flew, I could taste my own rising in my throat. I gasped for breath, then steadied.

'What did I say?' yelled Henderson. 'What did I tell you?' His face contorted into jagged angles as he slumped onto the boy's chest, beating him with blunt fists, 'You've fucking ruined us all!'

Fitz reached out. 'Chick . . . stop this, now!' He tried to pull the chief super away but was thrown off balance, skidded a little then landed on his arse. His actions seemed to prompt the uniforms, though – they fell on Henderson, dragged him away. He kicked out, yelling, 'The stupid little cunt, he ruined us . . . fucking ruined us.'

Fitz slowly raised himself. He looked winded as he pointed the uniforms to the door.

The scuffles ended, and now the hall seemed eerily quiet, until Gillian fell to her knees and let out a pained, wounded cry. My eyes followed her as she slumped to the ground and lay sobbing – she wasn't acting now. I watched her whole body tremble. Her hands clawed at her face in terror, pulling the skin so tight her eyes bulged showing the red explosions of capillaries.

It was the last thing I saw as my feet lost their purchase on the stool.

The rope snapped tight.

CHAPTER 39

The *Hootsman* splashed with my story on page one. Rasher even paid me a visit – well, I was hardly mobile.

'I always knew you had some neck, Dury,' he joked.

I tapped the neck brace, nodded. Let him think he was the first to crack this one. 'That's very good. You should be on the stage,' I said.

'Ha-ha . . . so long as it's not the one you wrote about in the article!'

The story had caused a stir; I was pleased with that. It had been a long while since I'd had a decent page-one splash. If this was what I had to go through for them though, I wouldn't give a fuck if it was my last.

Amy appeared, carried in a bowl of chicken soup for me. She sat it down beside the settee. She smiled at Rasher, one of her *you're a man, I can wrap you round my little finger* ones. 'Have you heard any more about the police investigation?'

He grinned back, stray whiskers stiffened on his cheeks. 'Oh, aye . . . meant to say. They say the shit's hit the fan down at Fettes . . . plod being probed big time. Lot of suspensions . . . and . . .'

he paused for dramatic effect, raised an index finger to the ceiling, 'we had it confirmed this morning: the seventies hanging's being reopened.'

'That's good news.' I picked up the soup, stirred the spoon about a bit.

'You don't look too chuffed,' said Rasher.

Should I be? I raised an eyebrow, spoke, 'I've been strung up, my neck feels like it's a foot longer . . . forgive me if I don't get up and start turning fucking cartwheels.'

Amy blushed, looked away. There was a moment of dead air in the room. Rasher rose, mumbled his excuses and headed for the door, said, 'Well, I'm a happy camper . . . put thirty per cent on the circulation with that story. If you've any more like it . . .'

I stopped stirring, let the spoon clang on the edge of the bowl. 'I very much fucking doubt it.'

Rasher looked at the door, then turned, gave Amy a peck on the cheek, said, 'I'll see you both, then.'

I could barely manage a wave. I was beyond sickened. All those deaths, all that hurt and misery I'd seen on Gillian Laird's face – it wasn't about circulation figures for any of them. I felt a deep unease growing in me. I was unhappy being part of the human race.

When Rasher had gone, I sensed beady eyes on me. 'You didn't need to be so rude,' said Amy.

I eased a finger between the brace and my neck. 'I'm just a bit sick of everyone wanting a piece of me.' My mind flooded with thoughts of

Stevo again; I could still smell the stench of his blood. There was no way I'd ever be able to shake it. There was no way I'd shake any of this; even if I recovered physically, I was going to be scarred. All over. 'I need out, Amy.'

She tilted her head, looked down her nose at me. 'What about Hod? . . . He seems to think you're both in business.'

I waved a flat palm, cut the air with it. 'He's wrong . . . well and fucking truly wrong.'

'Have you told him?'

The brace was pinching again. I loosened the Velcro a notch, stretched my jaw. 'Look, Hod knew from the off this was a one-shot deal. I got him off the ropes with Shaky, he's in the clear . . . now he can leave me be.'

Amy flared, 'He won't be pleased.'

'I'm popping more Harry Hills than Pete Doherty here . . . I have the shakes, nightmares, and a craving for drink that takes twenty-four-seven concentration to ignore. You think I give a shit if he's pleased or not? He's a big lad, he'll get over it!'

Amy came over to the settee, sat down beside me, placed a hand on my arm. 'Okay. Okay . . . let's just get you well, and take it from there.'

She put those heartmelter eyes on me. Despite everything, she made me feel a little gladness in my heart . . . even if I didn't deserve her.

I took her hand. Couldn't help grinning. 'Rasher's right about one thing . . . I've some neck.'